The Painted Cave

GC Hennessey

ISBN: 978-1-0689948-0-7

CONTENTS

1 THE STORM

Clouds massed on the horizon in mounting processions like tribes of warriors presenting themselves for battle. Waves of angry, gray shadows mingled and darkened into billows that expanded over the Land of Salt Water and Thick Trees. On a calm day in Peskotomuhkati Bay, waves melodically rolled onto one another creating a soothing rhythm of energy that connected all families living with the Land. Early and unwelcomed winds from the south altered the measure, creating an anxious uneasiness in the air that was difficult to understand. Salty winds from the south collided with cold air lingering in the bay and churned the waters into swirling portals of blue that hid wonders and dangers beneath.

Momentum built from the cold water below, allowing the south winds to rip into the shoreline and penetrate the shield of trees lining the boundary of the Land. Sounds of trees thrashing and snapping ricocheted off the rocks and eddied into the sounds of waves crashing below. The new rhythm was erratic, disorganized and announced the arrival of a disturbing and unfamiliar presence. All families living with the Land could tell stories of storms that tested their faith in the Creator to protect them. Something unfamiliar about the winds and energy from this storm brought unrest and uneasiness to the Lands.

Olonatoq, a formidable and unsheltered red spruce tree on the Siptuk Peninsula, shielded the point from the headwinds and acted as a forewarning to the inhabitants of the Lands. The towering giant was also home to the lookout nest built by the Eagles for the sentinels. The silhouette of Olo, as he is affectionately referred, stands as a beacon of security, while his weathered and unearthed roots tell tales from storms of unyielding, unimaginable power and unrelenting force. Every branch, whether adorned with needles or bare, lived on the stem with enduring persistence to fulfill its purpose of providing refuge to the Eagles, who carried out their duty to protect and guard.

The Land of Salt Water and Thick Trees is defined by the watershed of the Siptuk River that empties into Peskotomuhkati Bay and encompasses the connecting shorelines and the hundreds of islands across the archipelago. Boundaries of the Land were defined by rugged cliffs on the water side of the peninsula and bountiful coves and inlets on the land side that could be described as havens of food and shelter. Across the cove, the jagged shorelines reach up to the rolling and vast Red Forest that burned over one hundred years ago. The Great Fire cleared the Land and scorched the soil but spared Olo and his family. Protective older siblings towered over the peninsula and provided seeds to bring life back to the mainland. The enduring red spruce still provide a windbreak to shelter younger trees, until they put down centurion roots able to withstand the storms that threatened the cove.

Across the bay, the Lakauwok River watershed defined the western boundary of the Land and etched pathways of life to every corner in the Forest of Peace before ending at the Great Mountain. The dense and lush vegetation of the understorey provided refuge and food, and the canopy above offered protection to the inhabitants of the Forest. Some of the trees, like those with quaking leaves, are connected by their roots to young trees, carrying the same knowledge and wisdom of the original mother tree throughout the entire forest. There are many examples of this across the Land where the animals, birds, fish and humans together survive the oftentimes harsh conditions summoned by Mother Earth. The culmination of these experiences taught lessons in balance, and its importance in maintaining relationships between the living things and the Land on which they survive. Imbalance in the Land can lead to conflict and destruction, while balance required only the observance of a simple set of natural laws that were maintained by the Fire Council at Siptuk.

The vast territory is governed by the Council that meet with the seasons around a fire at the base of Olo's trunk. There is an understanding and ever-evolving peace amongst the families that is reaffirmed with the seasons by gathering in the shadow of wisdom and knowledge provided by the crown of the old spruce. It took over a century for Olo to put down the roots he needed to withstand the winds that shaped the surrounding Land. He endured many of the storms that were captured in stories of bravery and survival that were passed down in the lessons learned around the fire from father to son and mother to daughter.

He was a solemn witness to the celebrations in times of feast and the desperation in times of famine and understood that for there to be peace in the Lands, there sometimes must be conflict to restore the balance. For everything that appears to be beautiful, there will be something about it that is equally unappealing. Olo understood there was sometimes suffering in the Land when the power structure between the families breaks and creates inequality amongst them.

The ancient red spruce had befriended many young Eagle sentinels standing guard in the lookout nest. Olo shared the knowledge and wisdom from his two-hundred-foot perspective with each sentinel that perched in his branches. The old tree often found his stories created more questions than understanding and felt the concepts he shared to be beyond the comprehension of the young fledglings that were commissioned as sentries, until recently. There was one promising, yet aggravating exception to this general rule, and his name was Tuwiye. The young sentinel intuitively extrapolated the messages Olo wove into his captivating and inspiring stories yet patronized the old tree for trying to distract him with juvenile lessons.

Often, Olo reassured nervous young sentinels with stories of legendary storms from the past and their phenomenal power to distract them from the light breeze that was tossing around the lookout in the moment's storm. Tonight was not one of those nights. Olo felt a menacing wave of uneasiness hover above him as he swayed more vigorously back and forth in the strengthening storm. The timing and strength of the storm made little sense and he knew none of the families in the Land were prepared to move. Gusts of wind tested the limits of his trunk and Olo worried he would succumb to the power trying to twist and snap him.

The taste of salt water reached beyond his lower branches and climbed high into the top of his crown. The taste of salt so high above the water was a warning for something Olo had forgotten. Although he was unsure of its meaning, for the first time in his memory, the usually calm and resilient spruce worried about whether he would survive the storm. He was eager for the on-duty sentinel to be relieved, so he could talk to his more intellectual replacement.

"Where is Tuwiye? He should be here by now. Maybe you should go look for him," suggested Olo to the probationary sentinel.

"I was told to stay at my post until I am relieved by my replacement," looking inland, he observed, "He is flying up the cove right now."

"Thank you, young sentinel. You can head home now," said Olo, as he hurried the timid Eagle from the nest.

Olo watched as Tuwiye skillfully navigated the shoreline of the peninsula towards him and circled his crown to pay respect before landing softly in the lookout nest. The young Eagle skillfully shook the cold of the storm from his feathers to prepare for the evening watch. Although only three years old, he possessed the maturity of his white head and tail feathers, an honour usually saved for older Eagles. While he was viewed as respectful and helpful, he regularly rejected the role his family expected him to fulfill. To sway his thinking, Tuwiye's father secretly asked Olo to tutor the young captain with his two hundred years of wisdom and knowledge about the Land. He was desperate to help him accept his path in life and embrace his destiny as the future leader of the soar. The wise old spruce found the request to be an onerous task, as these types of tasks often are when you are trying to convince someone to follow a path they did not build for themselves.

"Hello, my Elder brother Olo. What tale do you have for me this evening?" asked Tuwiye with a playful squawk.

He arrived at his post early, as usual, and greeted Olo with his nightly request. The stories Olo told were the most wildly entertaining accounts of battles and tragedies mixed with tales of love and devotion. Tuwiye hung on every word and sometimes got lost in the details and needed to be reminded of the meaning camouflaged in the excitement. Olo never tortured him over the higher meanings of his stories, rather he led him down the path straight to it. Nothing like the conversations he endured with his father. Tuwiye enjoyed his time with Olo, as he felt a deep connection with the Elder that he hid from the other sentinels, and his father. While he considered himself smart, he felt more comfortable in the role of warrior, instead of the leader his father wanted him to be. He found satisfaction as a captain and readily accepted responsibility for protecting the soar and training the fledglings. It was a respectable position in the soar and it was enough for the young Eagle. He resisted the push he felt towards the path constructed for him by his parents.

Olo stood stoically quiet and for a moment said nothing in response to the young Eagle's question. As opposed to answering, the majestic tree offered only silence that was lost in the ominous creaks and cracks emanating from his trunk as he stood firm against the force of the storm. The pause allowed Tuwiye a moment to hear the wind and feel its power pushing back against his beak. He realized the winds had changed and grown stronger since the night before. Tuwiye recognized something more was bothering his old friend, something beyond the looming storm. He sensed the danger that was radiating through Olo and the negative energy focused his thoughts.

A close strike on the shoreline below startled Olo into asking, "Have you spoken to your father?"

Tuwiye is son to Mako, the hereditary leader of the soar of Eagles nested within the imposing red spruce of the Land of Salt Water and Thick Trees on the Siptuk Peninsula. Tuwiye was his only offspring and avoided spending any unnecessary time with his father. Although he had been promoted to the notable position of captain, Tuwiye still felt his father belittled and insulted him at every turn. Sometimes he thought his father was trying to control every decision he made, while demanding he forge his own path in life. Avoiding his decided destiny only strained the relationship between Tuwiye and his father.

Before becoming obstinate in choosing his own path, Tuwiye tried to reason with Mako and explain that the idea of being anything beyond a sentinel captain did not speak to him. When his father would not listen and instead dismissed his concerns and vulnerability, Tuwiye challenged the older Eagle with an ultimatum. The insubordinate young Eagle demanded the ability to decide his destiny for himself, otherwise he swore he would not speak to him again outside of his duties as a sentinel. He would put all his energy into avoiding the role his father defined for him.

"I have not seen him tonight. He said to find him at the end of my sentry," pained Tuwiye. "I was hoping to get some sleep and find him."

"Find him right away," cautioned Olo. "It cannot wait. This storm is different and unlike any I have ever stood against. There is something your father needs to tell you. I will take your sentry while you go look for him," instructed Olo. "I am worried this is only the beginning."

Tuwiye could barely hear Olo over the howling winds and crashing sounds from the ground beneath them. "I cannot leave the lookout!" he shouted back. "Do you remember this past winter? When I thought for myself and left the lookout? The Ravens from the Forest of Peace created a distraction to lure me from my post, and I took the bait. While I led the fledglings on an attack to defend the lookout, they sent a detachment of Ravens to raid our food rations. I will not be making that mistake again. Can't you just tell me what is happening?" Tuwiye asked impatiently. His father's contradictory words told him to think for himself, while his actions showed he didn't trust the young captain's decision-making abilities. Tuwiye would rather hear whatever he needed to know from Olo.

As if on cue, Mako landed on the edge of the nest, opposite Tuwiye.

"Olo, what did you say to the boy?" he demanded harshly.

Mako was the oldest male Eagle in the Land of Salt Water and Thick Trees and the hereditary leader of the soar, just as his father before him and grandfather before that. From birth, Mako was raised with a singular focus to follow in his father's footsteps to protect the soar, while fathering and mentoring the next hereditary leader. Watching his father drown as a young Eagle prematurely aged Mako and pushed him down the path towards a life with a single purpose. Blaming himself for his father's tragic death, Mako hardened his heart from love and compassion, while abandoning any hope of happiness or peace for himself. It made his life simple and detached with the sole objective of protecting the soar.

"Nothing, Mako," snapped back Olo. "It is not my place to tell the boy about his life path. Time is not on your side, my friend. You and I both know this storm could be a sign from the Spirit World and you are not giving him any time to absorb what you need to tell him," Olo countered with indignation. Annoyed with his usually far more pragmatic friend, Olo creaked back and kicked Mako off the nest using a gust of wind to camouflage his intent.

With confidence and poise, Mako rapidly thrust his wings back and forth to land back on the nest beside Tuwiye and said, "The first storm of the season has arrived early, Olo. Stop filling the boy's head with nonsense." His attention focused on Tuwiye, Mako held his wing up as an instructional pointer and gave the young captain an order as his commanding officer. "Gather the eaglets and get them into the nests on the leeward side of the peninsula. Winds are strong and coming from the south," he pointed out. "It means we need to move the soar now even if the nests are not ready. It is too early for these winds with so much cold air in the cove."

"Is that safe? The inland nests are still under construction, and there won't be enough food on the other side of the island. The northern soar is still there preparing for the first storm winds to carry them home for the summer. Besides, Olo said there was something you needed to tell me?" questioned

Tuwiye.

"Why must you always question what I say? Sometimes I wonder if I shouldn't have left you behind with the other fledglings and choose not to promote you to captain. I knew you weren't ready. Part of being ready for responsibility is the ability to make difficult decisions to benefit the entire soar," Mako stated flatly. "Moving everyone is the correct decision. Why can't you see that?"

The commander saw the pain his condemnation caused and broke his stare to stop the sadness in his son's eyes from penetrating any deeper. The dejection and swirling anger in Tuwiye's eyes unearthed a deeply buried memory of an eerily familiar exchange Mako had with his own father years ago. Paralyzing emotions flooded his memory and Mako found himself unable to hold them back. As he succumbed to the memory, Mako heard the last conversation he had with his father replay in his head.

At the time, his father was the hereditary leader and the young Mako, a probationary sentinel. There was a harrowing windstorm that threatened the nests constructed too close to shore. With the next flash landing dangerously close and a roll of thunder above them, Mako was pulled back deep into the past and found himself sitting in the lookout alone with Olo years ago. Prior to that fateful storm, Mako had been sentenced to permanent night-watch for disobeying a direct order from his commanding officer, and father, by leaving the lookout nest without approval. The distraction of a burning tree combined with a daringly heroic rescue had lured Mako away from the lookout that night, abandoning his post. His dereliction of duty was discovered by Olo who reluctantly reported the abandoned post to his disappointed father.

Mako arrived at the burning tree to discover the nest had been evacuated and the fire long extinguished. He instantly regretted his decision to leave the lookout and returned to his post as fast as he was able. As he approached the lookout, Mako recognized his father's silhouette sitting in the nest on watch. From that night forward, his father had been punishing him to instill the importance of following orders sent down through the chain of command without question. The events leading up to the night of his father's death were no exception.

As Mako continued to replay that fatal night in his mind, he could hear his booming voice ordering him that, "Under no circumstances are you to leave the nest! Do you understand? It is going to be a powerful storm this evening. Are you sure you can remember my instructions? I can't be distracted worrying about you. Just stay here and keep your beak down!"

Mako still remembered the anger he felt at his father for how he treated him. All that night while on watch, the anger burned into his mind with rageful thoughts. While imagining awful things happening to his father, Mako could hear his voice, faintly beneath the howling winds and crashing bolts.

"Mako? Can you hear me, Mako? Please help me," he thought he heard his father faintly call out. Mako hastily dismissed the cries for help as a trap. In a recent training session for new sentinels, his father tried to lure away trainees from the lookout with a decoy; an eaglet stranded on a ledge with a broken wing. If the trainee abandoned his post to save the eaglet before a search and rescue team was dispatched, his father removed them from the program. He assumed his father was putting him through the same challenge and swiftly disregarded the idea his father needed help. A leader does not admit weakness, and his father exuded fierce independence and trained his sentinels to value self-reliance above all else, except loyalty.

When roving sentries discovered his father missing in the morning, a search party was dispatched. It did not take long for his body to be discovered on the rocks along the water, far beneath the looming silhouette of Olo. For the rest of his days, Mako would forever connect feelings of guilt and shame with his anger and rage for not saving his father. Full of self-loathing, the experience resulted in confusing exchanges between Mako and Tuwiye that forever poisoned their relationship as father and son.

'If only I had answered his calls for help. Or at least dispatched search and rescue,' he lamented to himself. 'I was so angry at the thought he was trying to trick me with such a juvenile test,' he thought. 'If I had answered him, maybe he would still be alive.' When he could sleep, the same loop of regrets haunted Mako as he relived the final moments with his father "A fleeting moment of pain is a small price to pay for a lesson that could eventually save the soar or himself," thought Mako as he forced himself back into the present moment and turned to face his son.

"Yes, sir," Tuwiye obligatorily answered.

As the young captain waited for the sting of his father's words to fade before taking off, a jarring crack of lightning shattered a large branch on the red spruce tree behind them. Although the nest in the treetop escaped the destructive bolt, flames erupted below, posing an immediate threat to the two defenseless eaglets within. Mako and Tuwiye simultaneously sprang from the lookout and hurled themselves into the chaotic winds that were feeding the flames climbing towards the baby birds. While in perfect cadence with one another, each wing flap thrust them closer to the burning tree. Without a word spoken between them, Mako and Tuwiye both hovered over the nest to scoop an eaglet in one of their talons and promptly touched down to ricochet to a nearby tree for safety. Off in the distance inland towards the cove, another bolt struck and appeared to incinerate the immense red giant in a cloud of flames and smoke. Strikes crashed all around them, followed by claps of thunder that shook the ground beneath the mighty trees.

"Now, do you understand the gravity of the situation? Can you just listen to me and do as I say? I do not have time to explain everything to you right now. You need to get these eaglets to safety while I find your mother and the other egg sitters," instructed Mako, trying to be heard over the storm. "Once everyone is safe, return here to the lookout. I have more to tell you about this storm and what it means for the soar." Mako paused for a moment and the distinguished Eagle twisted his head to gaze out into the menacing storm on the horizon before looking back at Tuwiye. "Well, what it means for you and all our brothers and sisters. Even our human brothers and sisters on the ground below." Maybe the boy was ready, but the old Eagle was worried.

Tuwiye was abruptly annoyed. His father always spoke in an Elder's code that was exhausting to decipher repeatedly. When Tuwiye could not figure out the significance of what his father was saying, Mako would badger and insult him until one lost their temper. The relationship was defined by this unspoken language and hidden meanings buried in a code that Tuwiye could not break. Even when he thought he understood the significance of what his father was saying, Mako still seemed angry and displeased with him. To avoid a debate, Tuwiye simply nodded and grabbed the eaglets, one in each talon, and took off from the nest. Because he refused to speak to his father outside of his duties as a sentinel, every conversation between the father and son ended the same way, causing their hearts to harden that much more towards one another.

As he flew across the peninsula, Tuwiye thought, "Why can't he just say what he means? He makes me feel so small when he talks to me like that."

The young captain was ignorant to how desperate Mako needed him to become a leader and trust his teachings. Even Mako did not understand the extent of the push driving Tuwiye down the life path ahead of him. All Mako could offer was his knowledge and experiences leading the soar since his father died. At times, even he did not understand what was driving him. With all his wisdom and knowledge, Olo could not accurately predict what the early storm meant for everyone and everything living in the Land of Salt Water and Thick Trees. While Tuwiye flew the eaglets to safety, the fledglings were carrying out his orders to evacuate the Elders and other juveniles. Mako flew over the operation and could see it was organized and efficient with the Elders being carefully guided to safety. He smiled to himself, knowing he raised a confident and capable leader. "Tuwiye just needs to accept his destiny," thought Mako. He shook his head in frustrated pride as he landed on the edge of his own nest.

"What is wrong now? We are experiencing the storm of the ages and you have kept me sitting on these eggs with no sign of evacuation. What could go so wrong for you that you are shaking your head?" questioned his mate Nika. As Mako's partner, Nika was the head egg sitter and responsible for the care of orphans, or eggs dropped by predators when challenged by the sentinels.

"Nothing. You are right. We need to get you and the eggs to safety. The nest isn't quite finished and there are still several sentinels working on it. You head there. Tuwiye and I will get the rest of the eggs to you right away," offered Mako, hoping to avoid any further discussion concerning his unfortunately witnessed headshake.

Life became complicated when he was paired with Nika. With intelligence beyond which she displayed, Nika was the recognized leader of the egg sitters. The union was initiated from practical considerations and grew into one of caring, deep respect, and passionless love. An unspoken understanding between the formidable pair allowed both to dedicate themselves to individual vocations, egg sitting and their son. Mako dedicated his life to Tuwiye's training and development into the next hereditary leader, while Nika was the devoted mother for all orphaned eagle eggs discovered in the Land.

"Excellent attempt at avoiding a fight. Wait, no, not a fight…rather, a discussion. A heated and very one-sided discussion. I will leave it at that only because this storm is building and I need to get these eggs to safety," she conceded. "The egg that arrived before the first full spring moon is close to hatching. I think she is from the Forest of Peace, but no one could track down her family. We are all she has in the Land and we cannot leave her alone. I will take her with me and you send Tuwiye to me with the others. I will keep your spot warm," she said and offered an affectionate nuzzle before gracefully exiting the nest.

Mako let out a long, sad whistle that trailed off into the storm behind Nika. As the hereditary leader of the soar, Mako knew what he needed to do, but as a father he was incapable of doing it. Nika could do it. She had the strength and patience to field Tuwiye's questions and talk him into understanding what role he needed to play in the soar. She was a skilled leader and could command the entire soar with ease. More notably, she was brave enough to tell her son the truth. There is so much more about being a leader that Tuwiye needs to learn.

"That old spruce is right. This could be the storm that changes everything," thought Mako.

He and Nika were the only Eagles that knew their son was marked with a sign from the Spirit World. The pair, together with Olo, hid the marking from the Fire Council until they understood the message. So much tragedy surrounded those born marked that Olo thought it best to hide the symbol, both to avoid a fearful reaction from the Fire Council and to prevent fear from spreading across the Land. The decision was made not only for the soar but for all inhabitants of the Land. As a rule, any bird, animal or human marked by the Spirit World would be expected to make a pilgrimage to the Great Mountain to learn of their destiny in the Painted Cave. Pilgrimages were often darkened by loss, as the journey to the Great Mountain is a long and arduous one. Losing so many loved ones, pilgrimages were not commissioned lightly and signs from the Spirit World were often ignored or hidden. Nika was adamant that her son was not to be sent on the voyage. Few Elders could even remember the way and only recalled the arduous nature of the journey that took the lives of several brothers and sisters.

Many years ago, an eaglet was born in a neighbouring soar with what Elders interpreted as a symbol from the Spirit World. The council commissioned a pilgrimage to send the young Eagle to retrieve a message from the Painted Cave. Tragedy struck the pilgrimage when the path to the Painted Cave collapsed from falling rocks and several monstrous boulders. The Elders that had accompanied the marked Eagle were trapped inside, while the young bird was crushed at the entrance. It was the last pilgrimage initiated by the soar and any messages from the Spirit World were lost to the ages and died with the Elders trapped inside the Great Mountain. Word of the tragedy spread across the Land to other soars and the Eagles did not speak of the Painted Cave again.

When Tuwiye was born, he was never told that the skin on his chest was emblazoned beneath his adult, brown feathers with a white mark in the shape of a flame. It was hidden from him and everyone in the soar hoping another tragedy could be averted. When Tuwiye eventually discovered the symbol on his chest, he would need to hear the message from the Spirit World himself. When Mako saw the mark on Tuwiye's chest, he was simultaneously filled with pride and fear for being chosen to raise and protect him. Seeking counsel from Olo and Nika, Mako rendered the final difficult decision to hide the marking from the Fire Council.

Mako allowed the memory to fade from his mind and distantly supervised the migration of the soar to the inland stronghold, where they would be safe during the season of big storms. Satisfied everyone had been moved safely, Mako headed back toward the lookout to meet with Tuwiye. Unburdened of the worry and pressure of the early relocation, the hardened and unsentimental leader shifted focus to his son. Tactically brilliant yet dispassionate, Mako was still uncertain of his approach with Tuwiye and pined for Nika's help. Fearful their decision to ignore the marking angered the Spirit World, Mako worried the early spring storm was only the beginning.

As Mako effortlessly negotiated the swirling winds of the storm, he could see that Tuwiye had already returned and was fortifying the nest against the shelling winds. The storm was building and moments before rain fell in sheets from the sky, one final thunderbolt erupted above Olo. It summoned phenomenal power and commanded a deafening volume as the crack threw Mako backwards in the air. The solid bolt came crashing down into Olo's massive crown with a cascading fire that consumed his needles and fine branches. With force only capable in the Spirit World, the energy from the bolt surged through the old spruce and exploded out of the trunk at every branch, including the branch supporting the lookout. The branch holding the fortified nest sheered from the trunk of the mighty red spruce and hurled down towards the ground below. Shockwaves from the bolt knocked Tuwiye unconscious and hurled him with the nest down to the rocky shore below.

Mako arrived at the lookout to watch as his son tumbled to what he was sure was his death.

2 THE MEETING

Leaving all the living things in the Land of Thick Trees and Salt Water, we join the humans on the Jackfish River reservation in northern Minnesota in the present day…

When bulldozers and drill rigs arrived at McIntosh, the Elder's Circle demanded a meeting with the Chief and his council. The Elders could not understand how someone could build a road through McIntosh and cut the trees without meeting with the tribe. We decided what happened on the Land, especially at McIntosh. We still could not find Ethan or Gwendolyn, and the office on the reservation was emptied and locked.

We learned in the news that Weyerhaeuser had signed an agreement with the Governor's office, reclaiming control of the state forest licenses we were managing. With their new authority, the company licensed the subsurface mineral rights to a mining exploration company in search of gold. Weyerhaeuser was clearing the trees and taking them to their mill, while building the road to a proposed mine north of McIntosh. When we contacted Weyerhaeuser, their staff referred us back to Chief Trout. He is still Chief until the end of the month and Chief Stonefish has no powers until he is sworn in.

I pushed the Elder's Circle to call an emergency meeting of the tribe to discuss the matter in the Roundhouse at McIntosh. An unsanctioned meeting in the Roundhouse showed a lack of respect and confidence in our leadership. It set a path forward that could have serious consequences for the Elders who stood in defiance of the Chief. Fearful of the consequences of going around the Chief, I secretly wished Ethan would surprise me and somehow find his way to the meeting with Gwendolyn in tow, of course. Our small boat carefully navigated us to the place we called the Narrows, where the Jackfish River meets the Broken Mouth River before spilling into Bamaji Lake. When we reached the lake, the boat carved to the far shore towards the sandy beach. While the boat was filled with my fellow Elders, we were too young to remember the traditional migration our ancestors made every year to the sacred lake for the spring hunt and summer gathering. By the time most of us were born, the world had changed and our parents were forced to settle in our winter encampments and traditional journeys to Bamaji Lake were lost.

Elvis Ottertail piloted our boat around the last bend in the lake before we could see the clearing that was home to the newly constructed Roundhouse. A member of the Otter clan, Elvis worked with youth in the tribe and taught traditional hunting and gathering techniques, along with our ceremonies and rituals. He is a central Elder in the Circle and arranged for the boats to bring everyone on the journey today. Every year, he organized overnight outings that follow this same journey to teach young men and women our traditions before they are lost as our tribe loses the Elders. While the road built by Devlin Forest Products accesses the sacred site, it was decided the Elders would follow the traditional route taken by our ancestors to the gathering. As we watched the trees that camouflaged the clearing fade behind us, the Roundhouse emerged from behind their protection and came into view. The stunning structure was the centrepiece of the shoreline.

"You were worried no one would show up, Gloria," Elvis said with a wide grin that exposed several missing teeth on the bottom. "We're over an hour early and look how many people are here," he pointed out. "Everyone listened. I think the Land might be the only thing that connects us now," he reflected. "Some families live on the reservation and others live in the city, but everyone comes home for the gatherings in the Roundhouse. The Land brings us all back," he continued, gesturing to the gathering crowd. "Regardless of the usual jealousy and spite that divides the tribe."

We could see tribe members walking on the beach, while others tended to the fire and prepared food. Elvis aimed us for the dock and threw a rope to his cousin, Mason Yellowhead, who was waiting for us. "Hey Cuz, what a good turn out, eh? The fire inside the Roundhouse is started too and the drummers have been practising. Sounding pretty good, eh, nee-hee," he said with his characteristic laugh trailing at the end. "Food is ready if you want to eat before the meeting, Gloria," Mason informed me as he helped us out of the boat.

It was hours before the meeting was scheduled to begin, and it looked as if everyone in the tribe had turned out. Kids were running around chasing each other while parents tried to corral them for a meal. As we disembarked from the boat, the other Elders walked towards the Roundhouse to get ready, while others talked to their family members who were arriving by road. I couldn't help but search the crowd for them.

"They aren't here," Mason told me as he rested his hand on my shoulder. "Neither of them," he continued as he shook his head. "They didn't come."

"Maybe they didn't get my messages," I offered as an explanation. "We can't find them. Anywhere. Neither of their cell numbers work and soon after we heard about Weyerhaeuser's agreement, the Lands and Resources office was shutdown," I said trying to hide my disappointment. "If Gwendolyn knew what was happening, she would have come," I confirmed. "She convinced all the

Elders she was passionate about the work we were doing to protect the Land." Instead of doubting my friends, I want to find out what happened and why they left. "That's why we are here today," I reminded Mason. "We are going to find out what happened and try to understand why the Governor took the Land back. At least Gwendolyn left us a message before she went looking for Ethan," I continued. "But I know they would come back if they knew McIntosh was threatened."

"Gwendolyn found Ethan. I know it," Susan countered from behind us in the only language she knew. "When she hears what happened, she will bring him back. He will come back to help us."

"In the Roundhouse, Ethan promised us he would protect the Land, and especially McIntosh. When we showed him where the children were buried, he promised he would help," Evelyn said in our traditional tongue as she joined the conversation. "Ethan told me what he would do to anyone from Devlin if they didn't listen to him," she said with a knowing smile. "He is a warrior from the Wolf clan and he will come. He will know to come."

"Not if he isn't listening," I answered back in Ojibwe. "We hurt them, and he may not answer any message, from us or the Spirit World," I explained. "Gwendolyn's voice told me she was hurt and angry," I explained. "We must assume Ethan feels the same way." Susan and Evelyn Turtle were two of the oldest remaining Elders in the circle. They lead our gatherings as knowledge keepers and protectors of the past. Both fell hard for Ethan at our very first meeting, and Evelyn saw his animal spirit even before Ethan joined us for a ceremonial sweat. "And we aren't dealing with Devlin anymore, Evelyn," I reminded her. "This company is far worse, or at least they employ people with different values from Ethan and Gwendolyn." Both warned us in their own way about the differences in how their competitor approached the Land compared to the tribe. Gwendolyn trusted me with stories about her father, who works for Weyerhaeuser, and gave me plenty of evidence to support her warnings.

"It doesn't matter because everyone else came," Elvis said, pulling me from my thoughts. "The whole tribe is here to listen to you, Gloria. We are all here and I want to help," he said sincerely. "Tell me what to do."

I desperately wanted Elvis to speak for me. What was I going to say to the tribe? I thought for a moment about what he could do, what any of them could do, to ease the burden of my task. The Land, and especially McIntosh, was too important to give in to my fears of public speaking or for what punishment awaited me from the Chief and his council. "Stand where I can see you, Elvis," I asked him. "When I am speaking inside," I continued as I pointed to the formidable structure, "make sure I can find your eyes." I squeezed his hand and made my way inside to prepare.

The hours I thought I had to prepare disappeared, as people hurriedly finished their meals and made their way inside the Roundhouse. People were eager to learn what happened, and as people gathered, I overheard several asking when Ethan and Gwendolyn were arriving. Most of the tribe was familiar with them and expected them to attend the gathering with an update on our operations and explain why the machines were here. Realizing I would lose the attention of the crowd as it grew, I gave the drummers instructions to start and asked Susan and Evelyn to smudge me before speaking.

The familiar smell of sweet grass cleansed my thoughts and allowed me a moment to request strength from the Creator and wisdom and guidance from Mother Earth. Still trembling with nerves, I was comforted by Elvis' presence and steadfast commitment that what we were doing was right for the Land. With a look, I summoned Elvis to the head of the Roundhouse. "Elvis, I am so scared. Can you please open with a prayer and one of your stories?" I asked him. "Maybe you could lull everyone to sleep and make this easier for me, nee-hee," I said ending with a nervous version of my laugh.

Elvis had a reputation for being long-winded. He took the criticism well and never missed the opportunity to confirm it. After a brief pause, Elvis turned towards the entrance and started speaking, loudly, "The shores of Bamaji Lake were once rich with moose and caribou and the waters were full of pickerel, whitefish and sturgeon," he started. People in the growing crowd looked up and stopped their individual conversations to listen. "This lake was our summer gathering place and where our people gathered for thousands of years during the warm months to hunt, fish and celebrate with feasts. As the ice melted from the lakes and rivers, geese and ducks arrived and signalled to the clans to start the trek north. The first clan to arrive at Bamaji Lake, often the Otter clan, nee-hee," and Elvis paused for a laugh, "would kill enough birds to feed the tribe as they arrived and each would join in the effort. The clans would celebrate a successful hunt in the Roundhouse with drumming, singing and dancing. Meetings here allowed the clans to settle disputes, arrange marriages and discuss important matters with their Chief," Elvis explained and paused again in silent protest of his absent Chief.

"The original Roundhouse was built with cedar and spruce logs and was protected by birch bark. It served as a sacred space where we celebrated ceremonies and observed rituals, many that we have lost over the millennia. These ceremonies often involved the sharing of knowledge and teachings passed down from the Elders. It was a place where we came together to honor traditions and strengthen bonds with each other and with the Land."

As I listened to Elvis describe how the new Roundhouse helped the tribe rediscover traditions that were lost since encountering the first travellers to our Land, I remembered the importance of sharing our stories, even difficult and ugly ones. Everyone in the crowd was smiling and nodding along with Elvis, even chuckling at his jokes. I laughed and felt a peace wash over me. I finally knew what to say. Seeing Elvis looking for a reason to stop talking, I waited for a pause long enough to interject and caught his eyes with my smile.

"Thank you, Elvis. I appreciate you warming up the crowd for me, nee-hee," I said while the crowd joined me in laughing. "Before the drummers start, I want to share my story about McIntosh." Everyone in the Roundhouse turned quiet, and I immediately felt their eyes find me. Elvis made his way into the crowd and positioned himself across the Roundhouse directly in front of me.

With my focus only on him, I started to speak. "The men with stars on their belts came early in the morning when I was only five years old. I remember because it had just been my birthday, and I was still excited from the day." A fleeting smile danced across my lips as I touched the last memory of my mother and father before they were killed. "When they came, I heard my mother arguing with the men and she tried to stop them from coming into the teepee. At gun point, the men told her the government was creating a wilderness park, and the tribe was being moved to something they called a reservation. All the children were being taken away from the tribe and being sent to the boarding school at McIntosh," I continued, keeping my eyes on Elvis. "My mother demanded they wait for my father to return and refused to leave or let them take her children. She wrapped her arms around us and held onto me like a mother bear and her cubs." I stopped to let the memory of her flutter in my heart and then leave so I could continue.

"She squeezed me so hard that I couldn't breathe and I remember being scared. One of the men pulled me away and knocked my mother to the ground as he turned away from her. I remember looking up and seeing my father rush into the teepee to help her. The man carrying me outside put my head into his chest and as he walked towards his horse, I heard two loud bangs before I was handed to my older sister sitting in the back of a covered wagon. Later, my sister told me that my father and mother were shot by the men and they died." To fight the tears forming in my eyes, I pretended my heartbreak belong to someone else. "I remember being very scared and confused. I just wanted my mother. Then, when the wagon started to move, my big sister grabbed my hand, and we went back inside to get the baby from his bed and we ran into the trees to hide. We ran as fast as we could and for as long as our legs would keep moving," I said, remembering how brave my sister was that day. "I don't remember exactly where we went. We hid in a part of the forest where we were not allowed to play, so it was new and scary. As it got dark, the men found us and we ended up at McIntosh the next day. Stories people heard about the school were all true. The time I spent there taught me how to live *on the Land* and taught me nothing about what our people knew of how to live *with the Land*. I was taught to fear everything. I feared the animals we rely on for food; I feared the mushrooms and plants we ate for medicine, and I feared the language we spoke. The priests and nuns would beat us and tell us that if we didn't stop speaking the devil's language, we would end up going to hell for eternity. Instead of learning about the Land that connected all of us, I learned to fear and, at five years old, learned that evil existed in the world. It changed me and it changed all of us."

Still only focusing on Elvis, I continued with the most difficult part of the story. "I loved my big sister, and she was very good to me. She brought me food and brushed my hair the way my mother did. She talked to me in our language and told me stories about mother and father, the animals and the Creator. She made me happy and a little less scared," I said with tears welling as I continued. "During our first winter at the boarding school, the headmaster moved my big sister into his home to help his wife care for their son. One day, my sister told me she was running away. She was going to have a baby and needed to leave before anyone found out. I did not make it easy on her to leave. She said she could not take me and that she would come back for me. I remember crying and asking her to take me with her." I tried to shake the memory of her tears from my head so I could finish. "We were both so young when it happened. Now, looking back, I understand how terrified my sister must have been with the awful choice she had to make. If she hadn't run away, the Sherriff would not have come to the boarding school after they found her body, I would not have been rescued from McIntosh. I might have been one of the children buried underneath the church we are trying to protect."

Everyone in the Jackfish River tribe knew about the boarding school at McIntosh and every family in the tribe was touched by it. Most of the Elder's Circle attended the school and have memories that are theirs alone to share. Although several of them have documented their experiences with researchers that have visited the community, I have never shared mine. "I shared with everyone today to explain why I am here, and every one of you has a reason for being here. McIntosh is only one part of our story," I said to the attentive crowd. "Before we start the meeting, I would like the drummers to welcome everyone into the Roundhouse and bring you all into the meeting circle. I encourage everyone to take part in the welcoming and open your minds and hearts to what we will hear today," I finished and nodded at the Head Drummer to start.

The Head Drummer started by striking the centre of the drum and accompanied his rhythmic beat with a chant that invited the other drummers to join, one by one until all of them were contributing to the sound that vibrated the floorboards. The rhythm and melody of the drumming motivated the crowd to stand up as they were invited to join the meeting circle; first by age and then by clan until everyone was standing and shuffling to the heartbeat of the Roundhouse. The foundation of the building was wood constructed over the Land below with a large opening in the centre that allowed those speaking to touch Mother Earth when addressing the tribe. As I stepped onto the wooden floor of the Roundhouse, my feet could feel every stroke of the drum and the unified cadence of the community that vibrated the floor.

Satisfied everyone was welcomed into the Roundhouse, the Lead Drummer signalled to the other drummers to bring their beating tighter to his. With a series of calls and chants, the Lead Drummer increased the volume and speed of the drumming to draw everyone into the meeting and force out any thoughts or distractions from outside. The beat of the drum found its way inside everybody in the Roundhouse until everyone was moving and beating as one. It continued until the Lead Drummer signalled the end with a series of longer beats, eventually hit a crescendo of noise that left everyone breathless. In the silent moments that followed, Susan and Evelyn opened the meeting with a prayer, as other Elders and tribe members walked around with smudges.

After they finished, I smudged again with a bowl from Elvis, who winked at me and said, "Everyone is listening. We'll handle the hecklers; Mason and I have your back. Before you know it, we will be home and waiting for Bingo to start, nee-hee," he said in a stage whisper that most of the other Elders overheard. "The Chief isn't here but some of his supporters are standing by the entrance."

"Chief Trout and his council sent me to supervise the construction of the Jackfish River Road with Devlin Forest Products," I explained. "The road was important to the company because it accessed new harvesting areas. It was significant to the tribe because it provided year-round road access to our most northern settlement here at McIntosh. It meant a safer route to avoid travelling on the ice road and allowed us to rebuild the Roundhouse. While most of us viewed it as a positive development, others did not," I challenged and paused long enough for those with a differing viewpoint to interject. When no one did, I continued, "During the project, I met Ethan Travers and Gwendolyn Leavitt and invited them to the reservation. Most of you first met Gwendolyn here, in the Roundhouse, about two years ago. At that meeting, she told us about her connection to the Land and asked us to trust her by signing the agreement with Devlin to manage the forests in our Lands," I said and paused to look around the room. After finding some confused faces, I asked, "What does that mean? *Manage the forests?*" and answered my own questions. "I asked those same questions and Ethan took us to the Land to answer them," I recounted and smiled. "He agreed to take all of us, the entire Elders' Circle and whoever else wanted to come. Gwendolyn even brought lunch, and she finally got it right on the last trip and brought fried chicken, nee-hee," I said with a genuine laugh, remembering the sad submarine sandwiches she brought at the beginning.

While I have lost count of the number of meetings and ceremonies I attended in the Roundhouse, this was the first time I shared my connection to McIntosh with the tribe. Surprisingly, all my nervousness left me as I continued to speak uninterrupted. It was easy to speak because Ethan was a good storyteller and explained everything to me in a way that I could retell it to my people. When I recalled that day on the Land with Ethan, Gwendolyn and the Elder's Circle, I could hear his voice in my head, as if we were standing together that day on the shores of Bamaji Lake, close to where the Roundhouse stood. I did my best to tell an interesting and entertaining version of events to take the tribe back to that day. I started by recounting the sidebar conversation away from the rest of the Elders.

In the past, on the shore of Bamaji Lake in Northern Minnesota near the Jackfish River reservation…

"From the comments I have gathered so far, I understand the Elders dislike clearcutting," Ethan said as we stood next to each other looking at the calm water. Relocating to the Land was Ethan's attempt to overcome what he suggested were just language barriers, not impasses. We spent the morning driving and flying above harvesting operations and some of the Elders pointed to the sites, said *clearcut* and shook their heads in disagreement. The tour stopped at Bamaji Lake for a lunch break, and while Gwendolyn was serving food, Ethan and I discussed our thoughts. As the Chief's representative in negotiations with Devlin, it was my job to ensure everyone in the community understood what signing onto a partnership agreement meant.

"I want them to understand that Devlin can harvest the trees in a different way. We don't have to clearcut," Ethan explained. "There are different harvesting methods and I need to understand what is acceptable to the Elders. Can you help me explain this to them?" he asked and then stopped himself, "Wait." With a brief pause, Ethan said, "When we get back together as a group, ask me again about the clearcuts. To keep away from explaining anything to them, they can tell me how they want to cut trees."

Instead of continuing with the planned field tour, Ethan spent hours listening to the Elders' Circle tell stories about horse logging, how the community would set fires to renew blueberry fields that became overgrown and heard an account of a massive wildfire that burned as far as they could see in every direction. Their stories spoke of the human experience to big changes on the Land like fires, floods or storms that destroy all the surrounding trees. He didn't interrupt, he didn't ask any questions and let everyone speak until there was nothing left to say.

"I guess that's it, Ethan," I told him that day as I asked one last time for any final thoughts, for the tenth time. Elders can often be a quiet group but once we get going, we are difficult to stop.

"Thank you for everything you shared with me about your life experiences on the Land," Ethan replied with troubled emotions. "I don't expect you to believe me or trust anything I am saying. When I heard what the Indian Agents did to your tribe, setting fires to drive you from your homes, and the state flooding your land for hydroelectric developments, I don't expect any of you to trust a white man who visits your Land." Ethan stood up from his seat around the fire. "Your relationship to the Land is not something that I am going to claim to understand. Not yet, anyways," he finished with a slight emphasis on *any*.

"*Any*ways?" I asked him. "You have been spending too much time with us Nish, nee-hee," I laughed, which caused the entire crowd to join in the teasing. Ethan was familiar with our slang that meant Anishinaabe or the Good People.

With a good chuckle at his own expense, Ethan waited for the laughter to subside before he continued. "You have watched the Land change over generations and your oral history accurately explains old scars across the landscape without the data or maps that we use," Ethan recognized. "You should continue to manage the Land, so tell me how to do it," he said and waited for a response.

"What do you mean, Ethan?" I asked him when no one else offered an opinion.

"I understand you don't like clearcutting, right?" he asked and looked across the crowd to see most of us nodding. "We don't clearcut then. What's next?"

"We have been asking Devlin to stop clearcutting for decades. We have blockaded your roads for years. What makes you think the old man is going to agree to that?" asked Elvis, who started out as one of the more vocal naysayers in the community on the Devlin agreement. "He met with us once and cried poor at the thought of having to give up clearcutting."

"He will agree to it because I will tell him to agree to it," Ethan confirmed. "Before we head down that line of thinking, I have a couple of questions," he started. "What if there was a threat of a forest fire? Could we clearcut those trees to create a break in the wood feeding the fire? Or, if there was a bug that was spreading too fast, could we clearcut an area to slow it down?"

The Elders all started discussing the different scenarios Ethan raised, all with differing opinions and arguments. I was surprised Ethan posed the questions the way he did, losing control of the group to several smaller conversations. He left them to discuss the topics amongst themselves for a long while. They continued until one of the Elders noticed Ethan was just listening.

"It doesn't seem any of your examples have an easy *yes* or *no* answer. Everyone has something to say in each scenario and the outcome is different every time, depending on where this would happen. Sometimes the scenario doesn't change their minds at all," the Elder observed, "and it is always a *no* on clearcutting."

"That doesn't sit well with me. There are other things to consider before having a hard *no* on *all* clearcutting," another Elder offered. "I want the community protected from forest fires. If that means clearcutting trees around the community, I understand that."

"We can protect the trees. We can suppress the fires and protect the community without clearcutting our Land," a young woman from the tribe challenged. "We have been here for thousands of years. We don't have to explain to Devlin how to manage the Land, we should manage it for ourselves. The state licenses that were issued to Weyerhaeuser should be expropriated and given back to us, along with the private land around McIntosh."

A small group of Elders murmured in agreement with the young woman and looked back to Ethan to see how he would respond.

"I agree," Ethan conceded, surprising most of us around the fire. "But I can't get the old man to agree to that," he admitted and paused before continuing. "So, if I take that message back to him, nothing changes. Devlin continues to operate without consulting the Jackfish River tribe and you continue to watch others manage and use your Land. If you negotiate an agreement with Devlin, you will have a seat at the table and decide how we manage the forests on your Land."

"Can you write it that way? Can you recognize we are entering a partnership to manage the forests in *our* Land with equal say," I asked. "Can you write it in a way that we understand? Because if that is what the agreement says," I said and pointed to the papers beside my chair, "I don't understand it."

"Yes, that is where she comes in," Ethan said and pointed to Gwendolyn who was sitting on his left, down from Susan and Evelyn.

Returning to the Roundhouse at McIntosh on the Jackfish River reservation in the present day…

Leaving the rest of that day in the past, I continued with my remarks to the tribe, hoping everyone would take a moment to recall their experiences on the Land and why they attended today. "When Ethan and Gwendolyn returned to the community with the final agreement, it said everything they promised it would. Even his commitment to refer to the Land as *ours*," I pointed out. "The Elders' Circle unanimously endorsed the agreement and recommended that the tribe sign the agreement with Devlin Forest Products," I said and took a breath before continuing. "Even after Mr. Devlin refused to sign the agreement, Ethan kept his word. He somehow persuaded the Governor to transfer the state forest licenses to the tribe, a historic first for Minnesota," I said, letting the significance of it sink in.

"Afterwards, he and Gwendolyn joined forces with us and came to work directly for the tribe, and then everything changed. We learned the tribe signed a new agreement and the Governor transferred the forest licenses back to Weyerhaeuser," I said waiting for the questions and murmuring in the crowd to quiet down. "We went from being managers of the Land to nothing. No explanation for what happened to Ethan or Gwendolyn or why machines are parked at the end of the road into McIntosh. The Chief and his council have refused to meet with the Elders Circle and I believe they are hiding something from the tribe," I accused and tried to refocus my eyes on Elvis, who was not standing where he had been earlier.

A scan of the crowd revealed some commotion by the entrance with Mason and several other tribal members rushing towards Elvis who was leading the way. As I looked back to the entrance, I saw Chief Trout standing in the doorway with his arms folded in front of him. He was accompanied by several of his supporters in the tribe, who headed straight towards the head of the Roundhouse where I was standing with Susan and Evelyn. Elvis, Mason and their growing pack intervened to prevent the disruption. Unable to get across the Roundhouse, his supporters watched as Chief Trout stepped forward to address the crowd. "This is an unsanctioned meeting in the Roundhouse that did not obtain the required approval through a duly passed tribal council resolution. The meeting is over and I ask that everyone exit the Roundhouse immediately," he instructed in a stern and thundering voice.

Chief Trout sense hesitancy in the crowd to leave and continued in a lighter tone. "There is a lot of food left, so please take some and head to your homes. I also asked Roberta to hand out dividend cheques from casino proceeds a little early this month. She has a table set up beside the food. We will update you on the forest license at the next tribal council meeting," he finished and started ushering people out of the Roundhouse.

After we lost any chance of finishing the meeting, Elvis and Mason came back for instructions. "How do you want to handle this? I think he is going to stand at the door until you walk through," Elvis observed. "We can walk out with you."

With a look over to Chief Trout, I decided we would all make him admit to whatever he did. "No, Elvis. Mason, gather the Elders around the drum and bring some food and water," I instructed. "Elvis, we are going to have that meeting with the Chief and council, right now. He has enough councillors with him for quorum. He has no excuses left. Everyone is here. Tell him to gather his council and join us at the drum."

Confident we would finally get answers, I sat with the Elders waiting for Chief Trout to return with his council. Calmly deliberating our approach, it was decided Susan would lead the meeting. She would start the meeting in Ojibwe and make the Chief speak our language. "He is comfortable speaking English and will continue to lie to us. If we are speaking in our traditional language, maybe some truth will slip out, especially here in the Roundhouse," Susan decided.

Several anxious minutes passed before Elvis returned with only the Chief. "Gloria, Susan, Evelyn, would you join me for a moment? I would like to speak to you before I bring in my council," he demanded.

Looking at Susan and Evelyn, both agreed with a slight nod. As we walked away from the group, the Chief started in English, which he knew only I would understand. "I am not sure what your intended outcome for today was," he accused me through a clenched jaw, "but there is nothing in our election code that allows you to hold a tribal vote to remove me from office early," he stated knowingly. "I have four weeks left to serve before the new Chief is sworn in and I intend on serving every day of my term. Understood?" he asked with disdain. "I'll leave it up to you to translate it for the others," he finished and stormed off towards the entrance.

"So much for our meeting with Chief and council," I noted with frustration. "Did you two get enough of that?"

Susan nodded slowly and eventually said, "Sounds like we are at war," in her traditional language.

Evelyn agreed with a single qualifier, "Sounds like we are winning."

After rejoining the Elders, Elvis was the first to speak. "I didn't like the look of that exchange. What did he say?" he asked. "Are they going to meet?"

"No, the Chief was more concerned that we were trying to end his term early," I informed them. "We need to look for our own answers. Let's send

Mason back to Devlin's office and see if he can dig up any more information," I suggested. "The sawmill is still operating, so there must be a manager onsite or someone who knows what happened to Devlin's staff. More specifically, where is Gwendolyn? Someone must have a phone number or new mailing address."

"What about our contacts at the National Congress? Were they able to track down an address for Ethan?" Evelyn asked. "Did anyone get back to you, Mason?"

"I'm not too hopeful," Mason exhaled. "When I explained that Ethan Travers and Gwendolyn Leavitt were not Native American, the congress investigators weren't eager to spend resources on finding a couple of palefaces," Mason responded.

"Why would you tell them that?" Evelyn asked. "You only need to search for Ethan because *she* will be with him. And he *is* an Indian from the Wolf clan," she reminded him.

"Ah, Evelyn," Mason started. "You just told him that as a negotiating tactic. I overheard the Chief telling you what to say that day," he confessed. "Besides, we have no proof and the congress won't just accept he's Indian just because we say so."

Evelyn walked over to Mason and reached up to his face with both hands. Holding his face and pointing his eyes down towards her, she read his face "You are Mason Yellowhead of the Bear clan and you are a healer of the Jackfish River tribe. Ethan Travers is your brother from a far away tribe. He is a member of the Wolf clan and a fellow protector of our people," she finished and released her hold. "Just as sure as I am that you are Indian, I am sure Ethan is Indian, too. You tell the investigators that Evelyn Turtle says he is Indian."

Fearful of a scolding, Mason nodded. "If the investigators put their full resources on locating Ethan, we should have an address by the end of the week," he confirmed. "The congress has an experienced team. They have been tracking down Native American families that were separated at birth for years. They are very good."

"What are we going to do with an address, anyways?" one of the Elders asked. "Write a letter and hope they read it? Just wait while those machines chew up the ground underneath the church at McIntosh, and all the graves?"

"No, we have to send someone," offered another. "As soon as we know where to send them."

While listening to the others chatter, I swiftly backed away from the drum before someone looked at me to agree to travel to wherever Ethan had moved and ask him to come back. If I was being honest, I knew when we sent their information to the congress that I would eventually have to follow up on any lead. The Elders' Circle knew Ethan couldn't say *no* to me, but he couldn't with any of the Elders, especially the women.

Gwendolyn was the wild card and most assumed she controlled him. I knew the truth, and I was certain she would be with him wherever he was. Fixated on the entrance, my eyes found a new carving of a bald eagle perched above the doorway. It looked like a new carving or at least newly painted. Something about it was familiar and I couldn't remember where I saw it before. The colours were magnificently natural and shone in the sunlight peaking in through the roof of the Roundhouse. As I concentrated on the carving, Mason walked over to me and said, "You don't recognize your father's carving, do you?"

"The one from the old community hall?" I asked. From a closer look, I could see the fresh paint covering some of the scars the old carving endured while it presided over monthly tribal meetings, and bingo every Wednesday night.

"Chief Trout asked me to commission a new carving for the Roundhouse. He was very specific about what he wanted," he said and looked up at the carving, "and it needed to be an eagle. Your father rescued that carving before the old hall was torn down to construct the new tribal office," Mason informed me. "When he died, I put the carving into the storage room at the new office," he confessed. "So, when the Chief asked for a new carving, I knew the old eagle that watched over the tribe for decades would be perfect."

His artistry on display at the Roundhouse overwhelmed me with pride and longing. When my father was Chief, he had the courage to face his people and answer their questions, as opposed to scaring three old ladies into silence, or trying to, *anyways*. "It is beautiful, so majestic. You did a wonderful job restoring his work," I told Mason with a smile and squeezed his hand. "When did you hang it? Has it been blessed?"

"No, the Chief was very specific that he wanted the eagle carving hanging in advance of the last meeting with Ethan and Gwendolyn," Mason explained. "I only hung him minutes before Elvis said the prayer."

"That is strange," I said. Chief Trout was normally a very traditional leader that strictly observed our ways. "There must have been a reason he requested the carving. Did he say anything? Why didn't he ask the Elders' Circle to bless it?"

"When I asked for more time with the carving, the Chief said no," Mason said with confusion. "He told me it needed to be in place before your meeting with Ethan and Gwendolyn about the agreement with Devlin. Even when I asked him about blessing and dedicating the carving, he said we would have time for it later," he continued. "An eagle visited him during the ceremonial sweat with the new council and brought a message from Mother Earth."

I waited for a moment, expecting Mason to finish by telling me the message. Gesturing with my eyes to continue, he shook his head and said, "No, he didn't tell me the message." When he glanced up at his work, Mason said, "Maybe the Chief thought the eagle would preside over the meeting and repeat the message to your friends, nee-hee."

"Maybe, or maybe the Chief hoped the carving would command the respect of the eagle and provide a lost connection to the Spirit World and the Land," I countered with hope. "We need to decide for the Land, and we need to protect

McIntosh," I continued, certain of what we needed to do. "We need to find Ethan. It's the only way to negotiate with Weyerhaeuser, especially if the Chief will not help us."

"That is why you must bring him back," instructed Evelyn. "When the congress gets back to Mason with an address, you will bring him back. Wherever he is, you need to see him and explain what is happening," she continued in her traditional language. "He promised us. Even when Devlin didn't sign the agreement, Ethan found a way to take back the Land. He knows how to stop this and protect McIntosh," Evelyn insisted.

The Land at McIntosh was not part of the state forests and something else was needed to ensure the soil was left undisturbed. The old Indian boarding school site and the neighbouring forested areas were owned by the federal government and under the control of the Bureau of Indians. Ethan was working on a plan to purchase the land from the government but said it would take decades and the tribe needed to control what happened until then. He negotiated with the Bureau while Gwendolyn and I set up the Lands and Resources office on the reservation and hired the staff that would oversee the forest licenses. We left the details of signing the agreement and the protections for McIntosh with Ethan, and he always kept his word. If he said he was going to do something, it got done. We all trusted Ethan had succeeded, but we needed to persuade him to come back and set his plan in motion.

3 THE BRIDGE

"Can I get you something to drink, dear?"

The friendly stewardess repeated the same question, addressing everyone as dear as she made her way down the centre isle of the plane. A young brunette with a lovely smile, she eagerly went about her duties in the cabin. Alone in the small propeller aircraft, she handled the passengers with confidence and ease. When she reached my row, I could not help but smile. She was so friendly, and even though I was not thirsty, I politely responded, "Can I have a cup of tea?"

"Of course, anything in it, love?" she said without taking her eyes off the beverage cart.

"No, thank you," I said and lingered to catch her eyes for a moment.

When our eyes met, she could see I wanted to talk and obliged. "I'm Sadie," she said and pointed to her name tag. "Where are you headed today? Home? Or are you out adventuring?" she asked.

Her question sounded so silly. The thought I could be out on an adventure with the chaos around the tribe made me chuckle. "My name is Gloria and no adventures for me today. I am visiting friends," I answered. "They don't know I'm coming and I'm a little nervous."

"I am sure they will be happy to see you," she retorted automatically.

I didn't want to delve into why I was nervous about seeing them again. Gwendolyn's last message was so mysterious, and she sounded so hurt. I could only imagine how betrayed Ethan must feel. The spirits told me not enough time has passed but I am out of time and need their help, especially Ethan. "I am nervous because it has been a long time since we have spoken," I confessed, ignoring what was really bothering me.

Upon hearing about my nerves, Sadie made it her responsibility to ensure the rest of the flight was comfortable. Tending to the rest of the passengers first, she sat down with me for the rest of the flight. For the first few minutes, Sadie did all the talking and told me about where she lived and the man she was seeing, including her recent frustrations with him. I was enjoying the conversation when she turned the topic to me.

"Where do your friends live? Are they in Bangor?" she started.

"Oh, you must have other things you need to do," I offered, hoping to avoid the topic. "They are on Moose Island and I have an address, so I am hoping to hire someone at the airport to drive me there."

"The island is a beautiful spot and the ferry ride is so romantic. My boyfriend took me there last summer during whale watching season. I thought he was going to propose over a lobster dinner but that didn't happen," she lamented. "In the off season, everything is pretty much closed because the tourists aren't here until the whales are back. In fact, even the islanders leave this time of year for better temperatures. Are you sure your friends are home?" she asked.

Regardless of the congress' extensive network, it took a long time to track down where Ethan and Gwendolyn had relocated. Both of their cell phones did not work and neither of them answered their front doors. Eventually, the investigators were able to track down an address through contacts at the office in Bangor who found a local address with only a post office box. Ethan registered for a newsletter from the Passamaquoddy tribe in Maine, and the congress found a post office box that eventually provided a physical address. A tribe member on the Canadian side delivers packages to the American side of the island and snapped a picture of the delivery label for an Amazon package at 45 Deadman's Harbour Road on Moose Island under Gwendolyn's name.

"I hope they are," I responded. To end the questions about me, I asked one of my own. "Let's hear more about this boyfriend of yours," I enquired. "Do you want to marry him?"

"You hope they are home," she repeated. "Why don't you just call them? Feels like there is more to this story," the young woman suggested, not wanting to discuss her current relationship and where that was going.

I don't know why I answered her honestly. "I keep telling myself that I started my journey today because I need to ask my friends for help," I started and averted my eyes to the floor. "But I am not sure if I can call them my friends anymore," I said with embarrassment. Saying it in my own words out loud made it even more awful. "I am not sure if they will hear me out but I need to convince them to come back and help me fix things."

"It sounds like you are in a very difficult position," the stewardess said with compassion in her voice. "Have you thought about what you are going to say?"

Nodding affirmatively, "Every night, when I can't find sleep."

"It doesn't sound like it is going to be easy," she said and put her hand over mine. "But I bet getting on this tiny airplane will end up being the scariest part of your trip."

"It wasn't scary at all," I responded with a smile. "The planes we fly back home are even smaller. Besides, you distracted me for almost the entire flight."

With a knowing smile, Sadie stood up to resume her duties. "I forgot to mention, the ferry. Normally, cabbies don't like to go to the island and others aren't allowed because of insurance reasons. Stay on board until everyone else is off and I will call my friend's car service to take you there," she offered without staying long enough to hear *no*.

Within half an hour, Sadie was walking me from the airplane to the taxi line where she waved over a black Lincoln Town Car with tinted windows.

"Take my new friend here, Gloria, to 45 Deadman's Harbour Road. It's on the island. And take her straight there, Roland. No detours, I mean it," she warned him sternly. She leaned into the front seat and whispered, "Give her my flat rate deal too, Roland, and I will owe you," and with a wink, she spun around and headed back through the airport doors.

"To the island," Roland said as he turned off the meter and pulled the shift stick into drive. "I don't know how that woman gets me to do whatever she wants," he grumbled with obvious affection.

"I know someone like that too," I said. When I realized he was not looking for a response, I settled in for the journey to the island with my thoughts on Gwendolyn.

We drove away from the airport and soon had the city behind us. I opened the passenger side window and listened to the Land speak to me through the trees, water and birds as we passed. The Land reminded me she was still the same Mother Earth even though she looked different. While I was nervous, I felt excited as we lined up for the ferry. I was eager to get back on the water.

"How much does it cost to get on the boat?" I asked Roland.

"It's free, ma'am. The Canadian government operates the ferry. I forgot to ask you about a passport. Do you have one?" Roland asked nervously. "Oh wait, you don't need a passport because you're…," he struggled with finishing his sentence.

"Old?" I suggested and attempted to hide my smile.

"Well, yes, I mean, no! Age doesn't matter for a passport," Roland said awkwardly trying to make his point. "I mean, because you are Indian, or I guess it's Native American? You don't need a passport to cross, right?"

I could not help it any longer and released my old lady laugh. My nieces and nephews sometimes record me laughing and tell me I am trending on the internet. "Yes, Roland. I am Indian and I do not need a passport," I answered. "And, if you were a gentleman, you would have told me I was not an old lady. That would have been the polite response."

"Yes, of course, ma'am," Roland said with embarrassment.

"I am just kidding," I teased him. "It is our way of seeing whether you are a good person," I told him. "A good person can laugh at themselves and be open to kid back."

"When you say *our way*, you mean Indians," the driver asked as he looked for my eyes in the rearview mirror.

"No…old ladies!" and I laughed to let him know it was all good.

After a few more minutes of chatting and telling him how excited I was to see the ocean for the first time, we turned onto a smaller highway with fewer vehicles. It began to look more like home, except for a new smell in the air. While I have never seen the ocean, I lived my entire life on the water. We fished, we swam, we washed, and we gathered around the water every day. The water at home went on forever and I was excited to see how the ocean would compare. Roland pulled up his car to the landing and waited for the border guard to call us up, as the sign instructed.

"Roland, how are you doing today? Where are you headed?" the guard asked.

"45 Deadman's Harbour Road, Ricky" Roland answered. "I know most of the island but I don't know this address."

The guard shrugged it off and said, "Me neither. Lots of new people moving to Maine and the island since the downturn. Cheap land and old houses. We'll get to know them all, eventually. Who do you have with you, Roland?"

"Hello, I am Gloria Whitedeer," I answered and looked down at my feet. Conversations with men in uniform rarely offered anything positive. I learned the best approach was to look down and wait for the questions to end.

"Can I see your passports?" he requested.

"Jeez Ricky," Roland explained. "I didn't plan on heading to the island today. Can you just let me cross without it? I promised Sadie that I would take her to the right address and make sure she was safe. She asked me to take a picture as confirmation," he said as he rolled his eyes.

"Who are you going to see today, Gloria? Do you have any identification with you?"

"Just my status card," I told the guard without making eye contact. I gave Roland the card from the backseat so he could hand it to the guard. My hand trembling, Roland squeezed it before taking the card, "Don't worry. It'll be okay. This will just take a minute."

"I am going to see Gwendolyn Leavitt and Ethan Travers," I told the guard in the hopes it would allow us to board the boat. "They are my friends and I came here to ask for their help."

Upon seeing my distress, the border guard asked Roland, "Is anything wrong?"

"No, this nice lady is very far from home and would like to get to her friends' house. Isn't that right, Gloria?"

I nodded to avoid saying anything that could alter the mood of the situation.

"Alright then, carry on. Roland, you will need to check in on the American side when you go back in," the guard instructed as he lifted the old-style barricade to allow the car to pass. Roland nodded, passed back my card and navigated the car onto the ferry. As we drove by, I noticed the guard take his phone from his pocket and start tapping the screen.

The boat was small and rugged in appearance with only eight other cars on board. While I expected a bigger ship, the ocean surpassed anything I could have imagined. Before I arrived in Maine, I thought the water would be the same as the water at home. The lakes and rivers at home are plentiful and connected everyone and everything on the Land. Here, the ocean was something altogether different. The smell, the sound and the colour left me with no words to answer Roland's question.

"What do you think? You said you never saw the ocean before. Well, here it is," Roland said as he breathed the salt air deep into his lungs.

With a long pause, the words came to me, first in Ojibway and then in English. "It feels like home," I said, knowing Roland would not fully grasp the answer I offered. Even I was surprised by my answer. It was not the answer I heard in my head before speaking. A calm washed over me and it was easy to understand why Ethan choose this place as his fortress. While I was too old and experienced too much pain to be so naïve, for a moment, I felt the relief of knowing that everything was going to be alright. Twenty minutes later, we were leaving the ferry landing on Moose Island and driving towards Deadman's Harbour Road. Roland put the address into his vehicle and a computer-generated voice was guiding us away from the water. While I welcomed the distraction provided by the ocean and all its activity, I noticed Roland's eyes in the rearview mirror.

"Why do you keep looking in the mirror?" I asked Roland.

"Pardon, ma'am?" Roland replied, not taking his eyes off the reflection of the truck behind us in the rearview. As he reverted to an impersonal *ma'am*, I realized he was distracted.

"I think you should watch the road in front of us and not where we have been," I suggested as Roland met my eyes in the rearview mirror.

"There is a truck right behind us. It's kind of normal for people to chase each other off the ferry. Like it is a race to see who can get home first," Roland explained. "They aren't really chasing us though, just following really close."

As Roland shared his thoughts, which sounded like they were coming straight from his head, the navigation voice offered her direction, *in 100 metres, take the next right towards Deadman's Harbour Road.* "As soon as this vehicle gets close to Canada, the navigation system starts talking metric to me," Roland grumbled as he negotiated the turn, as did the white truck behind us. I soon realized my eyes were also focused behind us. "I think there is another truck following the white one," I said to Roland.

Agitated by the entourage, he picked up speed and approached the driveway marked with a blue and white 45 sign at the mouth. There were several warnings about trespassing and private property. I never really understood what that meant and I guess Roland didn't either because he turned in and drove towards the house. Apparently, the people in the vehicles behind us did not understand the signs either. We reached the house while I was still looking at the vehicles behind us. There were three trucks, all with at least two men. Big men. Big men with big arms.

"Are you sure your friends live here?" Roland asked without hiding his fear.

I turned in my seat to face the house and saw her. She was wearing the same outfit as when we met, work pants, boots, a big jacket and a ball cap. Her face misplaced her smile and the wild red hair I remembered was pulled back into a bun at the back of her hat that was barely able to hold her mane. She was accompanied by two dogs, one on either side. They did not look happy either. Still, when I saw her, I almost cried. I found them. She looked a little sharper and held a shotgun in her right hand. It was hanging at her side pointed towards the ground. While I was not concerned, Roland was getting very nervous because the men that followed us were standing outside of their trucks. They did not look so happy but their faces did not show any signs of frequent smiling, so I assumed it was their natural state.

Gwendolyn drew everyone's attention by chambering a round in her shotgun and then spoke. "Is someone going to explain what's going on? Jordan, what are you doing here? I heard the driveway alarm four times!"

"Well, we saw this blacked out Lincoln Town Car on the ferry and Ricky gave us a heads up you needed help. We figured there was trouble and followed them here," the young ferry captain answered.

"Well, that explains you and George. What about the Justason boys and old man Camick and his son-in-law? And who is driving the ferry?" Gwendolyn asked.

Not waiting for Jordan to finish his explanation, I opened my door to get out. Seeing me for the first time, the men that followed us altered their demeanour and walked over to help me from the vehicle. Roland, still frozen in his seat, stammered out an explanation but said nothing. Before I could say a word, the men had my bags out of the trunk and Roland hastily pulled out of the driveway and headed back to the captain-less ferry.

"Thanks, boys. You can all head home. I appreciate it and Ethan does too," Gwendolyn said to the men. "I'd invite you in but I now have a guest. Everyone, this is Elder Gloria…"

"Whitedeer," Jordan read from his phone. "Ricky gave me the details. He texted *Gloria Whitedeer is here for Ethan. Wife needs help*, I guess he can't spell your name" he said and looked up at Gwendolyn. The cell phone pinged in his hand and he looked down to read the screen. With a sigh, Jordan clarified by reading the text out loud, "*Gloria needs help, not the wife. Everything good. Little old lady. All good.*"

Gwendolyn set down her shotgun and walked over to me with her two dogs in tow. Firmly grasping Jordan by his shoulders, "Jordan, you did good. I am very glad you were ready for trouble, but does she look like trouble?" she asked and turned him to face me.

"Actually, I am terrified of my Nan, so yes, she could be trouble."

With an infectious cackle, Gwendolyn welcomed a smile back to her face and walked Jordan, along with his posse, back to their trucks. She talked with each of them and I watched as she comforted them with her genuine smile and warm touch. After I watched her put everyone at ease, I felt reassured in my decision to come. As she made her way over to me with her dogs, who were bouncing with playfulness, I was transported back in time, before the ugliness. I don't know if it was the way Gwendolyn handled all those men, or just her smile, but it reminded me of when Ethan described their first meeting, and his first scolding.

Ethan described the encounter more like a scene from a movie and I remember thinking how jealous I was hearing him talk about other woman that way. Even an old lady like me looked at Ethan with lusty eyes. Tall and dark with deep brown eyes, all I wanted to do was pinch his cheeks with both hands. His wide shoulders always looked like they were inviting me for a hug. He looked down at me with eyes that only showed kindness and compassion. Ethan patiently listened without rushing me when I hesitated to remember the correct word in Ojibwe and then in English.

Years ago, Ethan was sent by his boss to negotiate with my tribe to let his company build a road north towards McIntosh that would eventually cross the Jackfish River. Devlin Forest Products wanted to access the forest north of my tribe, and if the road increased access to the reservation, the company could apply to the state's infrastructure fund. For the first time, the northern parcel would be connected to the rest of the state by a permanent road and not have to wait until the winter to travel by ice road.

At the commencement of the Jackfish River bridge project, Ethan started the day he met Gwendolyn at the commencement of the Jackfish River bridge project with me. The bridge was the final piece of the project. To build trust with the Elders, Ethan invited the tribe to oversee construction, and I was selected as the tribal environmental monitor. The road was a life altering project for the tribe and I worked closely with Ethan to design the route. It was paramount to the community, and especially the Elders, that the road avoid our culturally sacred sites and prevent unapproved access to our sacred hunting grounds and fish netting areas. Ethan and I spent hours together traveling the route by boat in the summer and by ice road in the winter.

He was a wonderful storyteller, and I liked to listen to his adventures on the Land working for the old man. He talked about his office the way I would talk about my tribe and told stories about his staff the way I would talk about family. Whenever he spoke about the old man, he spoke with the respect of a son, not an employee. When I asked him questions about his own father, he always found his way back to talking about Mr. Devlin. Ethan and I travelled together to the worksite to watch the company blast away rock for the pilings under the bridge. I was with him when he took a call from the old man reminding him about a meeting later that afternoon.

A few years ago, at the construction site for the new Jackfish River Bridge before Ethan met Gwendolyn…

"Ethan here," he answered and then responded following a pause, "I will be there. The interview isn't until 3pm, right?" he asked and again stopped to listen. With a chuckle before answering the next question, he retorted, "I think I can handle the interview without a premeeting." Following another pause, Ethan turned away and said, "Yes, I read the file. All of it, yes, and I still don't think we need to meet before the interview." Just as Ethan finished talking, an enormous thundering crack shot across the sky and small rocks started falling off in the distance. "Shit," Ethan grumbled. "No, that wasn't dynamite. No, I am not at the work site. Talk to you this afternoon," Ethan stated and abruptly hung up the phone. With a turn towards me, Ethan explained his need to leave, "I need to head back if I am going to make a 3 o'clock meeting," he paused and looked down for a second before continuing, "a meeting I never intended on making."

"Sounds interesting," I said. "It must be someone important if the old man called about it," I offered. "I assume that is who you were lying to concerning your whereabouts."

"I wasn't lying, it is a company policy. The old man taught me never to admit my actual location. Keep the competition guessing," he smiled and winked before shaking my hand with both of his and walked back to his truck. Later that day, Ethan told me he returned to the office fashionably late at a quarter past three.

Later that afternoon in the Devlin Forest Products office in downtown Hibbing, Minnesota...

The secretary barely looked up in enough time to catch Ethan carefully skirting by her desk. "You, stop! Come this way," Gayle instructed. Quick to comply with stern instructions from a woman, Ethan stopped in his tracks and turned back into reception. Before he could explain that he was late, Gayle interjected, "You are late! And you're a mess. Take the back hallway to your office, get changed and get yourself to Leo's office. She is already here," she said in a hushed voice.

"What is with all the drama? We interview people here all the time," he quipped. "When I got promoted to vice president, I was kind of hoping it could be the end of my involvement with entry-level interviews," he complained sarcastically.

"Entry-level interview?" Gayle asked incredulously. "Did you read the file, Ethan?"

The look on his face confirming he had not, she sighed and continued, "Well, this should be fun," she chuckled. "Go ahead. The old man expected you to be there for the entire interview and they started fifteen minutes ago."

"They already started. On time? Exactly at three o'clock?" Ethan said with exasperation. "Only Ian starts an interview on time."

Ethan walked past Gayle's desk to the back hallway where he could get to his office without walking by the old man's door. Confident he reached his office undetected, Ethan opened his office door to find the old man sitting at his desk flipping through a file in his hands. Ethan walked to the closet to retrieve a clean shirt and pants before acknowledging his boss. "Leo and Ian can handle an interview until I get there," he informed him and draped the clothes over a chair at the meeting table in the back of the office. "The Jackfish River bridge project kicked off today. Jim should be done blasting today."

With a punitive headshake, the old man let his disappointment sink in before speaking. "I was very specific with my instructions," he started without making eye contact. Upon closing the file, he looked up at Ethan. "You were told to get the tribe to agree to the road and move on. Your days in the field are behind you," the old man reminded him. "I sent you there as the negotiator, not the road construction superintendent, and certainly not the cultural advisor. A long-term relationship with Jackfish River is not a priority for you today. Cement our relationship with the Governor!" he demanded. "He didn't exactly jump at your scheme to partner with Jackfish River to justify transferring the forest licenses to Devlin. Focus your attention on what is in front of you," he barked, continuing his scolding. "The company will not survive without controlling where the wood from those forests is delivered," he reminded his young protégé. "If you can't convince the Governor to fast track implementing the Supreme Court decision, he will renew Weyerhaeuser's licenses and they will keep redirecting the most economical wood to their mills. We will be forced to shut down *our* mills, one by one, until the company dies a slow death," he said with fists clenched. A self-made man, Ken Devlin built the company starting only with the family's farm in northern Minnesota, 75 miles north of Hibbing. "We need control of the forests. You have time for nothing else! Remember, time…"

"Kills deals," finished Ethan. "Yes Ken, I know."

"We are at war and you spent the better part of today, and probably this entire week, in the field blasting rock for a new bridge," the old man pointed out without raising his voice. "We need to confirm our leverage over the Governor!" he said with momentary excitement in his voice as he stood from the chair behind Ethan's desk. Collecting himself, the old man placed his hands on the desk and continued, "You keep reassuring me that everything is under control. Are there any details you can share with me that would ease my concerns? Because from my vantage point, we aren't exactly punching down," he observed and folded his arms in front of his chest.

"Every other forest company took a *wait and see* approach and let the Weyerhaeuser case force a decision from the highest court as opposed to accepting a role in consultation," he scoffed, "with Robert blindly in the lead." By observing the arrangement of the items on his desk, he could see the old man had read through every file and document. "Did you read anything that piqued your interest?" he asked. "The responses from the sawmill managers concerning the partnership with Jackfish River were particularly colourful. The strategy will work," he confirmed. "We need to play rope-a-dope with Robert just a little longer."

With a wave that dismissed both the explanation and cockiness, the old man continued unphased, "If Weyerhaeuser maintains control of the state forests, they will continue turning off the taps to our sawmills and every other independent sawmill in the state," the old man stated with certainty. "You need to make the Governor see what Minnesota's forest industry looks like, in the long term," he said, emphasizing his point with his finger on the desk, "under the management of monopolies answering to investment firms and hedge funds. All driven by greed, profits and short-term gain with no investment in the forests that feed our mills," the old man lamented as he sat back down. "We know the other sawmill owners and none of them have the balls to take a swipe at this beast the way we can," he said and reconsidered his words. "The way you can," the old man clarified by paying Ethan a rare compliment.

"Our end goal is front of mind," Ethan reassured him. "We aren't waiting for a state-controlled process or worse, something the feds design. Instead, we are taking on a tribe as a partner. The point being missed by everyone is that the justices unequivocally confirmed the duty to consult," he explained. "Every road, every bridge, even large harvesting areas all have to be reviewed with the tribes. And if a tribe pushes back or stages a protest, what will the government do, considering their track record with tough decisions?" he asked and continued before the old man could respond. "We can work with Jackfish River and use this decision to our advantage, by empowering them. If you want to grow Devlin Forest Products, you need to change your strategy with the tribes. Weyerhaeuser's strategy was to force the decision to the Supreme Court and have the state take lead on consultation. Before the Governor can assemble a task force, we will have our partnership in place and deliver a solution that also gives us control over our wood supply," he said with a certainty that overshadowed any possible counterargument.

"That sounds all fine and good," the old man interjected. "Even if your strategy is sound and you can convince the Governor, you started with the most militant and outspoken Indian tribe in Minnesota when it comes to development. They have blockaded the construction of the Jackfish River Road for over 20 years. While they wanted the access that came with the road, they didn't want Devlin crossing the Jackfish River."

"And the bridge is being installed as we speak," Ethan pointed out. "The tribe is dead centre in our wood basket and the reservation is wholly contained within the first forest license we are targeting with the partnership," he answered and sat back while he detailed the rest of his plan. "Tomorrow, the Governor will meet with his Attorney General to discuss the importance of recognizing the Supreme Court decision and point to the Devlin/Jackfish partnership as an example. The following day, he will meet with his campaign manager and there he will hear that the environmental vote is required to win back his seat," Ethan said confidently. "I have recently met with both these individuals. Both wonderful young women with minds open to influence and they will guide their boss down the Devlin path."

The old man shook his head and circled back to his earlier question. "What about our leverage? Is it in play?" he demanded.

Ethan stood back up to change and continued without acknowledging the question. "We need to go see Paul, together. Forget the in-house counsel. Paul can explain how significant the impacts of the Supreme Court decision will be on the sector, on any sector operating on government-controlled land. If we do this, Devlin can be poised to capitalize on not just forestry, but mining, oil and gas, transmission lines and highway construction. Our alliances with the tribe could put Devlin in the middle of every resource extraction project across the state," he countered while doing his best to hide his excitement. "Ken, they are debating the issue of free, prior and informed consent at the United Nations," he said with impatience. "The fact our industry wants to hide behind the government to avoid working with the tribes is embarrassing."

"We cannot trust the tribes, Ethan. They've screwed Devlin on every deal," the old man reminded his youngest vice president. "Before we arrived and violently forged this country, the Indian tribes spent thousands of years fighting each other for survival. Some tribes were peaceful, while other were brutal, especially when driven to war," he schooled Ethan. "A couple of hundred years later, we expect them to sit at a table with the industry and other tribes, and bury all that hate," the old man said with a headshake. "You convinced me to let you run with this, and I will continue to do so. Do not get distracted," he said, emphasizing every word. "It is critical that Devlin controls the wood that flows into our sawmills," the old man repeated. "If that means that you have to play whatever card you don't want to tell me you have, understand the future of the company, and your future, is in play."

"It is equally effective to convince the women around the Governor that the state forests are safer with us and the Indians; not in the hands of a bunch of hedge funds," Ethan challenged. "Let's give the Governor the opportunity to do the right thing," he suggested. "The next round of consolidations will introduce international competitors. We will be fighting corporations backed by foreign countries for sawlogs, while their governments covertly gain control over America's natural resources. We don't have a future in a world where all the Land is foreign controlled," he warned the old man. "If we air what we have on the Governor to win this battle," Ethan took a breath before continuing, "well, you can only destroy a man once."

"Companies do one of two things: they grow, or they shrink, and the latter leads to a slow death. I do want to grow," he countered Ethan. The old man understood that unwavering confidence was a requirement at Ethan's rank, he offered one last reminder to his heir apparent. "We are playing for keeps, son. Whoever makes this next shot, they take home all the marbles."

"Understood," Ethan conceded as he stood back up to change.

"Your days with the tribe are over," instructed the old man. "Send someone else to talk to the Indians. You need to be tied to the Governor's hip," he demanded.

Ethan met his eyes and dipped his head in affirmation. "Good," the old man said as he got up from Ethan's desk and handed him a file. "Flip through that one before you walk into Leo's office," he continued. As Ethan opened his mouth to answer, the old man held up his hand. "And don't tell me you read it. Because if you did, you would have been here this morning to prepare," the old man alleged.

"Why? Who are we interviewing?" Ethan asked. With the file opened in his hands, he scanned the paper for a name and did not hide his surprise as he read it aloud, "Gwendolyn Leavitt? What have we been talking about here? If anyone could threaten our plan, it's her. Why did you invite her to an interview?"

"For the exact reaction you just displayed," the old man said as he walked by his understudy. "Find me when it is over. We can debrief before the Governor's dinner. Just you, I won't need the others."

"Hold on, Robert's daughter? Lead counsel for Weyerhaeuser and likely the next CEO, if he gets his way," Ethan said with disdain. "Where are you going with this?" He heard what sounded like disrespect in his voice and softened the approach. "I understand you have a plan, Ken. Did you want to let me in on it?" he asked.

"I did," the old man answered with a smile, "this morning. You can wing it, as you say." Before heading towards the door, he said, "Remember what you have learned about her father and see how far the apple fell from the tree." As he stood in the doorway, the old man gave Ethan one last nugget of advice. "I have met this young lady, several times…with Robert. Do not make the same mistake as your colleagues and underestimate her." Lowering his voice slightly, he continued. "When you meet Gwendolyn for the first time, her eyes and smile cut through you and pull out the one thing you hide from everyone. That skill cannot be taught. Gifts that powerful must be earned and she earned hers through the pain of being Robert's daughter," the old man surmised. "It is that intriguing gift, camouflaged in only what she wants to show you that gives her power."

When Ethan was promoted from the field to vice president, he took over the annual negotiations for access to the Weyerhaeuser-controlled state forests. Ethan met with Robert Leavitt many times across the boardroom table and considered him an unworthy adversary. Most sessions were painful but necessary for Devlin to access the logs they needed to operate their sawmills. Ethan's strategy of partnering with our tribe to secure the forest licenses would remove the requirement of these negotiations. Ethan had not considered hiring Robert's daughter until the old man tabled the idea. "Well, her father is an asshole, so I guess I can start by telling her that," Ethan thought aloud to an empty office. Once his pants were buttoned and his belt adjusted, Ethan picked up the file and walked to the interview.

4 THE RAVEN

Leaving the humans in Minnesota, we join all the living things in the Land of Salt Water and Thick Trees…

The fierce arrival of the early Big Storm did not relent and any hope for an equally prompt departure was dismissed when the storm settled in over the Land of Salt Water and Thick Trees. Its roaring entrance was followed by a barrage of lightning and thunder, in rapid succession. The screeching winds and pelting rain continued long into the night, and eventually lulled all inhabitants of the Land into brief moments of exhausted sleep. Above the towering red spruce trees, menacing clouds blocked sunlight from reaching even the peaks of the Great Mountain in the Forest of Peace off in the distance.

Without daylight reaching the ground, it was difficult to survey the damage and delayed the search for the missing. In the fleeting brilliance of each bolt, destruction revealed itself in vivid images across the Siptuk Peninsula. Each burst showed the charred remnants of what was left standing of Olo's bole. The scorched remains of his crown that held the lookout was now resting on the shoreline below. Signs of damage across the peninsula and on the mainland could be observed in snapshots of jagged treetops and smoky billows marking lightning strikes.

The Big Storm did not grant quarter to many shelters and nests across the Land with damage visible to countless trees and throughout the dense understorey. Loss of life is expected in every Big Storm as the colossal power of the event renders it inevitable. It will be difficult for the Eagles to complete a tally of the damage and the missing until the storm subsides. Poor weather aside, Mako organized the Eagles into search and rescue teams to initiate early efforts to locate the missing. He strategically divided the Land into quadrants and gave the teams search grids. He dispatched the Eagles and held back one of the young captains he recognized from Tuwiye's commissioning ceremony to guard the command post. He delegated one additional and critical task.

"Before starting your sentry, retrieve the eggs left behind in my nest," Mako instructed, "and guard them here until I return. Nika will be beside herself with worry about those little ones. I will return them to her," he sighed. "No need for both of us to feel her wrath over having to wait all night for word. I am getting it one way or the other," Mako lamented as he sent the young captain on his mission.

Upon watching his son plunge into the water, Mako frantically searched for Tuwiye in the surging and crashing waves along the shore. The winds and erratic waves made flight a daunting challenge and made a water search a near impossibility. After abandoning his efforts, Mako flew up to the lookout and stayed with Olo. The distracted commander stayed with his friend long into the night until he stopped speaking, as he realized it took priority to accompany the Elder on his journey to the Spirit World. Unable to get word to Nika, he worried about her while comforting his dying friend. While she will be furious at first, Nika will agree that staying with Olo as he crossed to the other side was a higher priority. He was more concerned with her reaction when she received news of Tuwiye.

Nika understood her role as the mother of the next hereditary leader. An example for mothers and egg sitters, she offered her mentorship and guidance to others in the soar. She always maintained her composure, except when her fierce instinct to protect her children took over. When news of Tuwiye's status finally reaches the matriarch, she will need a moment to process the information before accepting support. Mako needed to get back to Nika and take her somewhere alone. He was torn between resuming the search for his son and getting back to tell the boy's mother. Not wanting to hurt Nika, he gambled and would concentrate on finding Tuwiye.

It will be easier to ask for her forgiveness for making her worry once he finds their son. Impatient to continue his search, Mako manufactured an imaginary lull in the storm to rationalize searching for Tuwiye over the open water. He took a moment to collect his thoughts and waited for the next burst of light to focus on the shoreline below and determine a starting point for the search. Mako held back the young Eagle that had arrived for his sentry duty moments earlier and enlisted his help in searching for Tuwiye. He turned to the timid bird and shouted, "Get ready, stay close and follow me down as I dive."

As he crouched down preparing to take flight, Mako heard a loud voice ask, "I understand you are willing to risk your own life over the open water, are you really prepared to risk the life of this young Eagle as well?" The origin of the voice eluded Mako, and he darted his eyes across the peninsula looking for the threat.

"Who is that? Olo? Is that you?" asked Mako as he waited for an explanation. Perhaps Olo had not crossed and was sent back to finish something in this world. The old Eagle took to the air and circled Olo's burnt trunk to get a closer look within the hollowed-out tree. He could see nothing in the stinging rain and deafening winds wreaking havoc on the peninsula. As

Mako strained to see in the darkness and chaos of the storm, he spotted movement deep within the tree and called out again, "Olo!"

"Olo? What? No, no! Just a moment," the voice said as loud tapping sounds erupted from the tree with a flash of red emerging from the newly punched hole. A vibrantly coloured pileated Woodpecker emerged from within the tree and continued to make the hole big enough for his entire body to squeeze through. Covered in splinters of char, the Woodpecker perched on a branch and shook vigorously, spraying Mako and the young Eagle with woodchips. The Woodpecker was a brilliantly coloured bird of adequate size that allowed him to maintain his composure while conversing with the Eagles.

"Where are you going in this storm? Most certainly flying to your death, and who does that help?" he challenged indignantly. Before Mako could offer an answer to the woodpecker, he continued, "Olo left me with some instructions for you, Mako," he said and looked straight at the older Eagle. "Olo has been our family's home for generations back to the beginning of our time here," the Woodpecker informed the Eagles.

The loud and erratic bird recounted the events from the previous evening and explained that Olo did not cross before Mako left. When the arc struck, the bolt hollowed a core within the revered tree almost to the base. The tunnel burrowed by the electrical power spared the Woodpecker's home and they were very grateful for Olo's protection. They explored the bole to ensure there was no one in need of help. In their journey, they stumbled into a cavity filled with pieces of very old birch bark. They were dry, brittle and required a gentle beak to handle. When moving them, the birds discovered strange symbols and pictures drawn on them.

As the Woodpeckers examined and discussed the symbols, Olo heard them and interjected, "Hello down there. Can you hear me?" he asked softly.

With strength drawn deep from within, he spoke slowly and clearly. He was unsure if he would have adequate time and energy to repeat his words. As Olo did his best to focus on the conversation, he realized the importance of the discovery. He may be able to pass down the messages to Mako and Tuwiye before crossing to the Spirit World. His life force dwindling, Olo needed to ensure the parchments were delivered to Mako.

"Hello, my old friend. I would ask how you are doing but we can see that you are suffering. How can we help?" asked the concerned Woodpecker.

"Do you see an Eagle on any of the birch bark pieces you found? Or maybe one with flames or a wolf?" asked the suffering giant. "There is a legend that was lost long ago and it is imperative that piece gets to Mako," said Olo as, his voice trailed off.

"We do not see any with the likeness of an Eagle or flames. There is a large, torn piece that has an image of a Raven, with mountain peaks above his head and the edge of another bird's wing reaching out to the mountains. It could be that of an Eagle," offered the Woodpecker. "It is the only piece of birch bark emboldened with the image of a bird," he informed Olo. The Woodpecker waited for a response that did not come.

"Those were the last words we heard from Olo," the Woodpecker said in conclusion. "We gathered all the scripted pieces of birch bark and sent them somewhere safe to be stored, as all of them have images we do not understand. Here is the piece that Olo wanted you to have right away," he said as the Woodpecker handed the large piece of birch bark to Mako.

"I hope you understand the significance of the symbols. Olo had more to tell us and passed into the Spirit World before he was able," explained the Woodpecker as he bowed his head out of respect for Olo. "Perhaps you could reach out to him in the Spirit World through the Fire Council on the first full moon following the summer solstice," he suggested. While not an expert on the ritual, the Woodpeckers were in the audience for several ceremonies where guidance was sought from the souls that crossed into the Spirit World.

"Thank you for that message, friend. Right now, I need to search for my son, Tuwiye. He was struck by lightning in the storm and fell along with Olo's crown down to the shore. I need to find him. You are right, I should not take this young Eagle with me," Mako conceded.

He turned to the young and confused Eagle and said, "Stay with the Woodpeckers and keep this piece of birch bark safe until the storm subsides. 'Olo knew I was protecting Tuwiye from a fate we didn't understand,' Mako thought as he handed the piece of torn birch bark to the young sentinel.

With his attention turned back to the Woodpecker, he spoke confidently to the smaller bird. "As soon as I find Tuwiye, we will decipher the clues you found."

"Stop, please," the Woodpecker said firmly and swiftly took off from his branch and landed right beside Mako, puffing up his chest to disguise his true size compared to the superior Eagle. "The storm has shown no sign of easing and your search efforts will be as futile as they were last night. Look at the symbols, perhaps there is a clue about this storm. There is no break in the clouds on the horizon and maybe there is something on this scroll that can help us," suggested the now calmer bird. "Olo mentioned the importance of this information to you and Tuwiye, as the Eagles protect all of us."

Mako was frustrated and growing increasingly impatient because the hereditary leader within him knew the Woodpecker was correct in his assessment and advice. He did his best to hide his true feelings, as leaders under pressure often do. The rational voice in his head clearly articulated his duty in that moment; to make good decisions for everyone in the Land. Fatherhood changed his priorities and challenged his ability to make decisions without pity or compassion for the outcome because it served the needs of many over the needs of few and the *few* was his only son.

"My new friend, you are right and someday in the future, I hope to repay you for your patience and persistence. You understand he is my only son. I need to find him. We also need to decipher what is on that parchment," Mako briefly hung his head in surrender and said, "I know somewhere we can all go to examine the symbols. It is not very far and it will be drier and much quieter."

He turned to the young Eagle, "What is your name, sentinel?" asked Mako.

"Nusopek, sir," answered the sentinel trying his best to hide the fear in his heart. The young Eagle was in a state of dread since the leader relieved him of his sentry and demanded he follow him on a search and rescue mission for Tuwiye. He was sure he would die tonight flying out over the vast water between the Land of Salt Water and Thick Trees and the Forest of Peace. 'I do not want to travel to the Spirit World while searching for Tuwiye,' thought the spiteful colleague. He trained with Tuwiye and was jealous when he was promoted to captain all because his father was the hereditary leader.

"You can stay here at the command post and make yourself useful," barked his commanding officer. Mako crouched down, took off in a swift springing motion with his legs and aggressively flapped his wings upwards. "Follow me," he shouted down to the Woodpecker as the two birds soared and undulated into the storm.

Once alone, the terrified sentry released all the air in his lungs in a blustery exhale. He contemplated how to describe the most terrifying night of his young life. 'Mako abandoned his search for Tuwiye to fly off and decipher an old, torn piece of birch bark with a Woodpecker. All because, before dying, Olo told them that Tuwiye was supposedly destined to save us,' thought Nusopek. The simple and envious Eagle grew angry and allowed the negative energy to control and guide his next decision. The prominent Olo was in the Spirit World and the wise Mako did not have a plan beyond finding his son. Nusopek felt everyone in the soar needed to know and the misguided sentinel left the command post and headed to the nests on the leeward side of the peninsula to spread fear and mistrust.

Across the water separating the Land of Salt Water and Thick Trees from the Forest of Peace, Tuwiye was awakened by a loud cawing sound. He opened his eyes to discover he was beached on a gentle sloping shore with the sunrise alive over the towering treetops. He did not recognize the trees and while trying to determine where he was, observed that he was encircled by an unkindness of Ravens. Surrounded by strangers and unfamiliar with his surroundings, he accepted whatever fate was in front of him and faced it with valor. He stood up, shook the debris and sand from his feathers and sought the Leader with a series of powerful whistling and piping calls. Surprised the young Eagle survived his epic swim, Kakik made his presence known to the castaway by dropping something to eat. Tuwiye recognized the food as a peace offering and bowed his head in thanks before ravenously eating what he thought was salmon. It turned out to be something entirely different, and he was shocked by the texture and taste. Not wanting to be rude, he furtively forced it down and thanked the Raven again.

"Thank you for the, uh, food," said Tuwiye. "Can I ask what that was?" inquired the castaway.

He took a moment to survey his surroundings with the hope he could determine where he woke up. The surrounding forest looked very different from the trees on the Siptuk Peninsula. Instead of needle trees, like the red spruce in the Land of Salt Water and Thick Trees, most of the trees here were leafy trees, like maple, birch and beech. Tuwiye knew these trees just in much smaller numbers. As he looked up behind him, he could see a magnificent mountain range in the distance that appeared much closer compared to the view he recalled from the lookout. There is still snow on the peaks with needle tree forests leading to the range. He must be somewhere in the Forest of Peace, in the valleys leading to the Great Mountain. He could not fathom how he travelled so far in one storm while unconscious.

The Raven smiled down at the young Eagle as he could see his mind racing to determine where he woke up. "That was moose meat my young friend," answered the time weathered bird. Tuwiye looked up at the Raven and noticed scars across his beak and body and the sprinkling of gray feathers in his otherwise jet-black coat. Kakik was not the leader of the unkindness, as Ravens are highly intelligent birds that work together and follow one another. Recognized as an Elder, Kakik was respected and honoured by the unkindness for his knowledge and experience across the Forest of Peace. His guidance is often sought when the younger Ravens encounter a difficult situation.

When they found Tuwiye, he was floating on the ocean propped up only by a large branch. Undecided if they should help, a scout was sent to find Kakik for guidance. He instructed the Ravens to pull the Eagle to shore and ensure he was guarded overnight.

"It is good to see you awake. How are you feeling? Are you hurt?" asked Kakik with concern in his voice.

"Thank you for your generosity. There is an awful pounding in my head and my wing is stiff but it isn't broken," said Tuwiye, as he moved his right wing back and forth and up and down to ensure he could fly. He turned his head to look behind his wing at his injury. "There is a charred, rounded wound above my shoulder but the bleeding has stopped. I must have been struck by a thunderbolt last night but I don't understand how I am still alive. Where am I? I must get back to the Land of Salt Water and Thick Trees," rambled Tuwiye.

As Tuwiye twisted his neck to examine his injury a second time, both wings left his body and exposed his abdomen with a large white patch in the shape of a flame that contrasted starkly against his chocolate brown feathers. Kakik discreetly took note and focused on answering Tuwiye's questions. Unsure of whether Tuwiye was aware of the symbol, he did not draw attention to it. The Elder of the unkindness recognized the symbol and could not place it in his mind. At the age Kakik had reached, his memory would not always allow him to retrieve images or information with the speed he was accustomed. He needed to get back to his nest and look through his archives for that symbol.

"You find yourself in the Forest of Peace and the foothills of the Great Mountain, so you are very far from your home. I know of the Land of Salt Water and Thick Trees and it is far across the great Peskotomuhkati Bay," answered the Raven. "The water is very dangerous, and in the Big Storm last night, you are lucky that our young Ravens found you," he said, turning his head awkwardly to recognize the Ravens that encircled Tuwiye. "If they had not, you would have surely drowned."

With a deeper understanding of the gravity of his situation, Tuwiye turned and tilted his head upwards to the old Raven and bowed to accept the debt in which he found himself. "I am so rude. Let me start again. My name is Tuwiye, son of Mako, the hereditary leader of the Siptuk soar of Eagles. I am in debt to you. I owe the entire unkindness for my life and I hope there is some way I can repay my debt."

Kakik smiled and hopped down off the maple tree branch on which he was perched. He gracefully floated down to the young Eagle on currents of the morning air and danced in and out of the sunlight as he ventured from the treetop. As Tuwiye watched the old Raven glide down to him, his black feathers took on sunlight and reflected a kaleidoscope of colours and patterns; something Tuwiye had not seen before. The young Eagle was surprised to see a multicoloured Raven and allowed his confusion to show.

The Raven landed softly on the ground nearby and strutted closer. He examined the young Eagle and mechanically cocked his head from side to side and awkwardly looked him up and down. "Did you see flashing colours when I was gliding down?" Kakik asked. The old Raven only knew the Eagles from the Forest of Peace to be able to see the hidden colours of their feathers. Confused and intrigued, Kakik trusted this Eagle as he pieced together the clues brought with him from the Land of Salt Water and Thick Trees.

"It looked as if you were wearing a coat made from the rainbow," babbled Tuwiye. "And I am not myself. It must be a lingering effect from the shock of the bolt," he offered. Tuwiye was uneasy and keen to get on the path towards home. "Can you point me in the direction towards home? I do not have my bearings and need to get back to help the soar."

"Of course," said Kakik. "I would like to show you something before you begin your journey back home," and Kakik took flight and encouraged Tuwiye to follow him. "It will not take long and obliging me this one request will see your debt paid in full," he said down to Tuwiye who was contemplating his next step.

The old Raven kept climbing up towards the sun until he was above the tops of the maple and beech trees along the shoreline. Tuwiye had little choice but to follow Kakik hoping he would shortly have him on his way home. He winced as he took off, as his head and wing still ached from his ordeal. Tuwiye was not sure if this old Raven was a charlatan or someone who could be trusted. The Raven was known as the joker or trickster across all the Lands and Tuwiye wondered if this was maybe a game.

While the shoreline looked familiar, off in the distance Tuwiye could see the foothills beyond the Forest of Peace leading to the Great Mountain that forged a green path upwards to its snow laced peaks. The sight of the mountains up close took Tuwiye's breath away, and he felt oddly small and insignificant. The feeling intimidated him and he pushed it down deep within to continue with what he hoped was his eventual journey home.

Kakik was true to his word, as moments later the two birds were landing on a massive and eerily intimidating yellow birch tree where Tuwiye waited with frustrated patience for what was next. While Kakik fully intended on sending the young Eagle on his way, what he found next would require Tuwiye to stay longer. He needed to learn the meaning of the symbol on his chest and understand why this Eagle was able to see the colours of the Raven.

"Cikia, this is Tuwiye, son of Mako, the hereditary leader of the Siptuk soar of Eagles. The Big Storm sent him to us from the Land of Salt Water and Thick Trees," he said to his wife as he motioned for Tuwiye to join them in the nest. The Eagle flew down into the nest and bowed to his hostess.

"It is a pleasure to meet you, ma'am," said Tuwiye. "I am sorry for the unexpected intrusion." He noticed Cikia was sitting on eggs while looking up at him. Upon noticing the symbol on his chest, she turned to Kakik and asked, "Is that why you brought him here?" With her beak, she gestured towards the flame on the impressive bird's chest.

"Do you recognize that symbol, too?" asked Kakik with excitement and hope in his voice. He hopped up and down waiting for her response. As his lifelong partner, Cikia was well acquainted with this dance of enthusiastic anticipation. She rolled her eyes and awkwardly looked him up and down.

"Are you about finished? Maybe then I could tell you what I remember about that symbol," calmly retorted the younger and fairer of the pair. Cikia only knew life with Kakik and was extremely loving and loyal to her reliable provider. Although lately his memory left something to be desired, Cikia had the patience of an angel with Kakik and his eccentricities, which were many. As his partner, she was often approached for advice before people would seek counsel with Kakik and she knew much of the information he kept hidden somewhere in his mind.

"Wait a minute, what symbol?" asked Tuwiye. He turned his head to look down each wing, turned his head around to look at his back and ended looking down at his chest. When he first saw the white flame, he brushed at his chest with his wing as if to wipe off the white dust that must have collected on his brown feathers. He looked closer at the symbol and realized the white colour continued beyond the end of the feather shaft and onto his skin.

As his eyes looked deeper into the flame emblazed on his chest, he felt a surge of heat pulsate through his body and images flashed before his eyes from a different time and place. A burst of convulsing energy accompanied each vision as it changed. It occurred so suddenly that he had difficulty processing all the images. He could only separate a few distinct images from the bombardment, which were a large fire, calm ocean lapping along the shoreline and what looked like a large black hole surrounded by mud.

Conscious of his odd behaviour, Kakik stopped hopping and asked, "Are you feeling okay, Tuwiye?" The Raven gawkily walked over to the young bird and put a wing on his shoulder. Tuwiye looked into the Elder's eyes and simply nodded. Unsure where to begin, the overwhelmed Eagle could not command any words to answer the question as he had too many of his own.

Cikia broke the silence and detailed what she remembered. "I remember seeing that symbol on an Eagle's chest drawn somewhere. There was a full moon and a flame above the Eagle and I also remember another animal in the image, and maybe a human." She closed her eyes to recall more information for Kakik, especially the location of the drawing. "I am so sorry but I am drawing a blank on where it is. Maybe the knot?" she suggested.

The knot was a large branch scar on the yellow birch tree below where Kakik built his nest. Once the branch fell off, the knot was hollowed out by woodpeckers into a large cavity in the bole of the tree. Kakik stored valuable artifacts inside, including many pieces of birch bark etched with stories. He could not remember the one Cikia described, but it was as good a place as any to start looking.

Kakik shuffled to the edge of the nest and hopped down to the knot to search through his treasures hoping to dig up an answer before sending Tuwiye on his way home. He was gone for only a moment before Tuwiye and Cikia heard, "Found it! I found it," shouted Kakik upwards to the nest. He reached down to expose the rest of the drawing only to discover that half of the image was missing, as the piece of birch bark was torn in half. "Oh no, the birch bark is damaged and only half of it is here," he lamented as he hopped back up to the nest. He placed the torn parchment down on the floor of the nest that showed only the silhouette of an Eagle with a flame branded on its chest.

"Well, we already have that part of the story. Where is the rest of it?" asked Cikia.

Something stirred deep within Kakik, drawing his thoughts away from the Forest of Peace and toward the Great Mountain. The birch bark laying on the floor of his nest contained a message intended to help everyone in the Forest of Peace. Tucked away in a forgotten hole, the stories were old and told countless times over a fire. They were replicas of drawings from a sacred place, made portable to transport them across the Land. It had been many years since Kakik or anyone from the Forest of Peace made the pilgrimage. Kakik would have no choice but to go back on his word to Tuwiye regarding a quick return home. If he wanted answers about the symbol on his chest, he would stay the night to accompany the old Raven on an excursion to find the Painted Cave.

5 THE INTERVIEW

Leaving all the living things in the Forest of Peace, we rejoin the humans back in northern Minnesota at the Devlin Forest Products head office continuing with the day Ethan met Gwendolyn...

Ethan made his way to Leo's office while flipping through the folder forced upon him by the old man. There was a resume with no covering letter, the normal diplomas and degrees and some work evaluations from Weyerhaeuser. Ethan was surprised to find the file's thickness came from pages of military service records, intelligence tests and psychological evaluations. He skimmed enough information to proceed and set the folder down on the table outside the office door. Combined with what he knew about Robert Leavitt, he was sticking with his original plan to wing it. I eventually learned 'winging it' was Ethan's only strategy. Even when we rehearsed for meetings, Ethan seemed to forget what he was supposed to say and took over the agenda but always in our favor.

Upon reaching the door, he looked down the hallway as he reached for the doorhandle. With no one in the corridor, he walked to the coffee room to find it empty with two full pots of coffee on the warmers. "Where is everybody? Is it Friday?" he thought. The room was almost never empty, as Devlin Forest Products operated 24 hours a day with caffeine a staple for survival within the organization. He usually wandered down to the coffee room around 3 o'clock to gather intelligence from the usual cast of characters hovering around the pot.

Before heading into the interview, Ethan called out to Gayle, "Can you bring me three bottles of water?"

"Well, there are four of you," Gayle countered, as she came around the corner, and dismissed her statement without looking at Ethan. "Three bottles of water, coming up." Gayle was new to Devlin and having a hard time acclimatizing to the level of testosterone and egotism in the company. In her first week, Gayle was reminded many times not to ask questions and simply follow directions. Ethan didn't appreciate how his colleagues treated the women at the company. He worshipped his mother and deeply missed her since she passed. I think Ethan was a little afraid of us old ladies, like his mother, because he did whatever we demanded and never complained. He reminded me of my son, the way he carried my bags and opened doors for me. I liked it.

Ethan retorted with a smile that was misplaced on the 6-foot, 4-inch titan. "I know. It is part of my strategy. If I told you all my secrets right now, how am I expected to impress you at the Christmas party?"

"Strategy, yeah right," Gayle jested. "Fifteen minutes ago, you thought this was an entry-level interview. Even *I* know who is in there."

Realizing she talked to Gwendolyn at reception, Ethan gently mined for anything she unintentionally gathered. "Did you talk to her?" Ethan asked, not wanting to overplay his hand.

Gayle shook her head and pursed her lips for a moment. "Not really. Just the usual reception chitchat. Except, she waited for me to finish with my phone call before walking up to the desk to introduce herself," she quipped. "The rest of you guys just barge in and make your demands. She seemed nervous," she offered. "As ridiculous as that may sound," Gayle said, emphasized with an eye roll.

"Why would that be ridiculous?" Ethan enquired. He expected her to be nervous. She was in enemy territory and alone, heading into an interview.

"Oh, I don't know," Gayle replied not expecting the question. "Her family, well, you know who her father is…I mean, it's not like she *needs* the job. What would she have to be worried about?"

With a knowing look, he left Gayle with her thoughts and opened the office door. Without knocking, Ethan walked into the in-progress interview and interrupted Gwendolyn giving what sounded like a sales pitch. She stopped speaking, looked up and waited for the late arrival to introduce himself. Before Ethan said anything, Gayle softly knocked and put three bottles of water on the table. After picking up one of the bottles and taking a seat next to the door, Ethan finally spoke. "Don't mind me, please continue. It sounded like you were making a presentation and here I thought I was walking into an interview," Ethan provoked.

"Actually, I was in the process of registering Devlin Forest Products as a Gold Member Sponsor of the research forest established by the university," Gwendolyn responded as she got up and walked over to Ethan. "My name is Gwendolyn Leavitt," she said and extended her hand. "I hope you can tell me why I am here because these two certainly weren't debriefed. Either that, or you are the one in charge and they couldn't start until you arrived."

Ethan accepted her hand with an overly firmer grip, a departure from his usual gentleness when greeting a woman. "Nice to meet you, Gwendolyn. Why don't you sit back down and we can start."

She met the pressure of his handshake and squeezed a little harder. "Aren't you going to introduce yourself? You know who I am, I would appreciate knowing who you are," the young forester demanded. Impatient and with arrogance that grated on every male nerve in the room, Gwendolyn continued, "Actually, if *you* are the one in charge, I would appreciate an explanation for why I am here, before we start. I did not apply for a job, nor was I looking for one; however, I was invited here," she insisted. "I accepted the meeting under the premise that Devlin reconsidered sponsoring the research forest."

"Well, Gwen, why do you think you are here?" Ethan baited. Passing control back to her to see what she would do with it, Ethan started throwing questions at her to see what would stick. Ethan told me he never needed a person's resume for an interview; it was too easy to lie on paper. Instead, he put candidates through a series of tests he fabricated on the spot to determine whether they were someone he could trust. I watched Ethan in many meetings. He could look at a person and determine whether they were lying. Even when the Governor reneged on our forest licenses, I am sure he knew it was coming. A quality that made people hate him, just as easy as like him.

"It is Gwendolyn, not Gwen," she shot back.

Already under her skin. Test one, check, Ethan thought. "Did you attend UMD? You mentioned the research forest," Ethan asked expressing little interest.

"You didn't read my resume either?" Gwendolyn questioned with irritation. "You arrive late and unprepared. Then, you don't introduce yourself and instruct Gayle to bring in three bottles of water when you know there are four of us," she paused and shook her head. "If we are done with the tests, can we talk about why I'm here?"

"I'll ask again. Why do you think you are here?" Ethan repeated. It was easy to get her to react, like winding up a spring-loaded toy. Ethan explained he found this tactic effective in most negotiations. It let his opponents expend all their ammunition on his questions, while he kept his powder dry for the meeting following the meeting. After interviewing Gwendolyn, he told me about her and how she impressed him when she scolded him. I saw it in early meetings with her too. She was quick to react and get defensive but learned to control her emotions, a little, during the time we spent together.

With a deep breath, Gwendolyn wound up and detailed her assessment of the situation. "Your colleagues, Leo and Ian, who have done their very best to keep me occupied until you arrived, already took us down the interview path, which we all know is laughable. Especially following my last experience in this office," Gwendolyn said with her eyes levelled on Ethan.

"Your last experience?" Ethan asked and glanced over at Ian, his senior and permanent junior in the company. Ian smiled smugly and tapped the folder on the table in front of him, which looked exactly like the folder the old man handed Ethan earlier.

Not wanting anyone to explain her early encounter, Gwendolyn answered, "I was invited to an interview shortly before I graduated and one of your VP's informed me I would never work for Devlin, nor would I work for any company doing business with the company, and so on and so forth,"

Gwendolyn detailed as she straightened up in her chair and shifted to its edge.

"But we are down the interview path, thanks to your colleague Ian, so let's talk that out," pausing only for air, Gwendolyn continued with her tirade. "Your company has a reputation for hiring only the best. Everyone enrolled in UMD's forestry program knows you interview the top ten graduating students every year and hire at least two. If I am here, you must need someone beyond the best and that would be me. I would be invaluable to this company, if you hired me," she paused before continuing to take a breath. "Since we all know that isn't happening, would you be interested in discussing the sponsorship? We are looking for corporate sponsors and donations to fund our annual symposium. Leo, you attended last year, remember?" Gwendolyn asked as she reached into her bag and pulled out a folder. "You gave a presentation on Devlin's silviculture investments and tree improvement program," she reminded him. "There is a brief prospectus of the research we are doing and a sponsorship form if you are interested."

"Hang on a second, Gwendolyn," Ethan sternly interjected. "Can I get a word in?" he asked. Accepting her lingering blink as an affirmative answer, Ethan explained, "I assume we are talking about Mike?" Ethan asked of Leo, his supervisor on paper, before continuing.

"Yes, Ethan," he confirmed. "Mike took it upon himself to bring her in when she graduated, shortly after the licensing negotiations that year. You remember, we couldn't agree on that block off Highway 642 and ended up in binding arbitration," he explained. "Mike blamed Robert for tricking the arbitrator…"

Before he could give up any more details, Ethan interjected. "That was Mike's style. Sharpening our knives on each other is part and parcel of working for Devlin. It was an atmosphere Mike took great pride in building and instigating," Ethan recalled. "Takes thick skin to work here."

When he told me about the interview, Ethan expressed sympathy for Gwendolyn. Putting himself in her shoes, he thought it must have been so hard to grow up having Robert Leavitt for a father. Ethan made room for the possibility that surviving her upbringing may have guaranteed her titan status, and a worthy ally. She seemed to handle herself where her colleagues often struggle. "Let's back this up and start over. My name is Ethan Travers and I am the Vice President of Planning, Mergers, Acquisitions and everything else that isn't nailed down," Ethan pointedly introduced himself and his ego.

Conscious of how far she overstepped in the interview, Gwendolyn accepted the offer to start over, "It is nice to meet you. Where do you want to start? It seems you know much more about me, especially about my family, which I hadn't realized. I am not sure what more I could tell you. That file is pretty thick," Gwendolyn observed, releasing a whiff of fear as her anger subsided.

"Agreed," Ethan said and stood up. "Let's pick this up down the street. Head down to the Fastlane and ask for my table," Ethan instructed. "I will be there as soon as I'm done."

"The Fastlane?" Gwendolyn asked and wrinkled her brow. "Isn't that a…"

"Peeler bar? No, that closed a few years ago. It's a sports bar now," Ethan answered. He failed to mention that it was all the same staff and customers from the previous establishment, which he also visited once or twice. He called it the perfect place to render straitlaced people just uncomfortable enough to let down their guard. Her hair pulled back into a loose bun and dressed in a grey pencil skirt paired with a white blouse, Gwendolyn tried to exude only business. At least that was Ethan's assumption given what little background he read.

"Okay, then. Will you be joining us?" she asked of Leo and Ian who had said very little once Ethan walked into the room. Having heard about the interview from both Ethan and Gwendolyn, separately, I still chuckle when I remember how they each described Leo and Ian. Ethan compared them to the two grumpy, old men sitting above the Muppet's stage heckling at everyone down below, Statler and Waldorf, I think. Gwendolyn said they were two talking heads without an iota of political acuity between the two. I liked Ethan's description better.

"No, they will not," Ethan answered for them. He would speak to Ian, again, about being a team player. Ian reported to Ethan and should have debriefed him about Robert's daughter being interviewed. While inconsequential to his career, Ethan worried about the effect of Ian's continued deceitfulness on the team. He decided that could wait and instead wanted to find the old man before heading to the bar.

"Thank you, gentlemen," said Gwendolyn and she walked over to shake each of their hands. "It was a pleasure meeting both of you," she said with sincerity and professionalism that surprised Ethan. "Regardless of my last name, the research forest needs the support of Devlin if it is going to be a success. I left the prospectus on the table, along with my card," she stated as she pointed to where she was sitting. "Oh wait, I don't have anyone's card," she realized, looking only at Ethan who was already making his way to the door.

"Ask Gayle for my card. She can give you the address of the Fastlane, too," he answered while still walking away.

"Oh, I know where it is," Gwendolyn informed them as she bent down to retrieve her bag and jacket. "I used to work there." Stopping in the doorway, Ethan turned and smiled at her. He looked at Leo and Ian who were also speechless, before guessing, "As a bouncer?" Looking up, she realized Ethan was enjoying the back and forth. She smiled and walked to where Ethan was standing in the doorway. "As a bartender," she said with a straight face. As she walked past him, drawing as little attention as possible, she paused for a moment to whisper, "Your zipper is down." She did things like that to save someone from being embarrassed. She did it for me too.

When Ethan brought her to McIntosh for the first time, it was August and the blueberries were ready. We were eating them before the meeting and Ethan found us to introduce Gwendolyn to the other Elders. Her smile made me smile and my teeth were purple with seeds stuck in between. Gwendolyn shook my hand, graciously chatted with me and as we headed towards the tent for the meeting, she leaned in close and whispered, "Gloria, you have blueberries in your teeth." She handed me a bottle of water and carried on drawing no attention. I liked her and I could always tell Ethan liked her too.

Ethan continued to watch as she walked down the hallway to reception, where the three men could hear her thank Gayle and converse with her a little longer than expected. Her chunky black heels clicking on the marble floor near the exit confirmed her departure. Ethan looked back into the office at Leo and Ian who both released the air in their lungs as if holding their breath.

"Is she gone?" asked another middle-aged man who stuck his head out of his office and into the hallway.

Before Ethan could answer, he heard other familiar voice from the coffee room that overlooked the parking lot shout, "Yeah, she's gone." The coffee room gradually filled up with the chatterboxes, ass kissers and complainers that Ethan usually mined for information. Today the topic of conversation was Robert Leavitt and his daughter, who very few could even name, let alone recognize. Certain there was little value to the information being exchanged, Ethan turned down the hall in search of the old man. On her way to the coffee room, Gayle said in passing, "He isn't in his office."

"He left his office but did he leave the property?" Ethan asked.

"I'm not sure. He got in his truck though," Gayle answered as she continued to the coffee room.

Retrieving his phone from the breast pocket of his shirt, he read the time aloud, "It's only 3:45. He is here somewhere." On the way back to his office, he noticed a line up of loaded trucks outside his window waiting to turn into the wood yard. As he followed the line of trucks, he found the old man's pickup parked squarely in front of the first one. "Well, I think I found him," Ethan muttered under his breath.

Headquarters for Devlin Forest Products was located on the same industrial site as the company's first sawmill. Originally opened in 1898, the old man purchased the shuttered mill that was closed decades earlier by the last lumber baron. While the original building was torn down to make way for a modernized facility, the front façade was preserved and integrated into the design of the office complex. Everyone who visited the office walked through the original bricks and mortar that stood for over a hundred years. Ethan told me he often looked up as he walked into the office every morning. It made him feel like he was a part of something truly significant, a purpose that overtook his own identity.

Outside in the wood yard, Ethan skillfully assessed the situation to determine whether his intervention was required. He could see the mill manager in a heated exchange with the truck driver causing the congestion. The old man was no where to be found. As the exchange escalated to a physical confrontation, Ethan inserted himself between the two.

"You, take a big step back," Ethan demanded of the driver. "Danny, what's going on? We're backing up traffic. Can we move these trucks off the street and deal with them in the yard?" Ethan suggested. By this time, the rest of the yard staff was walking over to the scene to support their boss.

"Get back to work! Stan, Al, turn around and get back into your machines. Now, I mean it," Danny shouted. "Normal problems, Ethan. Well, normal for Devlin. We've been having problems with Pierre's trucks," Danny explained by pointing at the driver. "Loads with too much balsam, the tops are too small and the wood is way too dry. It hits the saws and explodes. Shuts down the in-feed until we can clear it. Well, the old man came out and saw the latest load," the seasoned manager sighed. "He's walking the pile looking at the rest of the deliveries and the scales are closed until he is done."

Turning Danny away from the crowd, Ethan offered some relief. "Open the scales, get the trucks moving and we'll deal with the quality issues later," he said only to Danny. "There is a different way to handle this. You go back and explain to Pierre that I will meet with him next week to negotiate the final price. He can appeal to the old man if he is still unhappy."

"What about the old man? He just told me to shut them down," Danny said with hope in his voice that Ethan would deal with it.

"What about me?" the old man asked as he joined the conversation.

"Let Danny handle this for now," Ethan reassured the old man. "We'll deal with Pierre another day. We won't solve this by backing up traffic onto Lakeshore Drive and ticking off the neighbours," Ethan observed and signalled Danny to move the old man's truck.

As he looked over the rows of logs lined up to be fed into the mill, the old man spoke without looking at Ethan, "Well, that seemed to get everyone's attention."

"Yes, Ken. You have everyone's full and complete attention, including mine," Ethan conceded. "Especially Pierre's but we can talk about that later. Can we talk about your plan with this one? What do you want to happen with this girl?" he asked, knowing part of the answer.

"Do you know why Gwendolyn Leavitt did not follow in her father's footstep and attend Harvard?" asked the old man.

Frustrated at receiving an unrelated question in response to his, Ethan truthfully answered, "No, but I can tell you it wasn't because she couldn't get in. She is smart and quick on her feet."

With a knowing smile, the old man continued. "Correct. She was accepted by Harvard Law. Her father's alma mater," the old man stated and sighed. Everyone knew Robert Leavitt went to Harvard, he reminded everyone, somehow, in virtually every meeting. "Robert did not let her accept the offer. In fact, he had the admissions office send her a notice of rejection. She ended up accepting an offer from UMD, in forestry. Close to home and under his control."

Ethan attentively absorbed the conversation, hearing the old man express his hope to hire Robert's daughter to gain leverage over him. He hoped Robert would at least honor their agreements and, at a minimum, her engagement would keep him from sabotaging the negotiations Gwendolyn would eventually lead. Robert would stop at nothing to win and when Ethan was introduced to the negotiations, the scales were tipped too far in Devlin's favor. The old man had underestimated Robert's narcissism.

"You want her across the table from him?" Ethan asked, not looking forward to the answer. He liked the freedom of working alone or at least picking his own team. Given the calibre of the staff available at Devlin, Ethan planned on externally hiring someone to oversee the negotiations with our tribe. When Ethan told us he wouldn't be leading the discussions, I was nervous. When I saw an opportunity to speak with him alone, I requested Ethan hire a woman that reported directly to him. If Ethan wasn't always going to be available, I wanted to know whoever we were talking to was speaking to him.

"If you think she is up to the task, and that is up to you," he said without hesitation. "You met her. Can you control her? I won't ask you if she's capable, I know she is," the old man said confidently. "She wouldn't survive long in the Leavitt household otherwise."

"Capable, yes. Confident, able to defend herself, self aware? She's none of those things," Ethan offered as his initial assessment. "Being raised by Robert, I am not surprised. He would have only accepted perfection." He smiled at the idea of bringing Gwendolyn to a meeting. Continuing with his thoughts, *'The old guard won't see her coming and she'll do a tornado's worth of damage before they find her kryptonite.'* Ethan was confident he could capitalize on the chaos that would ensue and gambled on his ability to control her.

"What is so funny?" asked the old man.

With a firm grasp of what the old man had in mind, Ethan answered, "This is going to be fun, and wildly entertaining."

Satisfied Ethan was fully briefed, the old man offered one last instruction, "Make sure you explain the consequences to Miss Leavitt of joining Devlin Forest Products," the old man cautioned. Not needing to say anything more, the old man concluded with, "Let me know how it goes." As he walked away, he shouted back, "Remember, don't sell the farm but don't throw around nickels like manhole covers, either."

6 THE BAR

Continuing with the humans in Hibbing, Minnesota shortly after Ethan interviewed Gwendolyn…

Ethan arrived at the Fastlane within half an hour of Gwendolyn, who was playing pool with two servers. She was lining up her shot when Ethan opened the door, allowing the afternoon sunlight to explode into the darkened establishment. Upon his arrival, the bartender walked over with an uncapped Bud Light. "Figure you need this," the former dancer turned bartender said as she handed him the bottle. "Where did you meet Levey? Let me tell you, and remember it was me who told you," Sadie said as Gwendolyn joined them. "She is a wild cat and you better be careful or else you'll find yourself on the other end of that tail."

"Yeah, thanks Sadie," Gwendolyn cringed. "It's not what you think. I had an interview at his office this afternoon." Ethan enjoyed seeing Gwendolyn struggle as she deflected the romantic implication.

"Oh, right," Sadie said, sarcastically accepting the weak explanation. Whispering only to Ethan, she provided her regular with some unsolicited advice, "You watch that one. She'll have your job by the end of the month."

"Wouldn't that be interesting," Ethan replied loud enough for Gwendolyn to hear and took a lengthy drink from the beer in his hand.

"Wouldn't what be interesting?" Gwendolyn asked indignantly.

"Someone capable of doing my job," Ethan answered. "Sadie, can you order up some chicken wings? The usual times two. Another beer for me and whatever she's drinking."

"A refill on my water, Sadie. It's a little early for me and I am expected to report back on today's meeting," Gwendolyn confessed. "My boss didn't exactly prepare me for today. They want to know whether Devlin agreed to the sponsorship," she explained as she walked over to Ethan's table.

He pulled out her chair, then walked around the table to sit across from her.

"First, your boss wouldn't know where to begin on preparing you, and second, that depends. Do you want Devlin to sponsor the research forest?" Ethan asked as he raised his beer to drain the bottle.

"So, we're going to continue answering questions with questions," Gwendolyn concluded. "I had hoped a change in venue would render a change in your approach. Do you want to offer me any explanation for…whatever that was back there? Or am I expected to provide my thoughts first?"

To establish some initial trust, Ethan offered an olive branch. "It must have been difficult growing up with Robert for a father," Ethan conceded. "I didn't know my real dad growing up and my adoptive father, well," Ethan hesitated and stopped. "Let's just say the men who raised us are similar, so I like to think we are better off figuring out the world and our place in it for ourselves." Not wanting to confess much more over their first drink, Ethan started his pitch. "If you were to join Devlin, you'll find Ken has similar expectations and traits as your father."

"How well do you know Robert?" she asked, referring to her father by his first name. "I keep my distance from him and his work," she continued with her guard firmly in place. "After I failed to get into Harvard, conversations with him became unbearable with daily reminders of my shortcomings. I didn't want to hear any more about his work and tried to develop what I thought was a more typical father-daughter relationship."

"How did that work out?" Ethan asked knowingly.

"I imagine you know the answer," Gwendolyn offered. "You seem to keep up," she teased. "We don't speak often. I talk to my mom every day but he is never there when I call. He demands my presence at events when she can't attend, which is often. Actually, I am attending a political fundraiser with him tonight," she said, remembering where she needed to be later that day.

Firm in the belief that everything is connected, Ethan asked, "The Governor's election campaign fundraiser?"

With a slight nod, Gwendolyn swiftly surmised, "Yes, of course you would attend that as well."

Before Ethan could continued, Sadie set down his beer and napkins for the wings. "The wings won't be but another minute. Levey, are you sure I can't get you something to drink? The usual?" the bartender suggested.

"Sure, it might make this feel a little less like an interrogation," Gwendolyn conceded as she pointed back and forth between herself and Ethan.

"Whisky, neat. Coming up," Sadie stated and marched off back to the bar.

"That sounds good. I'll have one too but make them both Johnny Blue Label," Ethan called back at her.

"The good stuff? Are we celebrating something?" Gwendolyn asked.

To see how Gwendolyn handled the banter with a few drinks, he suggested the relocation to close the deal. Ethan explained to me several times that he rarely signed a deal in the boardroom that wasn't negotiated elsewhere, like the closest bar. He was eager to show the old man that he could handle her and that meant convincing Gwendolyn to join Devlin.

"I don't know, *Levey*. Hopefully we are celebrating you joining Devlin," Ethan offered, hoping she would share the backstory on her nickname.

Her eyes transformed into tiny slits as Gwendolyn searched for the right words. Sadie returned with two whiskies and two plates of wings and said, "Cheers you guys, enjoy."

Gwendolyn picked up her glass and took a sip to avoid speaking. After swallowing and sidestepping the question about her nickname, she stated, "I know Ken meets with Robert. They have been secretly meeting together for years. I don't think it's a secret but he wouldn't hide it from me if it was. He doesn't think I'm smart enough to follow his complicated business negotiations," she said with little emotion and laced with subtle sarcasm. Without taking a breath, Gwendolyn explained before Ethan could ask. "His daughter not being accepted into Harvard embarrassed Robert, me too. I wanted to go to Boston and never come back," she admitted and broke her stare. "Following my undergrad at Northwestern, I was lost. Eventually I ended up with an offer to forestry school at UMD," she said without elaborating on her decision. "Robert works for one of the largest forest companies in the country, so I didn't have many options for landing a job outside of Weyerhaeuser. Or anywhere else in the state after Devlin dismissed me."

As Ethan's gaze fixated on Gwendolyn, she continued to stare at her glass. "Even at the university, Robert controls the research I am doing through donations. He pulled me off my original project of investigating land rights and foreign influence in the North American forest sector." When Ethan did not engage, she tried again with more detail. "Foreign countries are incorporating American and Canadian entities to buy up publicly traded corporations with large private land holdings and mills with timber rights on state or federal lands." Certain she had his attention, she continued. "I thought maybe that's why Leo called because I cited Devlin as an example of an American-owned company with defendable land stewardship practices. But when I mentioned my work at the university, he dismissed it and carried on with his questions."

"How far did you get with your research?" Ethan asked. "Weyerhaeuser went public a few years back," he said. "It would be interesting to know who really controls the company now. Give me the elevator pitch on your paper," he requested.

"Elevator pitch?" Gwendolyn asked with a wrinkle brow.

"The Governor's office is on the fifth floor of the Minnesota State Capitol Building. The elevator usually takes between 45 and 60 seconds," Ethan detailed. "That is the time you have to pitch an idea to someone in politics," he explained. "It can't be any longer or they you risk the message being scrambled when the information is relayed to their boss."

"I need less than 45 seconds to answer your question," she shot right back. "The majority of Weyerhaeuser's stock is owned by BlackRock, the Vanguard Group and State Street Corporation, so basically, Weyerhaeuser is managed by a combination of investment companies and aggressive hedge funds. At least those companies are publicly traded, so you can influence Weyerhaeuser in the marketplace," Gwendolyn explained. "The foreign countries buying up North American mills and Land are depleting resources in a country halfway around the world with their own countries are a mess with pollution, corruption and chaos. They make it difficult to bore down into the actual ownership structure of the corporations they control," she pointed out. "I was tracking the ownership line of a company buying up mills in the Pacific Northwest when my research grant was pulled," she detailed. "The next week, the university sent me to work as an intern in the legal department at Weyerhaeuser, under the direct supervision of Robert, working on consultation requirements with Native American tribes."

Gwendolyn explained to me how difficult it was working as an intern at Weyerhaeuser under the control of her father and trusted Ethan with some details of her relationship with Robert. "I have very little in common with my father," Gwendolyn admitted to Ethan. "Since I was eight years old, I knew I was very different from my father, and I certainly do not mirror his ethics or values," Gwendolyn stated bluntly. "In my case, we are not cut from the same cloth and I want to work somewhere he has no influence." Gwendolyn hesitated before continuing. "Maybe somewhere I could continue my research and expose whatever connection Robert and Weyerhaeuser have to the foreign takeover of American Land and resources. When Leo called," she said and paused, "it all felt so convenient but seeing as you didn't know either…," she took a breath and turned inward. Looking beyond the other patrons, she looked towards the blacked-out windows while her mind wondered.

"Are you waiting for me to answer?" Ethan questioned. "Or do you have an alternate theory you want to share?" Maintaining her composure given the gravity of what she was sharing, her strength impressed him. Regardless, Ethan needed to find out how much she knew. "We have eminent threats to Devlin that need to be addressed, today. We can put on our capes and save the country next week," Ethan said mockingly. "The first lesson the old man will teach you is that time kills deals. What else would Devlin get out of hiring Gwendolyn Leavitt, who happens to be Robert's daughter?" Ethan asked, throwing down the gauntlet with a clock. "What do you know about the recent Supreme Court decision?"

Gwendolyn enthusiastically dove into the answer as if reading from a book. "It reaffirmed the government's duty to consult with Native American tribes on government-controlled Land, like the state forest licenses Weyerhaeuser holds and Devlin cuts under," she stated. "The decision is headed to the appellate court but it will be upheld. Eventually every state will have to develop policies for consultation," she said. "I haven't done the math but at least four Devlin sawmills are almost wholly dependent on logs from those state forests," she accurately calculated in her head. "Robert has always preached consultation is the government's responsibility," she continued aloud. "But I never understood why any company would want to leave such an influential relationship up to the government rather than aligning their interests. How could Devlin take advantage of that misplay? Maybe the work I am doing with the tribe?" Ethan was confused by her ramblings and waited for Gwendolyn to continue before interjecting his theory.

"No, that can't be it. You don't even know what I am working on," she said, dismissing the scenario as implausible. "The logs on those licenses are critical to Devlin's operations and having the state insert the local tribes jeopardizes the wood supply," Gwendolyn stopped and lowered her voice to a whisper. "Holy shit. You're going to steal them."

Impressed with her ability to connect the dots, he was a little frightened by the speed with which she did it. Ethan picked up a chicken wing and started eating to let her know she was in control of the conversation. She took a breath and kept working through the information in her head, "So, what's the plan? Devlin brings me to the table and you think Robert will play it straight? For my sake? Because screwing over Devlin would negatively impact me, my career?"

Later confessing to me the fear she felt that day, she said she found Ethan's eyes reassuring her to continue. Gwendolyn confirmed her desire to step out of her father's shadow by trusting Ethan with what she knew about Robert. "We can count on that not happening," she said as she tossed back the whiskey and placed the glass back down on the table. "Sadie," she said loud enough for the bartender to hear. "Two more, please."

Ethan followed suit and prepared for another. "You said 'we.' Does that mean you're considering the offer?"

"I wouldn't have come today if I hadn't considered it," Gwendolyn teased and picked up the glass Sadie dropped off. "Most of the exchange back there was for the benefit of your colleagues. When I figured out how little they knew, well, I took the conversation in a different direction," she confessed. "Besides, those two have already spun their own stories about me and what happened by now," Gwendolyn said and ate a chicken wing. Both sat silent for a moment before she admitted the ugliest part. "We both know my involvement won't control Robert," Gwendolyn confirmed without emotion. Not knowing Ethan well enough to share how she knew, she turned her sights on him. "I think it's your turn to share. What's your real motivation for offering me a job?" she asked.

Pleased with how she handled the exchange, he focused on closing the deal. He reveled in the thought of seeing Robert's face when she walked into the boardroom with the Devlin team and knew he had to make the offer today.

"You were right. Devlin is making a play for Weyerhaeuser's forest licenses and I am looking for someone to help me write an agreement," Ethan said while holding her stare, "more specifically, to write an agreement that no one has written before. It is not widely known that Devlin has been developing a relationship with one of the largest tribes in the state. We keep secrets at Devlin," he stated unapologetically. "That is how the company was able to grow and survive surrounded by giants, like Abitibi-Price, Weyerhaeuser, Domtar and Louisiana-Pacific, who all have long histories in the sector and much deeper pockets," he educated her. "We maintain an extensive network that feeds our team intelligence to guide directional shifts, where the giants stumble within their own hierarchies to react," Ethan finished. "You are going to spy for us. You are going to gather intel and bring it back with your theories. All your intel and all your theories," Ethan counselled her. "You know just enough to be dangerous and people will think you know more. You need to bring back everything so we can plug it into our network," he said as he further detailed the secret behind Devlin's success, "and protect you."

With a wrinkled brow at his final statement and choice of words, Gwendolyn countered, "Protect me? Protect my career or reputation?" she asked incredulously. "I don't have either. Robert makes sure no one takes me seriously, and those that choose to decide for themselves are punished," she stated with certainty. "Unless you mean physically, but then what are you talking about? Physical violence?" she asked without fear.

Ethan ate another chicken wing and cleaned his hands before picking up his unfinished beer and drained the bottle. "Why is it because we are dealing with trees and the Land that everyone thinks our industry is incapable of violence?" Ethan responded. "We buy and sell hundreds of millions of dollars worth of logs, lumber and residuals every year," he estimated. "The mob moves hundreds of millions of dollars worth of garbage and no one has a hard time accepting how Gambino dealt with his competition." Unable to elicit fear from her, Ethan continued. "The work you will do is covert and you will be safe at Devlin," he said. "It requires you to bring back everything you hear. Something that might seem irrelevant to you could be combined with something I know and," Ethan paused seeing she wanted to contribute.

"It may be the final piece of the puzzle that it makes little sense unless it is placed in the right spot," she concluded. "Network over net worth," Gwendolyn repeated. "I heard the old man say it to Robert as he was leaving the house once. I thought he was talking about data or computers," she admitted, a little overwhelmed and excited by the clandestine discussion. *'It feels like I have been training my whole life to work for this company,'* she would later tell me.

Sensing he had a deal, Ethan picked up his glass and said, "That calls for another shot. Sadie, another round please," he said towards the bartender who quickly obliged.

"Before we get too far ahead of ourselves, we should discuss the consequences of my employment with Devlin," Gwendolyn demanded. "We should also discuss timing. I need to wrap up one project with Jackfish River before I resign," she said and again surprised Ethan. "I have one more field trip to the reservation and a final session with the Elders' Circle to confirm some mapping. I don't think they would accept someone new at this point."

"Jackfish?" Ethan asked, frustrated at finding another puzzle piece the old man kept hidden. *'So much for the network,'* he thought. "You were using

Weyerhaeuser's donation to map Native American values on their forest licenses, while their position, which they took all the way to the Supreme Court, is that is not their responsibility. Explain to me how that works." Gwendolyn was connected to both Weyerhaeuser and the tribe Ethan had been meeting with for over a year, proving again that the old man was a shrewd schemer.

"Dr. Larsen and his team in the remote sensing department are doing the actual values mapping," she explained. "Technically, the approved project speaks only to collecting values information on the reservation alone, the federal Land," she confessed. "I expanded the scope of the project to include their entire traditional territory," she paused before finishing, "after Robert signed it," she admitted. "Now, I am sure you can appreciate the consequences of me accepting employment with Devlin." Ethan nodded, and she continued. "Neither Weyerhaeuser or UMD have copies of the tribal values data, just the standard forest inventory information and satellite imagery. The research team also collected geological information with some subsurface imaging," she continued. "Jackfish River has a copy of everything backed up on the server at the tribal office. I met with the Elders' Circle and created a naming system to hide the different values across the landscape. We even went up in a helicopter to collect data points instead of ground truthing by truck," she explained in detail. "We collected information on traditional foods and medicines in the area that fell within the state forest boundaries. The first version of the map is ready and I have a meeting with…"

Ethan interrupted her to finish, "Gloria Whitedeer. If you are talking about wild rice, blueberries and medicinal plants in the Jackfish River area, you are meeting with Gloria," Ethan concluded. *This one is just full of surprises,'* he thought while hiding a smirk.

"Yes, how did you know? Have you worked with Gloria?" Gwendolyn asked.

Ethan shot the replenished whisky glass in front of him and stood up. "We can discuss everything tomorrow morning at the office. You can meet with Human Resources and negotiate your salary and title," Ethan instructed as he pushed his chair in and made his way to the exit. "I am glad you understand the consequences of your employment, so negotiate accordingly." Side stepping the old man's instructions, Ethan would let Toby in Human Resources negotiate with Gwendolyn Leavitt. "Do you need any help with a non-compete clause in your employment agreement?"

She let out a snicker and said, "No, I technically work for the university, so they are only concerned with IP rights but possession is nine-tenths of the law," she responded by repeating Robert's favourite legal principle.

As he moved towards the door, he continued to enlighten his new understudy. "One fact about Devlin that we do not keep secret is our loyalty," Ethan said with pride. "When you represent Devlin, you have eleven sawmills and almost ten thousand employees in your corner. Everyone will have your back, and most of us are tougher than board nails and don't run from the train.

If you are loyal, you are protected."

"The position you are offering me, it doesn't exist right now, does it?" Gwendolyn asked. "Do I have a title? Does the position have a salary range?"

"Nope, it does not," Ethan answered. "And you won't be able to tell anyone about what you do. Good luck with Toby."

With little concern for negotiating her position and salary, she pressed Ethan. "You are fine with me continuing my values mapping with Gloria? What about the research paper I shelved? Can I pick that up too?"

Unable to hide his grin, "You must finish your values mapping. It will be what puts our proposal for the state forest licenses over the goal line," Ethan confirmed. "The Governor will have to table the same model for the other state forest licenses within the tribe's territory," he finished. "Leave your research paper until we have the agreement with Jackfish drafted," he said. "In the meantime, take what you've got on the paper to our investigators. They can do rest of the heavy lifting for you." Ethan could see that Gwendolyn was happy, which meant the discussion was over. Ethan stood up, observing another relevant lesson from the old man, '*know when the deal is done.*'

"What about the university? I need to give notice and train my replacement," Gwendolyn rambled while putting on her jacket and picking up her bag. As Ethan was not listening, she assumed those details were left with her. "Right, I will handle all of that. See you tonight then?" she asked before following him towards the exit.

"Tonight?" he questioned before he remembered the fundraiser. "Right, we will all be there and, if you are attending with Robert, we will all be seated at the same table. The Governor's office organizes tables by industry to keep the face time moving along to each paw shake and potential donation. So, you are often seated with your rivals," Ethan explained. "Even if we're not sitting together, it will be difficult to avoid one another," he conceded. "Tonight is not where I want your father to find out you're working for Devlin," he continued while thinking in his head, '*especially not the part where you are reporting to me but the old man is following his own playbook on this one.*'

"Understood," Gwendolyn said without hesitation. "Anything else?"

He noted the speed with which she agreed to lie to her father and filed it away for future exploration. While the ability to lie was helpful when employed by Devlin, the ability to lie to anyone, especially one's father, was a special skill that Ethan also possessed. Since they only just met, Ethan would wait for a more appropriate opportunity to mine into her relationship with Robert. He wondered if she knew her father intervened to sabotage her Harvard acceptance or if there was more to learn of her father's deception. Regardless, Ethan needed to be sure she was up to the task of working for him.

Heading out into the afternoon daylight, Gwendolyn squinted up at Ethan waiting for him to speak. As he made his way to his vehicle, he provided more details about the evening. "Tonight is a five thousand dollar a plate event that promises time with both the Governor and his Commissioner of Natural

Resources," he explained. "Everyone will be worried about capitalizing on the opportunity to speak with these two talking heads and focus on some law or policy that negatively affects our business," Ethan pointed out. "Few gunslingers are skilled enough to see the real opportunity is to gather intelligence and sacrifice a wounding shot tonight for a kill shot in the future. Tonight, you need to be convincing enough to deceive your father, while listening to everything and everyone around you, all at once and everywhere," Ethan instructed repeating the same words I said to him when I explained the importance of the Land and water to my tribe, although for a very different reason.

Gwendolyn dismissed the warning and retorted, "I have been attending these events with my father for years. Since I was a little girl, he would bring me onsite to harvesting operations and into the mills. On the way home, he would grill me for what I overheard and saw. I was a kid, and he expected names and flawless recall of conversations." With a knowing smile and confident stride, Gwendolyn walked towards the vehicle wrapped in the UMD crest. "I have been performing for my father for years," she flung back at Ethan over her shoulder, "tonight will be no different." Within seconds, she was on the road back to the campus to resign before getting ready for the evening.

7 THE MESSAGE

Leaving the humans in northern Minnesota, we join all the living things in the Forest of Peace…

Tuwiye struggled to understand the significance of everything that happened to him since speaking with his father ahead of the Big Storm. Olo knew something about a secret his father was keeping from him and he possibly died in the storm. Tuwiye remembered only short fragments of the night Olo was struck. Contemplating on what he did remember, he recalled a flash of light, energy sizzling in the air and a loud booming clap before being knocked out. The next thing he could remember coherently was waking up on the beach surrounded by his Raven rescuers.

Olo must have absorbed the energy of the bolt, otherwise Tuwiye surely would have died. While the strange sensation earlier in Kakik's nest, along with the barrage of images flashing behind his eyes all pointed to something more mystical behind the events of yesterday, Tuwiye focused on what he could understand. After the fact, he regretted not demanding answers from his father before leaving on the errand he tasked to him. The young Eagle had abandoned any hope of real sleep before their journey in the morning to the Painted Cave. In contrast to fighting his sleeplessness, Tuwiye focused on recalling the images that earlier flashed through his mind, while he looked for insight into what was happening.

Everything that transpired was out of a tale not unlike those told around the fire or while on sentry in the lookout. He remembered some of the stories Olo told him that were so incredible and far beyond logical explanation that Tuwiye wondered if all of them were true. Maybe all Olo's stories were true, even the ones about mythical heroes and harrowing tales.

He had little choice but to trust the old Raven and follow him to the Great Mountain at sunrise. If the Raven meant him harm, he could have inflicted it with little effort. On the surface, his intentions appeared to be altruistic and driven by a responsibility to pass along information vital to all inhabitants living in the Lands.

The Raven had given Tuwiye no reason to doubt him. Kakik was much older now, perhaps too old to undertake such a demanding journey. Unconcerned with his own safety, the old Raven did not hesitate to take the young Eagle on the journey to the Painted Cave.

"Are you awake?" said Cikia in a whisper from the darkness inside the nest. Tuwiye was perched on a sturdy branch just next to the nest where inside Kakik and the eggs remained asleep.

"Yes, I am sorry. Did I say some of what I was thinking aloud? I didn't mean to wake you," apologized the young Eagle.

"You didn't wake me. I haven't slept either. Likely for similar reasons why you are not sleeping," observed the wise Raven. "Come with me, please," she asked and swooped down towards the ground. Tuwiye obliged and followed without saying a word.

Both birds landed on the ground beneath the nest and stared out into the darkness in the direction of the Great Mountain that was hidden by the cloud covered night sky. After what felt like an eternity, Cikia turned to look at Tuwiye and broke the silence. "Our Elders taught us that what we are looking at is the Land of the Wabanaki, the land nearest the sunrise. You can see the sunrise even at this early hour. When you reach the Great Mountain, you will see the sunrise even earlier," she informed him.

"Sunrise?" asked Tuwiye, allowing his voice to raise slightly in surprise. Lowering his voice before continuing, he asked, "How long will we be gone?"

"The journey should only be a day, there and back but each adventure to the mountain seems to extend into an overnight trip that stresses the nerves of every partner left behind. Kakik knows the route, but he has not made the trek in quite some time," finding the right words, Cikia continued. "Before I start, I want to make sure this conversation stays between us. I do not want to embarrass Kakik," and she looked at Tuwiye for an answer.

"Of course, ma'am," he replied.

Cikia cocked her head to the right and then back to the left while giving Tuwiye an icy stare for using the word *ma'am*. Without correcting him, she continued with her request while softening the sternness of her stare. "You must promise me you will bring him back. He is older and will not survive the trip if you do not help him," implored the loyal partner.

"If this journey is too much for him, I will make sure he rests before we return. And I will not embarrass him," Tuwiye acknowledged and applied lessons learned in working with Elders from his soar, including his father. "I will make sure he gets back. I promise, ma'am," said Tuwiye.

"I promise, Cikia. Say it back to me. I promise, Cikia," the exposed Raven demanded, her voice breaking when she said her name for the second time.

Tuiwye did not know what to do or say. Her tears and vulnerability made him uncomfortable and questioned his impulse to console her. She did not shy away from his empathetic gaze and with her eyes, accepted the comfort. An immense feeling of compassion took control of his wings and he hugged Cikia while stroking the top of her head. "It will be okay," promised the young Eagle. While he was not sure, he knew she needed some comfort even if just from him.

"He is doing this because he feels it is his duty as an Elder and, for as long as I have known him, he always told me one day he would be asked to do something monumental," Cikia said and then looked out over the Great Mountain that was continuing to take shape with the rising sun. "I always respond the same way. I get close and force him to look at me so he would know I was serious and say, 'Kakik, you take care of me, our eggs and chicks every year, and you handle the entire unkindness. You are necessary, right here,' and it never seemed to be enough for him. I did not realize that all these years, he was right," she said with tears welling up in her voice. "You bring him back to me young Eagle," whispered Cikia.

The matriarch sprang from Tuwiye's embrace and back up to her nest before he could say anything else and before anyone saw their quiet exchange. The gravity of the situation weighed on his shoulders with questions tumbling through his mind adding to the load. Looking into Cikia's frightened eyes cemented the burden and forced him to feign certainty of a positive outcome. He was too young to truly understand what Cikia was afraid of losing, while mature enough to understand all he could do was reassure her that Kakik would come back.

The journey to the Painted Cave did not have the beginnings of a peaceful flight. With the weight of the mounting pressure, Tuwiye wanted to get home to see his mother and father again, along with all his friends and young Eagles he was training. He did not want to embark on a mysterious journey that would test him, especially when he did not feel prepared. He could not be sure he was ready for whatever challenges lay ahead. All his reservations aside, everything that happened since the storm pointed to a powerful yet misunderstood force in the universe pushing him.

"Good, you are awake," observed Kakik as the older Raven floated down from the nest and landed next to Tuwiye.

"I am," said Tuwiye. "Ready to go when you are," he retorted.

"Good, follow me and stay close. Our route travels through the neighbouring soar's territory and we are sure to encounter outpost sentinels," instructed Kakik. "It's best if they see me first so they don't perceive you as a threat." He looked over at Cikia and then turned his attention back to Tuwiye. "I don't care for long goodbyes, so let's be off," said the Raven as he swiftly took flight.

As the unlikely pair reached treetop level, Tuwiye heard an odd sound he could not place. "My understanding of Raven calls is quite extensive as an alliance with the local unkindness is helpful to any Eagle soar but I do not recognize that call. I am not even sure it is a Raven call but who else is awake?"

inquired Tuwiye.

"That is because the call is unique to Cikia and she only calls it for me," said Kakik and smiled as he pumped his wings harder and faster to reach higher into the expanse between the treetops and the clouds. Cikia and Kakik left many things unsaid in their relationship but 'I love you' was not one of them.

As he climbed, Kakik looked back at the Eagle and searched his youthful eyes, secretly hoping he knew something about the symbol on his chest. The old Raven convinced himself that Tuwiye was holding back and suppressing something that would help them along the journey. He had too because Kakik could no longer remember the way to the entrance of the Great Mountain. It was the last leg of the journey that concerned him most because there are so many caves carved into the Great Mountain that they could exhaust themselves looking and never find the right opening.

Kakik put his trust in a greater force intervening and setting them on the correct path and concentrated on the segment of the journey he did remember. Although now, he felt no urge to inform his travel companion of his orienteering issues. A few hours of uneventful flight passed and the two travelling companions exchanged life stories until their chatter was interrupted by the shrill of an Eagle high above them. Tuwiye searched the sky for a foe and spotted her high above them in attack-ready position. He repositioned tactfully between the presumed attacker and Kakik, waiting for the next move.

"Stop, Tuwiye," Kakik instructed. "We have officially crossed into her soar's territory and she is on sentry letting us know she sees us. She knows we are coming. I sent a reconnaissance party out ahead to clear as much of the path as I could…I mean, as much of the path as the young Ravens could remember." He was forced to lie to Tuwiye as the truth was, he could only send them as far ahead as he could remember, which ended here. "Thank you very much, as I now know you meant it when you promised Cikia you would bring me back," Kakik said sarcastically. "It was too bad you didn't add *alive* at the end of your promise," grinned the old Raven.

When both birds appeared to pose no threat, the Eagle sentry made her way down towards them. Elka was on roving sentry duty along the soar's outer limits. More of a lookout, Elka rarely engaged with birds crossing into the territory. She was stealth, extremely logical and rarely allowed intruders to see her. These intruders were different, as they carried with them an ancient symbol that unlocked a message hidden in the Great Mountain. Elka was eager to meet them and, regardless of her captain instructing her not to pester them with questions, she intended to do just that.

"Greetings and welcome to the territory of the Musquash soar. My name is Elka and my captain has instructed me to escort you safely through our territory, and not to pester you with too many questions," she jokingly confessed.

Tuwiye was surprised and a little dumbfounded at the sentry being female. There were obviously different roles in soars for the females and males. Young males served as sentries and young female were tasked with sitting on eggs until they were able to lay their own. In the brooding season, the females rule the division of labour and the males relieve them on command in the nest. Unsure of how to ask the question on his mind, Tuwiye ignored the impulse to ask why this young female was on sentry duty during brooding season.

As if reading the young male's mind, Elka offered an explanation. "If you are wondering why a young female is out on sentry, our young males have been dying year after year. There just isn't enough food to support everyone and the young males have suffered the most," she said with sadness. "There are no eggs for me to watch and I am not old enough for a partner, but I guarantee you I am a fully competent sentry," Elka informed them indignantly.

Tuwiye had yet to have any significant interaction with the females in his own soar, as he was not of the requisite age. While unsure how, he was quite certain he had angered her. He did not even pose the question that logically came to mind, and somehow she angrily offered an answer to the unasked question. Doing what most junior males do at times of insecurity with a female of their species, he feigned the inability to speak and looked over at Kakik in the hopes the senior male could smooth over the interaction. Tuwiye focused on flying, hoping Kakik would take over the conversation.

"No doubt entered our minds concerning your competence as a sentry. I have no doubts in your captain assigning you to guide us through your territory. And, regardless of his warning, please ask us all the questions you like," offered Kakik in the hopes it would reduce the tension between the two Eagles. "Why don't we hold up along the river below and take a rest? We could talk and go over our journey with you," suggested the tired Raven.

The unplanned break would let the old Raven rest his wings and get a drink while watching the young sentry manoeuvre and manipulate young Tuwiye. It was a long-awaited break with the benefit of entertainment. Kakik also wanted to understand what was happening to the Musquash soar, as he was unaware of their recent stresses.

"You picked a beautiful spot," Elka observed as all three birds landed on the shore. "It is an old fishing pool once filled with so many salmon that our hunters did not need to travel very far from our nests. But for many seasons, the spawners did not come back, and we saw fewer and fewer each year. So many of the rivers and fishing pools have changed that we are considering moving the soar," she confided. "The Elders were relieved to hear rumours of a pilgrimage to the Great Mountain. For as long as the Elders could remember, the soar has lived within the Musquash watershed and they feared the move. We are hoping for a message from the Great Mountain that will bring back the salmon," she said with optimism.

"What do you know of the Great Mountain?" asked Tuwiye. Eager to learn anything he could about the symbol on his chest, he hoped Elka would continue with more about what she knew of the story. If this young Eagle knew something about the symbol or the beliefs behind it, Tuwiye wanted to know.

"After learning of Kakik's journey, the Elders gathered the soar and told stories of past pilgrimages to the Great Mountain," Elka explained. "While the Painted Cave helped our ancestors and Mother Earth share stories across time with messages painted inside, the journey was challenging and many travellers did not survive," she continued. "After the last tragic expedition, the Fire Council was reluctant to commission another. Somewhere in the mountain are messages from the Spirit World and the flame on your chest is the key to finding it," the female Eagle detailed. "Some of what the Elders said was lost on me but my mother said she remembered the flame was a rare symbol used only by Mother Earth for messages significant to everyone across the Lands of the Wabanaki," finished Elka.

Kakik cringed as he realized just how crucial the knowledge trapped in his brain was to learn the details behind the message from the Spirit World. He felt the inevitable approach of the moment where he would have to confess to Tuwiye that he did not know the next milestone along the path. When he closed his eyes trying to remember the next landmark, he could see the cave opening that was obscured by a series of overlapping boulders. Frustrated by his mind failing him when it mattered most, he knew exactly where to go in the cave to find the images.

"My captain has released me from my sentry to accompany you to the edge of our territory. Can I please accompany you to the next landmark?" As Tuwiye shuffled on his feet searching for a reason to say no, Elka continued. "My Kokum was an Elder and represented our soar at the Fire Council."

"Your Kokum?" interrupted Tuwiye.

Elka paused to look at Tuwiye before continuing, "My grandmother. It is a traditional name for grandmother in our Elder language. She held an authoritative position in the soar and showed me as many sacred places in our territory as she could remember. Before she died, she took me to the entrance of the Great Mountain, without telling my parents, as only Elders were permitted. It is a difficult journey even for a young Eagle and many of the Elders stopped journeys to the Painted Cave," she told the two attentive birds.

She walked closer to the pair and lowered her voice. "There is no one in the soar that knows I have been to the mountain and, until today, I didn't realize its location was lost to our Elders," she confided.

Kakik could not believe what he was hearing and tried to hide his excitement. He completely stopped listening after she mentioned the entrance. 'If this young female can just get us to the next marker, I am sure I can find my way from there,' thought Kakik. As he turned his attention back to the exchange, he noticed Tuwiye's beak was moving. Before Kakik could happily accept her offer to accompany them, Tuwiye told Elka they did not need her assistance.

"Thank your captain for offering your help but it is a very difficult journey and we really don't need the help. Kakik has been to the Great Mountain many times."

Kakik hopped up and down positioning between the two Eagles. He could not hide his excitement and absolute need to be heard. Without wanting to admit he desperately needed help from the young female, Kakik explained why accepting her help would increase the likelihood for a positive outcome.

"I think we should invite her along. If Elka were to join us, we will avoid any confrontations in her territory and she could guide us along the fastest route. It would be the equivalent of having an escort through an unfamiliar land," cautioned Kakik.

"Unfamiliar land? I thought you said you have been to the cave before," questioned Tuwiye innocently.

The old Raven became defensive and overly embarrassed at the thought of having to admit that he could not remember the way. "It was so many years ago! How can I be expected to remember every twist and turn of the journey?" shot back the most senior of them.

Upon hearing his words, he wished he could manage his demeanor, as he held no anger toward the young Eagle. Much to the contrary, he was disappointed and humiliated he could not guide Tuwiye to his destiny. Whenever Cikia asked him something that evoked feelings of embarrassment, he made her suffer through the same outbursts and misdirected blame. She was wise and exercised patience when navigating Kakik's demeanour. Surprised by his reaction, Tuwiye searched for the proper response and exercised restraint. He realized he lacked both the experience and understanding to deescalate the emotions at play. Like most conversations with his father, Tuwiye first opted for silence and awaited the continuation of the tirade.

Then, Tuwiye went with surrender. "Whatever you think is best, Kakik. I was only concerned for Elka's safety," he said aloud. In his mind, Tuwiye confessed, 'And her natural ability to make me feel extremely uncomfortable.'

"It is settled. I am joining you on the journey to the Great Mountain," Elka said trying her best to hide her pleasure and maintain a professional decorum. "Are we ready to go? Do you need more food or water? I know a shortcut to the entrance and we can be there by midday," offered Elka as she prepared for the journey by stretching her wings and taking one last beak full of water.

Eager to get in the air, Tuwiye abruptly announced, "I am good to go. See you up there." He opened his wings wide and pumped them vigorously several times and ascended straight up into the sky.

Before joining him, Elka turned back to Kakik and said, "My Kokum told me about you. She respected you and even liked you, *for a pesky Raven*, she would say," laughed Elka. Kakik crouched down and hung his head. "You don't remember my Kokum, do you?" she asked. With enough respect for the old Raven not to force an answer, she continued. "That is okay. She would also say, 'becoming old is not for the weak, but weak is what we become,' and then tell me why it was vital for her to show me all the sacred places. She repeated herself often and I think that is something all Elders do, so we can hear their stories and lessons over and over, and commit them to memory," Elka shared.

Kakik valued Elka's willingness to share such a personal account with him, as well as the respect she showed him, which he felt he did not deserve. As Kakik contemplated the appropriate response, she leaned in and said, "When I heard where you sent the second reconnaissance team, I assumed the young Ravens did not know where they were going."

Kakik felt an uneasy feeling wash over him as she continued. "It is okay, I can get us to the entrance. Take over from there and lead us to the paintings. I was following my Kokum and mesmerized by all the drawings, so I didn't pay attention when she was explaining the different messages." As she finished, Elka pushed off from the shore of the Musquash River and set her sights on catching Tuwiye.

At a loss for a response, Kakik climbed into the sky and shouted, "Wait a second, from what you said, am I to assume there is no shortcut?"

Shaped by giant sheets of ice, the landscape below the birds was filled with rolling hills interrupted by large lakes and roaring rivers. Following the water system on the western portion of Elka's territory towards the next marker, they made their way along the path to the Great Mountain. Elka shared as much of the route as she could remember from the trip with her Kokum.

"We travel along the water to where the two mighty rivers meet and when we reach the headwaters, we climb as high as we can into the sky and head towards the tallest mountain we can see. We will know we are on the right path if we fly over water in the shape of a giant cloud," informed Elka.

After learning of the next marker, Kakik was flooded with memories of past pilgrimages to the Great Mountain. He instantly remembered the rest of the journey beyond the giant cloud lake. Not wanting to steal the young Eagle's thunder, Kakik kept silent on his recollection and felt a renewed sense of purpose and duty. As he plotted out the rest of the journey in his mind, he noticed Elka was flying in unison with Tuwiye while they conversed. 'He appears to have overcome his awkwardness with Elka. That was almost painful to watch but I remember my first encounter with Cikia,' thought Kakik and remembered the experience with the fondness of a much younger Raven.

A few hours later, the three birds found themselves at the base of the Great Mountain resting on several large boulders. Kakik was exhausted and knew he needed to press on. He had guided them through the final and more tricky twists and turns of the journey. They had to approach the entrance from the direction of the setting sun, unobstructed by cloud. Only at sunset is the entrance presented, as the rest of the day it is hidden by conveniently located stones and their shadows. Kakik looked across the horizon at the setting sun and knew they needed to head straight up the mountain before they lost the sunrays to unmask the entrance. The old Raven took as much time as possible to rest his wings and catch his breath.

Tuwiye looked at the weary guide and remembered what Cikia told him before they left. From experiences with his father, the perceptive young Eagle assumed Kakik would not accept his help without a little trickery. "There is still snow on the top of the mountain and I can hear the echo of falling rocks in the distance. We need to approach the rest of the journey with more caution. I think Elka and I should fly out front in a formation and have you tuck in behind us. We are flying into the territory of other predators and we should be out front. Kakik, your ability to decipher the message is too crucial to risk your safety," offered Tuwiye.

The old Raven was uplifted with relief and silently thanked his partner who outsmarted him yet again. He knew the draft created by his Eagle friends would carry his smaller frame up the mountain to the entrance. Kakik nodded towards Tuwiye and said, "I will follow your lead. There is a flat ridge just below the mountain peak that leads to the entrance. Hold up there and I can lead us inside," instructed the old yet rejuvenated Raven.

The two Eagles gracefully pushed off the boulders and generated speed as they approached the mountain. With as much momentum as possible, the two skilled fliers maneuvered their way above the last of the trees at the base of the mountain and started a near vertical climb. Kakik tucked in right behind their wings and felt as though he was being pulled along the ascent. As they climbed higher and higher, Kakik looked back at the setting sun and saw their timing was almost perfect. On the ground below them, the towering trees gradually thinned until there were only small trees and shrubs that changed into grasses and eventually was replaced by sand, gravel and the rock base of the mountain.

As they climbed even higher into the clouds, the winds churned around them and challenged the ascent. The Eagles tightened formation to withstand the wind and stay on course. Kakik was forced to pull up even closer to his two companions, which made it appear as though the three birds were flying as one. Tuwiye looked down and saw they reached the snow line near the peak. Shifting his eyes from left to right, he found the plateau Kakik described earlier.

With hope it was large enough to serve as a staging area, he motioned for Elka to follow him and the birds continued their flight formation to the ridge below. From hours spent talking along the way, Tuwiye was relaxed and feeling he understood Elka better. In a different place, he hoped to spend more time with her but he first needed to focus on the mission. As if rehearsed, the two Eagles landed simultaneously next to one another with a smile.

Kakik landed and was flooded with memories from his last journey to the sacred place. He found his legs shaky but not from weariness, rather from an overload of emotion and adrenalin. Memories of treacherous expeditions came rushing back to him and even part of the message behind the symbol flooded his memory. The complete image from the birchbark parchment flashed in his mind and he remembered the missing piece was a human attached to the wolf.

Spirits, Mother Earth and the Creator took the forms of humans and painted the stories on the walls within the Great Mountain through their own pilgrimages. It was a far safer journey for humans, as they could move the boulders that frequently fell to block the entrance. Kakik wondered if the humans were able to continue with expeditions to the Great Mountain or whether it was something that, like in his own unkindness, faded in importance over time.

The opportunity to reach the cave entrance was fading with the sunlight. Kakik walked over to the Eagles and said in a raised voice to be heard over the wind, "The cave is very close. I will lead us the rest of the way. The entrance is camouflaged when flying above it. This time, you both follow me," said Kakik with confidence.

Moments later, Kakik climbed the last few feet below the entrance and held up on a ledge to wait for the setting sun to reach the horizon. The old Raven scanned the mountain back and forth with his eyes, while his companions watched in silence. As the sun poured into the mountainside, Kakik began to worry. He was looking for a series of boulders that were placed by the Creator to obstruct the entrance to the cave. Just as he felt anxiety building, his eyes caught a shine off what looked like the cave entrance just above him. In the dying moments of the sunset, its last beams pulled back the shadows to illuminate the entrance.

In pursuing a closer look, he turned to Tuwiye and shouted, "Wait here, I think I see it but I want to make sure. I will signal you and Elka up once I find the entrance. Keep watching the rock face for an alternate entrance in the event I am wrong," instructed Kakik.

"I think it would be safer if we fly up together," suggested Tuwiye. An aggressive wind shrieked over the birds, bringing in angry clouds from off in the distance. The wind brought snow down from the peaks of the Great Mountain and filled the sky with a blizzard of its own creation. Conditions near the summit were deteriorating and Tuwiye knew once Kakik took flight, they would undoubtedly lose sight of him.

"That snow is becoming a problem and I want to make sure it is the entrance before we all fly up. You stay here and keep scanning the mountainside. We only have one chance to find the cave before the sun fully sets," argued Kakik.

Tuwiye watched as Kakik flew up through the swirling winds to what he thought was the entrance. The old Raven swiftly navigated his way along the wind gusts up to a large boulder he thought hid the entrance and lowered his head to power straight ahead. Inside the sacred cave, Kakik could hear the rushing sound of the waterfall deep within and could see the first few paintings on the walls.

As he walked into a different time and wanted to show respect to his Elders long since passed, he took a deep, cleansing breath to calm his spirit. Before finding the message deeper within the cavern, he went back to the entrance to wave in his companions.

Down below, the two anxious Eagles watched Kakik as he flew up to the entrance. "What is he doing?" asked Tuwiye. With growing concern for Kakik, he turned to face Elka and said, "He is flying straight for that rock." With fear in their hearts, the two Eagles watched the Raven aim for the boulder in front of him and fly right through it.

From their vantage point, it looked as though Kakik was flying straight into the large rock and instead of colliding, he disappeared into the boulder. Tuwiye and Elka looked at each other to confirm what they had witnessed and before either of them could speak, they could hear a faint voice in the wind.

"I found it! I am inside the mountain. Hurry! I want both of you to see it right away. Come up! Follow my path and when you get up here, you will see the entrance," called out Kakik into the wind.

The two obediently took flight and followed the Elder's path up to the peak. Up close, the setting sun illuminated a series of boulders that camouflaged the entrance with their shadows. Tuwiye heard a familiar sound but this time it was not in the distance. As Kakik waved his new friends into the cave, Tuwiye could see small rocks fall around him. The crashing and rumbling sounds grew louder and Elka was alerted to the danger as well.

"Quickly, get inside!" shouted Kakik, encouraging his companions to move with some urgency. Large rocks started falling around Kakik and crashing sounds echoed in the distance. Both Eagles hastened their flight while trying to gain the attention of the Raven to warn of his perilous location. Just as Kakik saw the Eagles were trying to warn him of something, he looked up to see a landslide of large boulders crashing towards him. Plunging into the cave for protection, Tuwiye and Elka were uncertain if Kakik was able to avoid the perilous landslide.

Determined to keep his promise, Tuwiye wasted no time in creating a plan to save Kakik. He motioned to Elka and shouted over the howling winds, "A cave of such significance must have a back entrance. We are so close to the top. Let's fly over and see if there is a way in from the other side."

Elka nodded in agreement and allowed Tuwiye to lead the way. Along with his new friend, Tuwiye thought he had also lost his chance to learn the truth behind the symbol on his chest under the pile of boulders at the entrance to the Painted Cave. Skillfully navigating the swirling winds, the Eagles powered up and over the peak in front of them and tucked into a screaming dive against the other side. Separately finding somewhere safe to perch, the determined pair scanned the mountainside for a back entrance. Tuwiye's quick thinking and willingness to act allowed them to get to the other side before the sun fully set. Elka squinted to see beyond the wall of snow pelting her beak when she noticed something sparkle in the darkness. Her eyes could not find it a second time and panic set in.

"Tuwiye, I think I saw it! There was something bright just above us," she shouted. "Look for a light. I think the sun is shining straight through the mountain. The opening must run the entire length of the peak. I lost it in the blizzard but I know I saw something shiny," explained Elka.

Not wanting to be wrong, Tuwiye lacked the confidence to say something earlier. "I knew it! I still see it. Stay here," he said while taking flight. "I will call you up once I am inside," he shouted down towards Elka.

With the dying moments of the sun still shining through the extensive tunnel in the mountain, Tuwiye landed inside and skillfully took stock of his surroundings. After a moment for his eyes to adjust, he listened for sounds beyond the howling winds outside. He could hear rushing water and concluded there must be a waterfall running somewhere in the mountain.

As he explored further inside, sounds from the waterfall grew louder and his eyes focused on the images painted along the cavern walls. The roar of the water was hypnotizing and focused his attention on the paintings surrounding him. Many of the paintings were familiar images and stories he remembered from childhood. There were images of Turtle Island and the Story of the Great Spirit and other legends he heard from Olo in the lookout. There were images of humans interwoven into the paintings, standing next to the wolf in each story. As he kept walking deeper into the cave, he came upon a very familiar image, part of it he had seen before.

"Were you ever going to come out and tell me you found the cave?" asked Elka, startling Tuwiye as he was embarrassed that he had forgotten her.

"I am so sorry. I was distracted by the paintings and the sound of the rushing water kept drawing me further into the cave," Tuwiye explained. With attention focused on the walls of the cave, he continued. "Each one looks more familiar until I saw this," he said and he pointed to the image in front of him, which at its centre had the flame that was emboldened on his chest.

Tuwiye hoped Elka would see his excitement and not be upset that he left her waiting outside, following his instructions. He continued, "We need to memorize the painting so we can explain it back to Kakik when we find him."

Tuwiye and Elka stared with amazement at the Eagle soaring above the fish filled water with Ravens and Woodpeckers scattered below, and a Wolf emmeshed with a human along the western edge of the image with large arms wrapped around everything. The only part of the image with colour was a red moon, while the rest of the image was done in black.

It did not take long for Tuwiye and Elka to memorize the drawing. Tuwiye was the first to speak. "Please take this message back and redraw it for my father in the Land of Salt Water and Thick Trees. As soon as you cross the Great Bay, ask anyone you encounter to speak with Mako. Tell them you have information about me and they will take you to him," Tuwiye instructed.

"Aren't you coming with me?" asked Elka. Aside from her uneasiness with leaving him alone, she also would have preferred to stay with Tuwiye. From the little time she spent with him, Elka grew to like the young Eagle and was concerned for his welfare. "I know what you are thinking, and you cannot go looking for Kakik alone. It is not safe, and it is not smart. I can stay and help you look for him," she offered.

"It's essential that my father delivers that painting to the Fire Council so they can interpret its meaning," he rebutted. Tuwiye could see she was going to argue, and he became frustrated. The proud male refused to admit he was scared and dreaded the thought of splitting up with her. Elka's intelligence and knowledge of the Great Mountain could help him find Kakik, but he knew the message was of greater importance compared to himself or the missing Raven.

"You need to go, right now!" he shouted at her. Shocked at hearing his father's voice coming from his beak, he stopped and hung his head in remorse. After a short pause and without looking at her, Tuwiye tried to explain. "I cannot face Cikia without at least an answer for what happened to Kakik. I refuse to go back and face her without him. If I must carry his body back, I will," said Tuwiye as he headed off deeper into the mountain. "Get going, please," he said over his wing. "I will come find you when I get Kakik home. I promise."

Elka watched as her new companion lumbered away, enveloped by the darkness clinging to the surrounding walls. She took one last look at the image in her mind and made her way to the exit. As she was retracing the moon and stars above the Eagle in her mind, she focused on the silhouette, and realized there were two birds, not one. She could see the weight burdening Tuwiye's conscience and did not want to add to it. Regardless, she knew what she needed to do and turned around back inside.

"Tuwiye! Please wait!" she shouted into the darkness of the cave.

"Elka?" Tuwiye said. "I told you to leave," he said with relief in his voice. The sight of the young female electrified him and gave his confidence a much-needed boost.

"No, Tuwiye. I did not leave. I am staying here with you. We will find Kakik together and all fly back to the Land of Salt Water and Thick Trees together."

8 THE FUNDRAISER

Leaving all the living things back in the Great Mountain, we join the humans in the present day on Moose Island off the coast of southeastern Maine…

The memory of Gwendolyn's voice describing her first encounter with Ethan echoed in my head and ripped me from the past back to her driveway on Moose Island. Her enthusiastic and excited voice didn't belong in the present moment. As the second truck pulled out of the driveway, Gwendolyn finished waving and turned her attention back to me. Escorted by her two Goldens, she walked towards and I took the opportunity to speak first. "Hello, Gwendolyn. It is so good to see you." Reaching down to pet the dogs, the bigger and darker of the two licked my hand and ran around me to push his head between my legs, forcing me to ride him like a horse! Almost tipping me over, Gwendolyn had to steady me so I didn't fall.

"Archie, no! Archie, stop it. Archie, sit!" Gwendolyn tried to heel Archie, and he was having nothing of it. While Gwendolyn tried to attach his leash, the other dog tugged it away from her and ran off. "Edith! Sit!" she demanded. "Bring that back, oh whatever, these dogs don't listen to me. Especially when we have company," she complained and helped me off Archie. "Hello Gloria, would you like to come inside?" she asked.

"Archie and Edith? Like that television show? I can't remember the name but I remember the lady's voice," I said with a chuckle.

"*All in the Family*," Gwendolyn said with a sigh that suggested she heard the question before. "Yes, I let Ethan name the dogs. Well, he named Archie and then convinced me to let him name the white one Edith."

We walked down a gravel path that led to the wraparound deck of a small, blue metal clad house. Built tall into the rock, the house looked as if it would withstand a hurricane with large posts supporting the deck and securing it to the ground. As I listened to my hollow footsteps on the cedar deck boards, I looked up and saw a rugged landscape of giant spruce and pine trees leading my eyes down to the ocean. It was a protected cove full of water and birds with fishing boats off in the distance. I could see Land just across from us with a big, open body of water and then more land beyond it.

"It's an archipelago called the Fundy Isles. We look straight across at the Pleasant Point reservation and next to that is Eastport," she informed me. By the look on my face, she could see my amazement at the sight of the ocean so close. "I had the same reaction when Ethan first showed me this property. We can sit out here," she pointed to chairs facing the ocean view. "I will put on the tea and be right back."

Now that I was here, staring at the ocean from her deck, I wasn't sure where to begin. When she came back outside, I started with something positive. "You handled all those men with such skill. It reminds me of Ethan talking about the first time you met him and how you handled the situation," I said. "He described your first encounter after you and I had met, so it was engaging to listen to him describe your skills. It showed me Ethan was a good person. He was able to take the scolding and see you beyond it."

"He was a good sport that day. I can hear my voice in that interview and I cringe," Gwendolyn confessed. Flushed with embarrassment, she continued. "The same way I just waltzed into your community with the idea you needed help to protect what was yours," she laughed before continuing. "I'm not sure I would be able to laugh at myself if it wasn't for meeting you, and Ethan."

Remembering the tea, Gwendolyn stood up and said, "Let's head inside. Later in the afternoon, it is chilly in the shade." She waited for me get inside before asking, "Two cream and a sweetener, right?" She took my smile as confirmation and continued, "It is chaga, so I am not sure if you would like to have something more traditional, maybe with a little maple syrup?" I nodded and she turned towards the stove to pour the tea. We sat down at the kitchen table and Gwendolyn continued as she handed me a mug.

"Although when I think about my interview, it wasn't so much a scolding but a schooling," she said through a smirk. "I'm not saying I didn't scold him occasionally, and inappropriately, but I saved the best ones for when we were alone. He handled it just as well," Gwendolyn recalled. "Actually, I scolded him later that night, at the fundraiser I attended with Rob-, my father..." she stopped. "I don't think you attended the dinner, but you and the Chief were invited," she recalled correctly. She averted her eyes for a moment, and I saw the pain on her face at the mention of Chief Trout.

Before that, telling stories over a cup of chaga felt familiar and effortless. I felt relaxed for the first time since leaving the reservation that morning. I'm not sure what made her stop, so I prompted her to continue, "Please, continue. I don't think you told me that story," I tried to remember.

"When it happened, I don't think I would have been able to share that experience with you," she admitted. "I was so embarrassed by everything that happened, including the scolding I gave Ethan in the parking lot afterwards. For some reason, Ethan took pity on me or," she paused and I interrupted.

"Fell in love with you, instantly on the spot, like the ending of a romantic movie," I said with a smile and raised my eyebrows.

A spontaneous laugh erupted from within that surprised even her. "That would all come later. It would have been a far easier journey compared to the one we took to get here," she said ruefully. "It's a miracle he was able to look beyond that night."

I settled into my chair and listened to Gwendolyn recount the rest of the day she first met Ethan Travers. As soon as she started talking, I could see she was transported back in time. Everything around her slipped away into the background, the oceans, her dogs and even me. Time melted away, and she was back in the ballroom of the Prince Arthur Hotel years ago. As if talking to herself, Gwendolyn took us back to the evening of the Governor's re-election campaign fundraiser.

In the past, in Grand Rapids, Minnesota shortly before the Governor's fundraiser…

It was a few hours after she parted ways with Ethan at the Fastlane. Given the formality of the event, she made an appointment at her girlfriend's salon to have her hair styled before driving to Grand Rapids. The entire appointment was really her excuse to see her girlfriend, the owner, and have a couple of drinks to vent before spending the evening at Robert's side. Once her long, red-dyed hair washed and dried, Gwendolyn changed into her outfit for the evening.

"How many of these does he expect you to attend?" Cheryl asked as she zipped up Gwendolyn's dress. Not expecting an answer, she continued her questions, "How is your mom? Is she feeling any better?"

Gwendolyn found the stylist's eyes in the mirror and shook her head. It was so hard to explain that her mother would never get better. Not if Robert kept her swimming in morphine and allowing her to ignore her doctors. "She has good weeks and bad. This week is bad, and she asked me to go in her place."

"I don't understand. Why can't he just go alone? He works with those people," Cheryl continued.

Holding back a smile, Gwendolyn wanted to tell her friend everything. She wanted to admit she was eager to go. These events were usually so boring with pointless conversations between politicians and lobbyists. Everyone lying to one another, while trying to advance their own interests. She found most agendas were personal with only a few selfless and strategic enough to affect any real change. Excited to see Ethan again, she hoped he was right about sitting at the same table. As Cheryl nattered on, Gwendolyn gave her a glimpse into the event and let down her guard by sharing her secret.

"I'm not really attending with Robert tonight," she started. As she registered confusion on her friend's face, she explained. "Well, I am going there with him but I'm also attending because of my new job," she confessed. "I was just hired by Devlin Forest Products."

"Oh! That's amazing. I didn't even know you applied," she exclaimed. "Let's have one more drink before you go, to celebrate."

"Cheryl, you can't tell anyone. Not even your husband, and especially not your parents. I want to tell Robert but not tonight. He isn't one for surprises," she reminded her.

"I don't understand. Why don't you want to tell Robert tonight?" Cheryl asked innocently. "He's your dad. He'll be excited for you and maybe want to brag about your accomplishment." Gwendolyn didn't talk about her family with anyone and never discussed her relationship with Robert. The Leavitt house was ruled by its skeletons and she understood the consequences of airing family secrets.

"It's complicated," Gwendolyn explained. Never speaking about Robert's work, she offered just enough to pacify her friend. "Devlin is a competitor, so I want to give him some time to accept me working for the enemy."

"Who am I going to tell? I just do hair all day," she joked. Taking a few steps back to look at Gwendolyn's ensemble, she commented, "You look amazing," she clicked her tongue against her teeth and concluded, "Whatever your reason for going, you are going to turn some heads."

"Are you sure? I have a black dress as well," Gwendolyn told her. "I'm not sure this look is me." She looked in the mirror, wearing a long, red dress with a tasteful neckline and second-guessed her choice. "The Governor is a democrat, so maybe I should have gone with blue."

"You look gorgeous in that dress," Cheryl retorted while shaking her head. "It defies party lines. Only necktie colour signifies party affiliation. Dresses are apolitical. Don't you dare change," her friend instructed as Gwendolyn gathered her things to leave. "Tell me all about it next month when I touch up your roots," she said and squeezed her friend's hand before cleaning her station.

With bolstered confidence, Gwendolyn left the salon and headed for the hotel to meet Robert. She followed Robert's instructions and arrived just as the symposium started. Unable to find him in the lobby, she proceeded to the entrance of the ballroom with her invitation. As she walked up to the registration table, she heard a familiar voice behind her. "Good evening, Miss Leavitt."

Turning her head towards the voice, Gwendolyn saw Ken Devlin walking across the hotel lobby towards her. It had been a few years since she last saw him but recognized him, nonetheless. Not a tall man, Gwendolyn towered over the old man in her heels and felt uncomfortably self-conscious. He was dressed in a classic tuxedo, complete with wingtips and a fedora. While the hat was his moniker, the tuxedo was a stark contrast to his usual attire for the field or a shift in one of his sawmills. Considered a recluse amongst other industry CEOs, few people would take notice of him in public or understand his wealth and influence.

"Mr. Devlin, it is a pleasure to see you tonight," Gwendolyn responded and held out her hand to shake his.

"It is a formal event, my dear," Mr. Devlin explained as he gently pulled her hand up to his mouth and kissed the top of it. "Gentlemen do not shake hands with ladies at a formal event," he corrected. "In the boardroom, it is a different story." Before she could form a response, she saw Ethan emerge from the ballroom.

"Come on, Ken. Young people don't do that anymore," he teased. "Look, you are making her uncomfortable."

"Isn't that the point?" the old man asked, almost under his breath.

"Hello again, Miss Leavitt. You look wonderful," Ethan said as he shook her hand that was still outstretched from earlier. "Shall we?" Ethan asked and motioned towards the ballroom entrance.

"Mr. Travers, nice to see you again." As Ethan led the way, Gwendolyn watched his swagger and looked him up and down. She realized she was staring and looked around the room to find other women doing the same. It was hard not to notice Ethan, even in a room full of other giants.

"Why don't we get a drink before we sit down?" Ethan suggested as he walked towards the bar. "Whisky, neat?" Ethan asked Gwendolyn who nodded in response. "Water for you, Ken?"

When Ethan turned back for a response, he saw the old man shaking hands with some guests who were arriving. "The old man is shaking hands with our in-house counsel, Patrick Dempsey and his wife," Ethan pointed towards the entrance. "I can never remember her name."

"Amanda, but I think she goes by Mandy. It was always Mr. and Mrs. Dempsey growing up, so I'm not sure what she prefers in professional settings," Gwendolyn offered. She noticed Ethan was somewhat perplexed and explained further. "They lived in my old neighbourhood and I went to high school with the eldest son."

Before Ethan could respond, a flamboyantly loud voice filled the ballroom. "Gwen, my dear! How are you? You look absolutely amazing!" the voice echoed. Looking up to see who was walking across the room towards them, Ethan saw a young man dressed sharply in a designer tuxedo complete with novelty socks that peeked out from beneath his pant legs with every step.

Before Ethan could react, Gwendolyn introduced her acquaintance, "This is the Governor's Chief of Staff, Jared Williams. He helps me organize the university fundraiser gala every year."

"Are you going to correct him? Tell him that is Gwendolyn, not Gwen?" Ethan asked only her.

"Jared, how are you? You look pretty sharp yourself," Gwendolyn complimented him as they briefly embraced and kissed each other on both cheeks. "Have you lost weight?" Gwendolyn asked knowingly.

"Oh, aren't you sweet? I wish," he sighed and batted at her softly with his right hand as his left hand wrapped around her shoulder and leaned in closer. "Tell me, who's your friend," he said in a conspiratorial whisper.

"Jared Williams, this is Ethan Travers. He is second in command at Devlin Forest Products," she ad-libbed.

"Hello Jared," Ethan offered his hand. "I'm Ken's VP, Mergers and Acquisitions. I'm surprised we haven't met sooner. You're with the Governor's office?"

"Nice to meet you, Ethan," Jared said accepting his hand. "Yes, I was just promoted to Michael's Chief of Staff about a year and a half ago, and fundraisers are my specialty," he said with the same energy as his greeting for Gwendolyn. With a more serious tone, "I leave Senior Policy Advisors to deal with their respective lobbyists. If you are with Devlin, you must talk with Eric. He deals directly with Michael on all state land issues."

To switch topics, Jared asked them, "How do you two know each other?"

"I met Mr. Travers earlier today, at his office," she explained. "I was pitching the importance of Devlin's sponsorship for the symposium," Gwendolyn answered plainly.

Jared chose to save his follow-up questions for later and prodded Ethan instead. "Given your persuasive powers, Mr. Travers undoubtedly offered you gold level sponsorship from Devlin," he said with a wink.

"Of course, Gwen can be very convincing," Ethan agreed and raised his brow towards Gwendolyn. "How could Devlin refuse? And the two of you?"

"Gwen and I dated back in the day, for like a New York minute," Jared revealed. "But I need more time and a few more drinks to tell that story," he said with a wink for Ethan. "Well, Gwen, I must work the room," Jared said while squeezing her arm. "People's cheque books won't jump out of pockets on their own. I am off to raise some money," he whispered in an octave above normal and strode away.

"Before you ask, yes, I know he is gay," Gwendolyn stated abruptly. "We grew up together and, as strange as it sounds today, being gay was socially unacceptable when we were in high school," Gwendolyn explained. With too much detail, Gwendolyn continued, "And I am a gay man magnet. Gay men are attracted to me as a safe friend," Gwendolyn said and wish she stopped a sentence earlier.

"For the record, I did not ask a single question," Ethan pointed out as he passed her a whisky and walked by her towards their table.

Sheepishly following, Ethan led Gwendolyn to the table at the front of the room across from the podium and head table for the dignitaries that would be in attendance. The entire ballroom was filled with roundtables of eight to ten people with uniformed hotel staff rushing back and forth between them. He pulled out her chair, which was to the right of his, and motioned for Gwendolyn to sit down. Robert had instructed her to come early and wait for him in the lobby, so she nervously scanned the room to see if he had arrived early as well.

"He isn't here yet," Ethan said as he pushed her chair closer to the table. Gwendolyn looked at the name on the seat to her right to find that Mr. Devlin was seated beside her.

"Well, he won't be able to miss me seated right between you and Mr. Devlin," she shot back at him. "Why did you change these? There is no way

Jared's staff would have seated me between you two."

"Not in that dress, no one will be able to miss you," Ethan observed, sidestepping her questions.

To brush off the compliment, Gwendolyn asked, "What happened to your strategy? I thought I would have time to tell Robert alone."

"Tell him what? That you are working for us?" the old man asked. "I told him, earlier. I phoned him from the car on the drive over," he informed her flippantly as he took his seat. "It was a short call," he stated and took a sip of water, "that he ended."

"Of course," Gwendolyn muttered. "I'm going to step out into the lobby," she said as she stood up from the table. "I would like to tell my father about my employment at Devlin before he sees me sitting here."

"Are you here working for us tonight, Miss Leavitt?" the old man asked.

"Technically, no. But I doubt that matters to you, sir," Gwendolyn ventured.

"You would be correct. So, given that you work for me now, I'd ask that you stay here with us."

As Ethan watched Gwendolyn calculate scenarios in her head, he was confident she would make the right decision. Without reacting, Gwendolyn picked up her whisky glass and drained it. "I need another drink. Does anyone else need one? Sir, can I get you something?" she asked the old man.

"No, I'm fine, dear. Ethan, accompany her to the bar," the old man instructed.

Already standing, Ethan escorted Gwendolyn back to the bar. "How are you holding up? We sharpen our knives on each other at Devlin and the old man is the master," Ethan reminded her. "Are you worried your father will make a scene? I'm not sure what you could say to him in the lobby that would smooth this over," Ethan concluded.

Hesitant to delve into her relationship with Robert, Gwendolyn deflected Ethan's question with another. "What is our mission tonight? Why did Devlin pay fifteen thousand dollars to attend tonight's dinner? Yes, fifteen thousand dollars because if I am working for Devlin tonight, then Weyerhaeuser is no longer paying for my plate. I will put the receipt on my first expense report," Gwendolyn informed him. "So, who is the target? And this time, whisky and water with lots of ice," she instructed.

"Two whiskies, tall glasses, lots of water, lots of ice," Ethan ordered. As they waited on their drinks, Ethan answered her question. "Robert is always a target and tonight was the perfect setting to see how you perform under pressure," he confessed. '*So far, so good, but the hard part is still coming,*' he thought.

She picked up her drink from the bar and walked over to a nearby high-top table. "Will the test be over tonight?" she asked.

"No, every day is a test," Ethan responded honestly. "Tonight is a test for me, too. The old man wants to see if I will keep my temper when Robert attacks you, which he is pretty sure will happen," he informed her against instructions from the old man. "Stay calm and keep your powder dry because this is an audience that will never forget your reaction."

Gwendolyn took a sip from her drink and looked out across the ballroom. "You may have worked for Devlin for the last decade under someone like Ken," Gwendolyn conceded, "most of the men here probably have." With her words void of emotion, she turned her eyes back to Ethan and said, "But I was raised by Robert Leavitt. You sit on Ken's side of the table at work," she observed. "He has no real power over you, no control over your life outside of work. He doesn't have the ability to decide for you or control where you go and how the world sees you," she explained, while realizing her words did not resonate with Ethan. To reach him, she grabbed his hand and said, "Close your eyes, please. Just for a second," she pleaded until Ethan conceded. "Imagine growing up with him under the same roof. Everything you did and every mistake you made was scrutinized by him. And in front of whoever may have been standing there," she detailed. "Now, remember you are a kid. Imagine you are 8 years old and just tiny compared to him. Do you understand how it's different than sitting across the boardroom table from him?"

Ethan opened his eyes and looked at the woman across from him. "So, this should be child's play for you," he countered coldly. "If you need someone to hold your hand, I'm not your guy. If you need someone to have your back, that's me," he stated with absolute certainty. "No one in this room knows your father as well as you do. Handle him tonight and handle him with as much grace as you can summon," he advised her. *'Which isn't much, I'm afraid,'* Ethan thought.

"Gwendolyn, get over here," said an angry voice that cut through the dull roar of the ballroom.

Stiffened in her stance, Gwendolyn moved back and Ethan touched her arm, "No, stay right here. Make him walk over to you," he instructed. "I will head back to the table and watch with the old man from there. If we see you struggling, we'll come over."

"No, don't come over no matter what, I mean it," she instructed. "I don't need to be rescued. Track down Jared and tell him to wrap up the symposium and start the introductions. Now," she said firmly.

As she watched Ethan walk away, Gwendolyn regretted dismissing him. Even though they only met earlier that day, she felt oddly vulnerable without him by her side. Robert Leavitt aggressively marched across the ballroom towards Gwendolyn. In his standard tuxedo that he wore to these events, the overbearing father locked eyes with his daughter, who he believed committed the ultimate sin. While she knew his playbook and was expecting a very public display of his dominance and power, she also knew his triggers. She felt oddly prepared, maybe because she wasn't alone. Without lowering his voice, Robert sparred with his daughter regardless of the people surrounding them.

"What in the hell do you think you are doing? Did you think I wouldn't find out? Devlin? Really?" he demanded. Not allowing her to interrupt, he continued to berate her as the people standing nearby backed away. "I fight with Devlin every year! I sit across from Ken and that cocky little shit he brings now, Evan or Edison. Doesn't know the first goddamn thing about respect!"

With the eyes of the room on them, Gwendolyn touched Robert's arm and asked, "Can we talk about this after? I don't want to do this here and neither do you. I didn't know Ken was going to tell you tonight. That wasn't the plan," she admitted.

"The plan? And since when is Mr. Devlin '*Ken*' to you? Where is he? I want to talk to him, right now," Robert demanded as he scanned the room. "I knew before he called me to rub it in. I told you, there is nothing you can hide from me."

"How could you possibly know? I didn't tell any…" Gwendolyn stopped and parked that question for later. "Can you please lower your voice? Look at me, Robert," she snapped, seeing only rage in his eyes.

"What did you call me?" Robert asked as he narrowed his eyes to slits. "Try that again," he said through clenched teeth. He reached across the table and took hold of her wrist in his hand. Gwendolyn froze and said, "Let go of my arm, right now Robert. I am not asking. If I jerk back and you don't let go, someone will level you," she warned him sternly. "Let go before we turn this into a media frenzy instead of a campaign event," she said as she did her best to hide the fear that was building.

Not sure what impulse would dictate his response, Gwendolyn braced for any reaction. Robert surprised the room and everyone watching by tugging his daughter to his side of the table and pulling her out the nearest exit into the lobby. Situated with his back to the door they just exited, Robert cornered Gwendolyn and mocked her threat. Without waiting for approval from the old man, Ethan took position on the other side of the door and listened as Gwendolyn sparred with her father.

"Where are they, Gwen? I don't see your bodyguards coming to your rescue," he gestured back inside the ballroom. "I cannot believe you are this stupid! What have I told you about thinking on your own? Gwen, what? What did I tell you?"

Without giving him the answer he demanded, Gwendolyn maintained her stare straight ahead at her father, which only egged him on. "Every time you think for yourself, every time, you embarrass yourself and worse, you embarrass me! I work with these people," he threw a hand behind him in exasperation. "All the senior managers from Weyerhaeuser are here. I mean, it was embarrassing enough for me when you didn't get into Harvard, now you accept a job with Devlin?" he questioned her with indignation. "Did it even occur to you they offered you a job to have something they could hang over me; leverage at the negotiating table?"

Before continuing, he looked away from her and around the lobby to see who was listening. "You could not be more clueless. You won't have a job in the morning. This was a one-time opportunity to make me look like a fool. It is so obvious that anyone can see they are just using you." Robert's words forced her jaw to clench and face to flush but she allowed him to continue. "I imagine Ken's goon told you he would have your back, so principled," he said with biting sarcasm. "He is full of shit. His first test and he is no where in sight."

Finally having her fill, Gwendolyn interrupted. "That's right, there is no one in sight," Gwendolyn said loudly so someone on the other side of the door could hear, assuming Ethan was a second away from busting through. "I told Ethan that under no circumstances was he to come to my rescue. I told him I don't need to be rescued," she schooled him. "We are not talking about this tonight. Instead, I am going back inside to sit with my new bosses. You are welcome to come back inside but if you are not civil, I will drop the gloves. Nothing will be off limits and the rule about our family's dirty laundry, I'll drop that as well," she explained.

She did not wait for a reply and started back into the ballroom through the main entrance. Before stopping at the door, she turned around to face Robert and said, "And that is the last time I let you put your hands on me. The only reason I didn't level you in front of everyone, was because someone advised me to handle this exchange *with as much grace as I could summon*,'" she advised him by repeating Ethan's words and strode through the open door.

Without making eye contact with anyone, she walked straight to the bar where Ethan was waiting for her and first addressed the bartender, "I'll have a…"

"Whisky, neat?" the bartender asked. "That looked intense. Can I make it a double, miss?"

Gwendolyn nodded and fought back every urge to break down and melt into a puddle on the floor. The image of Robert's face with the vein on his forehead pulsating was burned into her retinas. "Is everyone looking over here? All I can feel on the back of my neck are eyes," she told Ethan.

"Well, not everyone is looking over here," he replied as he took a drink from his glass.

Without turning around, Gwendolyn asked, "How long do I have to stay? Is there a time limit to this test or do I have to endure Robert sitting across from me all night?"

"The hard part is over," Ethan observed as he stood next to her at the bar. "You held your own. Most of the ballroom overheard your exchange with Robert or got it second hand," Ethan said without looking at her. Turning to find her eyes, Ethan shook his head and continued. "These talking heads and suits love this crap and they love juicy gossip even more. You can't imagine the enemies your father has made over his career and how many people would like to see him fall," Ethan enlightened her. "Let's park the topic of your father and try to salvage the rest of the evening. Besides, you still have your one-on-one with the Governor during dinner," Ethan sprung on her.

"Pardon? I thought this was a fundraiser. Buy some tickets, support the Governor, and ask for a favour later," Gwendolyn detailed. "What's the one-on-one?"

"The Governor mingles from table to table securing votes from the different industry lobbyists and union leaders," Ethan detailed. "It's all quid pro quo to ensure the Governor stays in office. We're seated at one of two tables of forest sector reps, including our friends from the homebuilders' association, who are lumped in with the sawmills," Ethan pointed out. "The Governor will focus on you, right away, for sure," Ethan predicted. "And your connection with *Mr. Fundraisers are my specialty* doesn't hurt either," he teased. "Turn the discussion to something relevant to the Governor in the upcoming election cycle and give your thoughts," he suggested. "We don't expect you to make any points with him tonight," he reassured her. "This is about getting you used to talking to these people. All the way to the highest office," he explained and turned his head to look at her. "If you can handle the Governor, you pass and the evening ends, to answer your original question," Ethan informed her with a smile and picked up his glass.

"And, if my aunt had balls, she'd be my uncle," Gwendolyn sighed as she shot the drink poured in front of her and started back to the table.

Back to the present day on Moose Island…

My laugh interrupted Gwendolyn repeating her anecdote and ripped us back to the present moment. She joined in laughing and we didn't hear Ethan's footsteps on the deck boards. Waiting for a break in the laughter, Ethan's raspy and playful voice cut through the brief silence. "Can I tell the rest of that story? I am pretty sure I was there for that one."

Gwendolyn jumped up with surprise and walked over to the door. "I didn't realize you were done for the day. Here, let me take those," she instructed as she took a plastic crate from his hands, while simultaneously watching Ethan's face for a reaction to seeing me. "Looks like we are having lobster and scallops tonight," she happily observed. "How was it with Connor today?"

Before he answered, he bent down and kissed Gwendolyn on the top of her head to reassure her that everything was fine, "You know that kid. Doesn't stop moving, doesn't stop talking and refuses to drive anything under 55 on the island," Ethan detailed with frustration. "Just because we don't have any cops on the island doesn't mean we have to attract unnecessary attention."

Ethan took off his boots and walked into the house to where I was sitting. "Hello Gloria," he greeted and waited for me to stand for a hug. "It is nice to see you. Already enjoying the island chaga, excellent. Pour me some too, babe, on ice though," Ethan requested. "So, where were you in the story? We were at the bar and heading back to the table for the Governor?" Ethan looked out over the ocean view while he thought back to that night. "When Mr. Purple Socks called your name out across the ballroom again?" Within seconds, Ethan took over the role of storyteller to provide details I had not heard.

"No, please. You can just skip to our conversation in the parking lot. When you walked me to my vehicle, like the gentleman you were that night," she recalled fondly. "It was the reason I was walking Gloria through the rest of the day we first met. I wanted her to hear how you handled your second scolding of the day," she chided.

"A gentleman," scoffed Ethan. "I saw how much you had to drink that night. I was hoping to steal a kiss and a squeeze," he joked as he grabbed Gwendolyn's butt while she stood at the sink cleaning the scallops he brought home. With a jab to his stomach, she let Ethan continue without interrupting. "Gloria, you should have seen her that night, and I don't mean how she looked. She was the hottest thing in the room, no doubt, no question," Ethan confirmed by biting his bottom lip. "She was also the smartest person in the room. Well, second to me, of course," he provoked. "While I couldn't take credit for any of her training, I was so damn proud of her."

"Yes, yes, of course, dear," Gwendolyn conceded. "Let's skip ahead to the parking lot," she prodded him along. "That was the real Gwendolyn back then. The rest evening was just a performance."

"Of course it was, my dear. Everything is a performance except for the people we choose to show our real selves, everyone else knows a version of us," I offered. With my words coming close to a nerve, I circled back to the story. "So, you walked her out," I said and led Ethan back to his version of that night.

"I can still hear the sharp clack of her heels on the marble. You were fast in those things," Ethan recalled as travelled back to the hotel lobby. "She had just finished with the Governor," Ethan detailed.

Back to the night of the Governor's fundraiser…

"Gwendolyn…Gwen, jeez, hold up," seeing she was intent on losing him, Ethan sped up to a run to catch her. Once outside, he caught up to her and touched her left arm. As a reflex, Gwendolyn shook off his hand and swung around with her right hand, clenched. Barely catching her fist before it reached his chin, Ethan squeezed her hand until she lowered it to her side. With her pupils dilated in fear and quickened breath, he stopped to feel her hand shaking in his. "Gwendolyn, it's okay. It's over," Ethan said, trying to ease her panic. "You're safe."

With an agreeing nod, Gwendolyn relaxed her hand and Ethan let it go. Her eyes down, Gwendolyn turned away and walked to the tailgate of her truck where she doubled over. Ethan heard the whisky she drank earlier splash onto the ground and, after a moment, Gwendolyn walked back to where he was standing beside the driver's side door. She opened the door and pulled out a napkin from the centre console and wiped her mouth. Wishing the adrenalin fuelled panic would subside, the anxious young forester directed her remaining energy at Ethan.

"What was the point of that? To see if I could survive the humiliation? To see whether I would break down, run away crying?" she demanded. "Every day of my life growing up was like that. Just when I think I have enough distance from him and my own life, something sucks me back in," she whimpered. "You staged all of that, every part," Gwendolyn accused him. "And it all ends with *that*," her voice cracked as she pointed towards the hotel. "Why? So, you could test me? Or was he right? Was all this orchestrated so you could take a shot at him?" she ruthlessly accused him. "Who do you think you are?"

Desperately wanting to pull her in and protect her from everyone, especially Robert, Ethan numbed his emotions and dismissed her frailty. Aware he was being tested, he offered the response a mentor should give their protégé in a teachable moment. "I'll let you ponder that question," he toyed with her, "while you finish your tantrum. Where am I right now? In the parking lot with you and I had to chase you down. I don't chase anyone," he arrogantly informed her. "You got me to follow you out here and you think you're the one being played?" Ethan asked through a smile camouflaged by his wrinkled brow. Her eyes misting, he softened his tough love strategy because he wouldn't be able to continue if she started to cry. "You can't even see your own power," he said shaking his head. "That's okay. We'll work on it, starting tomorrow. Come this way," he instructed. "You can't drive home."

"No, I don't want you to drive me home. I am too angry and I..." Gwendolyn stopped as she saw where they were headed. He walked her back to the front of the hotel and called over the doorman.

"Can you call up Mr. Devlin's car?" Ethan asked and handed the young man a folded bill. "Thanks."

Turning his attention back to Gwendolyn, he could see she had collected her thoughts and suppressed her emotion, for the moment. "Jimmy, Mr. Devlin's driver, will take you home. We'll see you here for breakfast at 6 o'clock. Jimmy will drop you off tonight and pick you up in the morning to get your truck. Get some sleep."

Back to the present day…

Leaving the rest of the night in the past, Ethan found his way back to us in the house. He looked past me at Gwendolyn and asked, "Did you say anything else? Before I closed the door? I can't remember."

"No, you heard the rest from Jimmy the next day," Gwendolyn remembered perfectly. "As soon as you closed the door, the floodgates opened. I cried like an ugly baby, just uncontrollable sobbing. Poor Jimmy. He was as incapable of watching a woman cry as you," and while looking at Ethan, she continued. "Poor simpletons, you blubber whenever you see a woman well up," she teased. "At first, Jimmy didn't have an address and drove around for a while until I could answer him. I finally caught my breath to give him my address and asked him if I could use his phone."

"Oh right, I forgot about that," Ethan nodded. "You terrified Jimmy."

With an eye roll, she dismissed the statement and continued. "When Robert said he knew I took the job with Devlin, I couldn't stop working through how he found out. It came to me when I walked past the entrance to the salon in the hotel lobby," Gwendolyn explained. "I asked Jimmy for a phone so I could call Cheryl and tell her that night would be the last time I set foot in her shop."

Ethan smiled as he recalled the rest of the story. "That's right," he said as he remembered the rest of the conversation with the driver. "When he came back to the hotel to pick up the old man, he warned us both. *'Watch out for that one. She looks like a woman but she is something else. You put her in the backseat and she just fell apart when you closed the door. She couldn't speak…for blocks she just cried. I finally ask her for an address and she magically pulls it together. So well in fact, she asks for my phone and just destroys the poor woman on the other end of the line.'"*

"Okay, I think that's enough stories for now," Gwendolyn decreed and ripped Ethan from the past. I could see Ethan's account of that night pained her and assumed it stirred unwelcome memories. "Why don't you take Gloria on a tour of the property, Ethan? I can cook up these lobsters and we can all share a meal together before we talk about why she is here," Gwendolyn suggested. I hid my smile in praise for Gwendolyn's offer of food. She knew so little about Native American culture and our traditional ways when she came to us but she listened to the Elders' Circle and learned the importance of sharing food, especially when building trust.

Ethan turned his head towards the water and suggested an alternative. "It's low tide," he noted as he looked out the window. "Let's have a lobster boil on the shore and light a bonfire. The dogs need a run," he noted as he reached down and patted the smaller of the two dogs. "If Edith doesn't expend some energy, it's going to get ugly in here," he said while we all noticed Edith had Gwendolyn's shoe in her mouth. "We can take the side-by-side down to the shore and park where we can watch the dogs run in the mud. If we are lucky, we can watch the lobster boats working in the bay."

"That sounds wonderful, Ethan," I said, accepting the offer to procrastinate our inevitable difficult conversation. "I can't promise we are done with the stories though, especially around a fire."

9 THE SWEAT

A few minutes later, on the ocean floor in front of their property, Ethan built a large fire from dried spruce branches and driftwood. As Gwendolyn set up a propane heater and pot for the lobster, she explained the tide rises and falls over forty feet every six hours. The tide was at its lowest point and her dogs enjoyed exploring the newly exposed mud. The sky above us was painted with purple and pink clouds mixing into a fiery ball of orange that melted into the archipelago off in the distance. Within an hour, we were all sitting down to enjoy the lobster Ethan caught earlier that day.

I was surprised by the texture from my first bite and found the meat to be sweet. "I never had lobster before. Wait until I tell the ladies back home. Especially Susan. She will be so jealous," I informed Ethan before taking another bite. "She wanted to come with me. Before I left, we had tea, and she reminded me of the sweat at McIntosh," I explained.

"I remember," Ethan responded. "It was your idea to have the community meeting at McIntosh. You said it mattered to the Elder, though I didn't fully grasp the importance," Ethan said and gave me a knowing look, "until we arrived. We barely talked about the agreement; it was all about the sweat." I could see Ethan letting his mind wander back to that day driving into McIntosh. "I remember driving to the site with Chief Trout in my passenger seat," Ethan recalled. With the bonfire crackling in the background, he stood beside the swaying flames and took us back to the day when it all really began. "The Chief was sitting in the passenger seat of my work truck and he told me pull off the main road onto an overgrown trail towards the water," Ethan started.

"That's right, and I followed behind with Gloria and Susan in my truck," Gwendolyn added. "We all arrived together at McIntosh," she said as she recalled the day of the sweat.

In the past, driving north on the Jackfish River Road from the reservation to McIntosh…

Ethan negotiated several turns before coming to a clearing along the Jackfish River with several old buildings. While Ethan and Gwendolyn were both familiar with the abandoned structures from their many visits to the old boarding school site, a newly constructed sweat lodge surprised them. It was a small, unassuming dome structure with a large fire burning in front that drew everyone's attention. There were several Elders congregating in front of the structure dressed in shorts, some in sarongs made of deer hide, waiting to be smudged. The women were in white flowing dresses adorned with coloured ribbons. Everyone was barefoot and undertaking a purposeful task to help with the ceremony, whether it was tending to the fire or preparing food and tea.

While the gathering was small and modest, the scene in its entirety could intimidate someone unfamiliar with the ceremony. Through her research with the tribe, Gwendolyn was invited to take part in a women's sweat with the Elders, and with our permission, she documented her experience as part of the paper she was writing. When she asked me to review her work, I corrected the information her professor provided to explain the ceremony, and the rituals practised by our tribe. She asked me to present the paper with her, as most of the paper contradicted her professor's previous research and made for an uncomfortable seminar. Ethan was not familiar with Gwendolyn's paper or her own experiences in the sweat, and only heard stories about the sweat ceremony from our Elders.

"Are we roasting something on that fire?" joked Ethan as he exited his vehicle and walked over to the Chief.

"Of course," the Chief replied and paused while looking at the growing fire, "…you, Mr. Travers. It is how we deal with problem negotiators. The cleansing power of fire," the Chief said with deadpan humour that was difficult to detect.

While waiting for the other to react, eagles shrilled off in the distance. The prolonged shrieking broke Ethan's concentration and caused him to look up at the impressive birds hunting the waters in front of the peninsula where we stood. Lowering his eyes to the Chief, he realized he was looking up at the birds as well. Both men flashed each other an invisible smile that caused them to chuckle. Gwendolyn and I were chatting away about her sweat as we exited her truck and joined them.

As Gwendolyn approached, she asked Ethan, "Isn't this exciting? Gloria said this sweat is for you. The Elders use the ceremony to seek guidance and counsel from Mother Earth and others that have passed onto the Spirit World," she repeated from her paper. Ethan's obvious confusion led Gwendolyn to conclude, "The Chief didn't tell you."

Chief Trout was called away by an Elder and walked closer to the fire in front of the sweat lodge. Gwendolyn led Ethan away from the others and lowered her voice, "The Elders invited you to a sweat with the Chief and his council. You gained the trust of The Elders' Circle by meeting them here so many times. Especially the Elders that travelled here with you and, well, all the ladies," she said as she rolled her eyes. "They want the rest of the tribe to trust you, which requires you to sweat with them before they can sign the agreement," she explained. "Gloria said the lawyers gave them the green light," she happily informed her mentor. "You passed the legal test, now they want to put you through the traditional test."

"And why aren't you joining us?" Ethan asked. "I can't be left alone with these old Indian ladies. They are vicious," he complained lightly. "They pinch and grab, sometimes they even kiss." Gwendolyn understood right from the start that Ethan was a slight germaphobe and did not handle the overt physical contact with the little old Indian ladies very well.

"This sweat is just for the men," I answered, eavesdropping on their conversation. "Gwendolyn was invited by the Elders' Circle into our spring sweat. She wrote about it in her paper and I was one of her reviewers," I said with pride. "While everyone experiences something different in the sweat, we explained the ritual steps and what happens once you enter. Too bad you didn't read it before today, nee-hee." With my distinctive laugh, I tried to let Ethan know he needed to relax.

"Follow me, Mr. Travers," the Chief called to Ethan.

"This is a ceremony, not a meeting," Ethan realized. "I don't have any tobacco, not even a pack of cigarettes for an offering," he said. "I gave up Lucky Strikes right before we started our discussions," explained Ethan who was worried about offending his host before the sweat even began. In the first meeting, the tribe explained the importance of tobacco and, even before that, Ethan knew the plant was sacred to us. He said it was something he learned a long time ago, and it stayed with him.

"You are invited into one of the most sacred ceremonies practised by my people, Mr. Travers. We want to trust you because the Land warrants us taking the risk. The Elders have constructed the sweat lodge to cleanse and purify the knowledge we will exchange and the agreement we will sign. They have shared stories with you about the Land and they must trust you to protect those connections. The sweat allows you to open your heart to them and prepare you for your journey with us," explained the Chief as he stopped in the front of the sweat lodge and unbuttoned his shirt. "Don't worry. I have tobacco for the offering," smiled the Chief as he reached into his back pocket and pulled out an unopened bag of loose tobacco.

Ethan took in his surroundings and carefully observed what the Elders were doing around them. There was a large pile of river washed stone warming by the fire that were carefully being carried into the sweat, while others were changing for the journey. Ethan started doing the same when Susan, dressed in a flowing dress decorated with ribbons, came to stand in front of him.

"Hello, Susan. How are you doing today?" Ethan greeted her while holding out his hand.

"Nimkodawn," Susan said. Even with her remarkably small stature, she pushed Ethan back on his heels and took the advantage to allow her inquisitive eyes to evaluate every feature of his face, ending with his eyes. Her skin was only a little darker compared to Ethan's with deep wrinkles around her eyes and mouth because she liked to smile and laugh with her whole face. She repeated, "Nimkodawn," and nodded to encourage Ethan to comply.

"She wants you to bend down," I explained.

Ethan immediately bent at the waist and maintained eye contact with her. It wasn't the first time she took his face in her hands and felt every inch. "Ma'iingan Dodem," she said with confidence and clarity.

Without saying another word, she turned around and walked a few steps away towards a small fire with a tripod supporting a cast iron pot. She picked up a mug from the basket beside the fire, ladled a cup of hot liquid from the pot and filled the mug. It was a thick, dark beverage with an earthy, rich fragrance that reminded Ethan of coffee.

"Thank you very much. I don't drink coffee, Susan," he said regretfully.

"Chaga," said the Elder, and she thrust the wooden cup into Ethan's hands. She smiled and again said, "Nimkodawn," and Ethan obliged by bending down a second time.

She grabbed his face and cupped it in both hands, looked into his eyes and repeated her earlier words that he still did not understand, "Ma'iingan Dodem," and then looked over towards the Chief and nodded. She let go of Ethan's face and walked away from him but not before she sharply tapped him on the behind and giggled. While looking back at him over her shoulder, she motioned for Ethan to drink the tea.

"While I'm not sure how to take the slap on my butt, it reminds me of something from our last visit," Ethan said as he leaned down to me. "Susan took me away from everyone the last time we brought the Elders' Circle here, when we ended the field tour here. She grabbed my face and said those words to me. When we rejoined everyone around the fire, you started the meeting with a prayer," Ethan remembered. "I forgot to ask for a translation of what she said."

"Susan said you are from the Wolf clan," I translated for him. "She is a powerful medicine woman and a descendant from a line of ancestral Chiefs. She focuses on the Land to protect places where medicinal plants and traditional foods are gathered," I explained. "When you promised to stop clearcutting, she knew you would help us protect the Land, and she has been asking the Creator for help to convince the tribe. She is a vocal supporter of you with Chief and Council and the tribe," I told Ethan. "I would drink the chaga. It's a traditional drink, and it tastes nothing like coffee. Susan sweetens hers with maple syrup."

"Gwendolyn cranks up to chipmunk speak when she drinks it, so I assumed it was a high-test coffee," he teased. Then complying with my instructions, Ethan took a sip.

The Chief turned to Ethan and explained, "The pat on your ass was because she thinks you are cute. Indian women, especially the older ones, are incredibly…," the Chief searched for the most appropriate word, "flirtatious."

Ethan was thankful he stifled the laugh welling up inside, as the Chief was not joking. "Thank you for the warning about horny, Ojibwe women. Although, I was already aware. This is not the first time I have been manhandled," Ethan offered sarcastically. Circling back to my earlier words, he repeated, "The Wolf clan, as in she sees me as a threat? Does she look at me as someone attacking the tribe?"

"Amongst the Ojibwe, the wolf is usually a protector of the tribe. The wolf can also be a leader or pathfinder, it depends on the tribe. It's a strong clan, and the wolf is a fierce defender," the Chief acknowledged. "You never told me you were Indian," the Chief pointed out. "Things may have been easier if you had shared that with us earlier."

"I wouldn't know if I was," Ethan replied. "I was adopted." Without breaking eye contact, the Chief's stare demanded more. Reluctantly, Ethan shared the few details he knew about his past. "Someone left me at the hospital where my adoptive mother worked. Local police searched for my birth mother or anyone who could identify me but, in 1969, tracking down someone who didn't want to be found wasn't easy." Ethan stopped in contemplation. "I have been looking for my birth parents since I was eighteen years old, when I was legally able to request my adoption records from the state," Ethan looked at the fire for a second and then offered more, "only to find my adoptive parents told me the truth. There was nothing in my file about my birth parents, where I was born or anything useful." Ethan paused as if pondering the thought of being Indian. "There's no evidence to prove it one way or the other," he concluded to himself.

When I first met Ethan, I wanted to trust him and felt comfortable speaking with him, even sharing my thoughts. I rarely felt at ease with white men and now I understood why Ethan was different. He was Indian. It made sense when speaking to Ethan out on the Land or on the reservation but I was confused with the person he became in meetings. There was something earnest and transparent about Ethan that disappeared when he was confined to a boardroom.

"Oh, you're Indian. Susan is never wrong. She cannot be wrong," the Chief stated flatly. "Regardless, it will come out in the sweat. Are you ready?" asked the Chief.

"Not sure if I am dressed for it, but lead the way," Ethan said. He had taken off his shoes, socks and shirt but still had his pants and belt on. Ethan appeared more concerned with the Chief's chosen words, *it will come out in the sweat.* His face questioned the wisdom of agreeing to take part.

"Before you enter the lodge, make your offering of tobacco on the small, flat rock there," the Chief said, as he pointed to the entrance. "Once inside, you can take your pants off and put this on," and handed Ethan a deerskin breechcloth. The Chief held back one side of the deer hide flap and motioned for Ethan to enter. He bent down and entered the sweat lodge with the Chief following behind.

The flap barely fell behind them before we heard, "Oh, my goodness, did you see him with his shirt off? Oh, I could just lick him all over!" my cousin Shirley shouted. She barely stopped skinning fish to detail what she wanted to do to Ethan, or more specifically, what she wanted Ethan to do to her.

"I was hoping they were going to change out here, eh? Nee-hee," said another cousin, Jeannie, followed by her infectious laugh that spread to all of us, except Gwendolyn.

Her eyes widened as the ladies piled on their fantasies about her boss and mentor. Gwendolyn didn't hide her shock at what she was hearing. She turned to me with her mouth open slightly and I waited for her to say something, but nothing came out. Gwendolyn didn't often struggle to find the right words. Quite the opposite, as she usually found plenty of words.

After Ethan hired her, we spent months together drafting the agreement on the reservation with Gwendolyn going home only on weekends. She eagerly confessed her captivation with the business environment at Devlin and excitedly told me about the happenings at the company. Every experience centred on Ethan and what she learned from him. She weakly hid her infatuation with the man we all found comforting and protective. The opportunity to work with them separately and then together gave me a different perspective on their relationship from the beginning.

"Gwendolyn, are you okay?" I asked but she was consumed by the laughing and chatter about Ethan. Almost as if she was hypnotized, she listened to the old ladies describe some very graphic goings on. As the conversations continued, everyone kept preparing food and tending the fire. I watched Gwendolyn start to smile and chuckle as she listened to the Elders try to best each other's fantasies. Finally, she let go and allowed a belly laugh to erupt.

Gwendolyn continued to listen as we bantered amongst ourselves. She was so much younger and didn't pretend to understand what it meant to be old. The first time she interviewed the ladies from the Elders' Circle, she asked us what it meant to be an Elder. She was surprised to learn there was no age requirement and liked the concept. While age can help and eventually comes to everyone, serving on the Elders' Circle required wisdom, knowledge and an open mind to accept messages from ancestors in the Spirit World and Mother Earth. She captured in her own words what it meant to be an Elder for our people and the unique role women played in the tribe. Her words described all the Elders, not just the women, in a powerful and influential light, and placed us above her western education, and even above tribal politics.

The first draft of her research paper combined our words with hers to confirm the tribe's hereditary role as stewards of our Land. Her conclusions put her paper in opposition with her professor, the businesses sponsoring her research and over a hundred years of colonial history. The concept that Native American traditional knowledge should be weighted equal to western science was not a popular opinion, and not one a newly graduated forester should be promoting. Her academic supervisor did not agree with her conclusions and demanded changes that Gwendolyn was unwilling to make. She tried to help her people understand our people, and where she failed, Ethan forced them to listen.

"You ladies are so entertaining and you tell the best stories, X-rated ones mind you but entertaining!" she said and allowed us to continue our banter.

"Come on, you must have at least one good sex story. It doesn't have to be with Ethan but at least a dirty one!" Susan requested excitedly in Ojibwe.

"Susan wants to you tell a…well, a sex story," I translated. "She is hoping for one about Ethan but you can just make one up," I whispered only to Gwendolyn, knowing most of her real experiences with men were negative. I learned from Gwendolyn that a woman doesn't need to grow up on the reservation to suffer. "Most of their stories," I said and pointed to Susan and Evelyn, "are so old, there's no one left alive to confirm if they happened, nee-hee!"

Gwendolyn squeezed my hand back as she answered, "You ladies have so much more experience with men and love, well lust at least," and winked at Susan. "I'm embarrassed to say that my recurring fantasy is about finding love, unconditional love. It is boring and simple, but I want it to be love. I want to know how it feels," she finished, surprising most of us.

"You must know what love feels like," one of the Elders asked as she looked up from the fish she was cooking. "Even if you haven't found passionate love, you know what love feels like. What about your family?" she asked with hesitation.

When she didn't respond, I broke the uncomfortable silence. "Would you like some chaga, Gwendolyn?" I asked and walked over to the pot. She avoided talking about her family, especially her father. Some of the stories Gwendolyn shared about her childhood suggested she would appreciate a topic change.

"Yes, please," she said in acceptance of the distraction. "Chaga is amazing and the cancer-fighting properties are shocking," she informed me. "I was surprised so few people knew about it. There are neurological benefits too and it's good for gut health," she continued to ramble. "I have been searching for it on my walks, but it's hard to see in the summer."

"It's easier to find once the leaves fall and the ground is white. The dark chunks stand out better," I confirmed. "You won't get sick if you drink some every day. We can gather some together. There are many good spots close to the reservation," I told her. "Wait, there is a good spot down the next road," I remembered. "We can go today."

"Are you sure? I would like that," she said. "We can take my truck whenever we are done here," she offered. "What can I do to help?"

"Oh, I was just kidding about making you prepare food. You are our guest, and besides, I made the Bannock last night," I told her. "We can go right now.

I will get a basket and find a tool we can use."

"Sounds wonderful. Let's take Ethan's work truck. It's a more comfortable ride on the gravel roads compared to my old beater," she told me. "You don't need to worry about a tool or basket. Ethan has every tool we could need and I'll grab the basket you gave me from my truck," Gwendolyn instructed me as she took me by the arm and led me to the truck.

She backed the truck from its parking spot and headed towards the main road where I told her to turn left. "I'm not sure if Ethan expects me to speak today but I would be surprised if he didn't," Gwendolyn predicted. "The first day we met, he put me in front of the Governor, unprepared. He is speaking first and always takes the meeting somewhere spontaneous and I am never prepared. Any advice for me?" she asked earnestly.

The trees, rocks and water flashed by the truck window as I looked out across the Land. After considering different ways to answer her question, I started with my own. "When you look at the Land, what do you see? As we drive through it, what do you see?"

As she pondered my question, Gwendolyn stared out the windshield as she drove. "I see trees, water, birds, air...," she stopped before finishing her list. She looked at me and turned her attention back to the road. "I like details, there is safety in taking care of every detail, so I list things, but I don't think that's the answer you want."

When I didn't offer any guidance, she started again. "I see those things individually on the Land and I also see them as one. The Land is home to living things that were here long before I was and will still be here when I am gone," she accepted. "Every living thing is connected to the Land and dependent on it for survival whether they know or not. Most people forget about their connection to the Land because they never see it. They live in cities and buy food at grocery stores, like me," she continued. "I'm lucky I stumbled into a life that lets me be on the Land and meet people like you. I feel like the best version of myself when we are here," she admitted to me. Before I was able to ask my next question, she felt it coming and continued. "I don't think I came to help you," she said and then reconsidered. "Maybe it started out that way, but I'm the one who needed help. As naïve as it sounds, I think we are making change. You and your tribe are going to manage the Land differently."

With a thoughtful pause, I provided Gwendolyn with some advice. "To help the Elders understand, I reminded them about why we took you to our most sacred sites. They understood it was our choice to share them with you, but if we didn't show them to you, how could we protect them? If we created maps with our oral history, we could protect what is most sacred to the tribe," I repeated to her. "You and Ethan helped us record the information we have about the Land and explained how we can use it to protect Mother Earth," I reminded her and thought about what I said. "That is how I explain why you are doing this. You are helping us protect the Land because you feel her too."

"I have different answers to that question because the more I learn, the more I challenge how we do things. That is the most personal answer I can share with the tribe about my connection to the Land and why I am here," she said and waited a long time before speaking again. "There is something else that motivated me to work with the Jackfish River tribe." Gwendolyn confessed. "The research I was doing before reaching out to you found evidence of foreign companies buying up Land here and, more troubling, gaining control over state and federal forests."

"Control you think the tribe should have over the forests," I remembered from an earlier conversation.

"Exactly. The Jackfish River tribe's territory overlaps multiple state forest licenses that are issued to the mills," Gwendolyn pointed out. "The location provides an excellent opportunity to test the recent Supreme Court decision on consultation and also an opportunity to challenge my father with protection from the tribe, which is a secondary concern now that I work for Ethan," she said comfortably. "I can't share everything with the tribe, and the part about the foreign companies in the United States is a dangerous topic," she warned. "I wanted to make sure you knew everything in the event I speak tonight in the Roundhouse."

Before continuing, I noticed we were approaching the turn off to Burchel Lake Road, "Take the road coming up on the left," I instructed her. Taking advantage of her words *you knew everything,* I asked another tough question. "Ethan, you love him, don't you? Are you two together?" I braced myself, expecting she might resist the personal nature of my question. But with just the two of us there, I felt comfortable enough to see how open she might be.

Gwendolyn navigated the turn and stole a quick sideways glance before speaking. "How far in before we reach the birch stand you want to show me?" she asked, sidestepping the question.

"At the split in the road, take the first left and the chaga stand isn't too far from there," I answered and awaited her response. Gwendolyn drove in quiet contemplation, as I am sure she was weighing whether she could trust me with the truth. After taking the left, Gwendolyn slowed the truck to a stop and placed the vehicle in park. She sat back in her seat and looked at me before answering.

With a serious tone, she explained her situation before answering. "Ethan Travers is my boss, and my job at Devlin is amazing. I have never felt this way about work, or anything for that matter. I feel wanted and needed," she continued. "I am proud to say I work for Ethan and Mr. Devlin," she added. "Aside from the secrecy and adrenaline of it, I feel so safe." She looked out her window at the forest that surrounded us. We were both distracted for a moment by the birds soaring and singing around us, including a woodpecker whopping off in the distance.

Before getting out of the truck, she turned back to me and said, "I respect and trust Ethan, and I think I love him," she admitted, "but I don't really know what love is yet. I know I wake up every morning and I can't wait to get to work to see him," she said with building excitement and emotion. "Even though the first task of the day is a cage match with the old man and the other vice presidents at breakfast," she chagrined. "Those sharks are ruthless and attack me every morning, and Ethan doesn't save me, which I actually love even more," she revealed. "There isn't a task I wouldn't do for him and I want to talk to him all day because I learn something every minute. He sees me in a way that I never could." Her smile fading, she answered my original question, "We are not together. I can't risk this job or my new life at Devlin, and working with your tribe, over a fling. I finally feel safe and I know Ethan will protect me and I can't risk losing that."

I could see tears welling in her eyes and reached for her hand across the seat. I was right. She loved him, just as sure as I was that Ethan loved her. With the understanding we still had much to do that day, I squeezed her hand and said, "Susan will be so happy to hear you two aren't a couple, nee-hee! There is still hope for her and Evelyn." She responded with her own laugh and casually wiped her right eye with the cuff of her shirt.

"Let's find me some chaga, Gloria," she prompted. "You lead the way and I will carry the basket and tools."

Returning to the present day on the shoreline of Ethan and Gwendolyn's property on Moose Island in Passamaquoddy Bay…

Remembering what happened on our way home, I pulled back to the bonfire and tried to end the account with Gwendolyn and I starting the chaga hunt. "Gwendolyn and I were gone when the sweat ended," I deflected. "I can't remember if we found any chaga, but we all ended up at the Roundhouse later that afternoon."

"Yes, you two were gone…getting into trouble only Gwendolyn could find," Ethan lamented. He assumed the storytelling role and explained that it was hours later when he emerged from the sweat with Chief Trout. "The Elders led the Chief and I back to the fire where chairs, water and food were waiting for us," Ethan explained. "I didn't realize how thirsty I was until I accepted a bottle of water. Then, someone offered me a plate of food. I wasn't hungry, but I took the plate, *anyways*," Ethan paused to smirk. "We organized every meeting around a meal and you always ordered enough to invite the entire tribe," Ethan remembered with a smile. "It wasn't fun explaining those charges on the company credit card." He continued to describe what happened as Gwendolyn and I settled back into our seats around the fire to listen to the part of the day we missed.

Returning to the day of the sweat at McIntosh…

"Thank you very much. Smells amazing," said Ethan as he accepted a plate of food from Evelyn. It was clear she did not understand his words. "Without Gloria here, I am going to need some help so I don't offend Evelyn," he said to the Chief.

"Chi-Miigwetch is thank you very much in Ojibwe," the Chief taught Ethan. The Chief noticed Ethan's hesitancy in picking up the fork to start his meal. As he accepted a plate from Evelyn, the Chief instructed Ethan, "You might not feel like eating but you need to. It will help you recover."

With his mind racing, Ethan obligatorily grabbed the fork and tried the pan-fried fish that was netted hours earlier and cooked over the fire in front of him. Ethan recalled drinking the tea earlier and thought nothing of it. The tea had an earthy aroma with a subtle peat-like taste and he didn't think it could be the explanation behind the images and voices he encountered in the sweat. Ethan rationalized what he saw to the seed Susan and Chief planted before the ceremony started. It was what the wolf told him that neither Susan nor the Chief could have known.

"Are there any hallucinogenic effects from drinking that chaga tea?" Ethan asked the Chief.

The Chief finished chewing and swallowed before answering Ethan and started by shaking his head. "Chaga is not a psychedelic. When I drink the tea, I find it gives me a boost of energy and a cleansing effect, but nothing else. Why do you ask? What did you see?" asked the Chief as he shifted in his seat to face his guest.

"I saw myself all alone with these ladies. And it was terrifying," quipped Ethan as he continued to eat his meal.

"Did you hear any sounds or voices? Sometimes people will tell stories about colourful images, or animals invading their thoughts or even speaking to them. Some have reported watching images of people carrying on conversations and sometimes in a different language," the Chief said.

As the Chief waited for Ethan to speak, one of his councillors arrived with the tribal Police Chief and interrupted the conversation. "Chief Trout, we need to speak with you, alone."

"Yes, of course, David," the Chief said as he stood and walked to where the Police Chief parked his cruiser. Chief Angeconeb looked characteristically somber as he walked away from the crowd. It was not unusual for him to request input from the Chief for policing matters on the reservation, so no one was concerned with his presence. Except for Ethan, who turned around in his chair to see what was happening and saw an additional police vehicle arrive.

When he saw me in the front seat, Ethan jumped out of his chair and rushed over. "Gloria, are you okay? What's going on?" Ethan asked impatiently. Still shaken from being run off the road, I couldn't answer him. He could see the fear that remained with me and it heightened his reaction. Anxiously scanning the crowd and not finding Gwendolyn, he demanded an answer, "Where is Gwendolyn? Someone talk to me, right now!"

Chief Trout heard the apprehension in Ethan's voice and offered what he knew to reassure him. "There was an incident on Burchel Lake Road that resulted in their truck leaving the road and they hit a rock outcrop," the Chief explained. "She needs a few stitches and a possible concussion. She is being treated at the Nurse's Station."

Ethan clenched his jaw and tried to hide his building anger. "You said there was an incident. Her truck leaving the road is an accident," Ethan corrected. "What aren't you telling me? And why did the Police Chief need to speak with you, alone?"

"The incident is under investigation and we won't have all the details until my constables take statements from Miss Leavitt and Gloria," Chief Angeconeb interrupted. "At this point, all we know is that Miss Leavitt's truck left the road and struck a rock that caused the airbags to deploy," he stated without emotion. "We have unconfirmed reports that at least one other vehicle was involved but we don't know who was driving or how it was involved in the incident."

When he heard another vehicle was involved, Ethan pieced together a version of what he thought happened and bolted towards his truck. Still wearing the deerskin, he changed directions and went back for his clothes and shoes. As he rushed to dress, I made my way to him to refocus his energy.

"Ethan, she is okay," I told him and reached for his arm but he brushed me back. Surprise took over my face and Ethan saw the fear in my eyes that lingered from the earlier confrontation. Ethan blinked and unclenched his jaw while letting out a long breath. "Gloria," he started with an eery calmness, "please don't stop me. We can discuss what happened after I see her," he finished.

Ethan was fixated on Gwendolyn's safety, so I complied. "I will take you to the Nurse's Station," I said with my hand firmly on his forearm. "Come with me and you'll see she is fine."

"Were you with her? In the truck? What happened? Take me to her," he demanded as he stood. "Let's take my truck," Ethan instructed as he headed to where he had parked earlier. "Wait, where is my truck?"

"Gwendolyn said your truck had better tires for the gravel road," I offered. We walked to her truck, and he helped me into the passenger seat.

"The one with Devlin decals?" Ethan bemoaned and all I did was nod in agreement. I was unaware he and Gwendolyn had an understanding that she would go no where alone on the reservation and not in the Devlin-decaled vehicle. Ethan continued to the driver's side door and climbed in. Striking his knees on the steering wheel, he yelled out in pain, "Ugh, she is so damned short!" He adjusted the seat and started the vehicle, simultaneously, and discovered Gwendolyn left the radio volume on maximum.

"Did you hear that, loyal listeners? It was the medley of traffic sounds, signalling it is time for The Drive at 5, where one lucky listener picks the music that will rock you from 5 to 5:30 on your ride home. The lines are open and I am looking for lucky caller number…"

"Oh my god, how does this girl drive with that noise?" he shouted to no one and pawed at the dash for the '*off*' button.

Given the circumstances, I hid the smile that wanted to come out. Even during difficult meetings with the tribe, especially when dealing with protesters about crossing the untouched Jackfish River, Ethan did not lose his cool. He didn't once show the anger I could now see he was capable. It was clear Ethan felt it was his job to protect Gwendolyn, and that was true for any woman in his presence. Given Ethan's reaction, it was unmistakable to me he loved her. Even if he didn't know.

"Head back to the tribal office on the reservation. The Nurses' Station is next door," I instructed. "The clinic moved into the new mobile trailer you saw delivered last month. It is up and running."

Not requiring any further direction, Ethan steered the truck towards the main road. Unable to speed through the reservation, Ethan did not hide his frustration well. There were children and Elders walking along the side of the road and there was no where to pass. With his knuckles tight on the steering wheel, I reached over and said, "Gwendolyn has a cut above her right eye from hitting her head on the rearview mirror. Nurse said she needs 3 or 4 stitches and was waiting for the freezing to work when I left," I explained and looked at him. "She asked me to bring you to her and made me promise not to tell you anything. '*Not one word*' she said, to be exact."

Ethan looked me square in the eyes and said, "If something else happened that you are not telling me and I find out, you and I are going to have a big problem. A problem I won't be able to get passed." He turned his attention to the road and finished with a specific caution. "There is something that you aren't telling me," he said with certainty. "I will let you do this once because Gwendolyn put you in the middle. I'll take that up with her," and shook his head slightly. "This is your one and only lie."

As we walked into the newly constructed Nurse's Station, we could still smell wet paint and hear vacuums in the hallway. Even above the noise, Gwendolyn's voice permeated through the walls.

"I am not telling you how to do your job. I am simply telling you that needle will not be going into my face," Gwendolyn said in a voice that made me cringe for the nurse. Unable to hear the response she received, Gwendolyn's voice clearly cut through the vacuums again, "Because, it is not sterile," she said emphasizing every word. We couldn't hear the nurse's retort before Gwendolyn answered, "Yes, you are wearing surgical gloves, but you touched both your face and the examining table surface before picking up the needle and running the length of it to check for spurs," she said with biting judgement. "You have contaminated the sterile field and the needle, so it will not be going in my face."

As we reached the treatment room, we met the nurse at the doorway in a hurry to leave. "Hi nurse, how is our patient?" I asked without expecting a helpful answer.

Forced to drive in from the neighbouring town each day, the nurse resented the tribe and provided substandard treatment that many thought was better than no care at all. Gwendolyn didn't see it that way. "If you could get me a sterile sutures kit, I will take care of this without your help," she called out to the nurse. We entered the room to find Gwendolyn standing with her back to us looking into a small mirror on the wall. She was cleaning blood from her face and neck with a wet towel, trying to avoid the wound.

Upon hearing my voice, she turned and said, "I'm glad you're back. I am not letting Nurse Pissy Pants back in here. Is she always that rude?" Gwendolyn demanded without pausing for an answer. "She didn't even flush the wound; she was just going to close me up. New protocols, my ass," she muttered with obvious annoyance. "Ethan, grab me that basin and a bottle of saline from the counter and put it on the table beside me," she instructed.

"I told you she is fine," I mocked Ethan, who hadn't moved since reaching the doorway. Gwendolyn was dressed in her pants, bra and a medical gown that was open in the back. Blood from the cut had poured down onto her face and matted her hair in place.

Not overly interested in dealing with the blood and stitches, Ethan countered back. "We should really let the nurse do her job, Gloria. Go back and get her and I will talk some sense into this one," he said and thumbed at Gwendolyn without making eye contact.

"No, I can stitch this myself," she answered. "It will heal faster and look better in the end." Feeling she was exposed, Gwendolyn asked, "Gloria, can you cover me up? Nurse Crabby Face wouldn't tie it up. I think it was her attempt to keep me confined to this room." As I was tying her gown, Gwendolyn whispered to me, "You need to get him out of here and let me finish. Distract him in the waiting room or outside."

"Not a good idea, dear. That truck could be driving around the reservation," I whispered back. "We need to tell him what happened before he hunts down those men."

"Ladies, stop the whispering and tell me what happened," Ethan instructed with his patience exhausted.

Before either of us could answer, the nurse returned with a new suture kit and tossed it at Ethan. "Here, maybe she'll let you stitch her up," she spat at him. "I am leaving for the day, so Gloria, lock the door when you leave."

"Thank you, nurse. That will be all," Gwendolyn said in sarcastic dismissal. While holding the disposable basin just below her cut, she poured the saline over the cut, causing Ethan to wince. "Don't worry, it's frozen," she reassured. "You missed Nurse Cratchit's injection skills. I can't feel my entire face. Come take this basin and bring me the suture kit," she ordered. Ethan complied and placed the kit on the examining table next to her.

She scrubbed her hands at the sink, donned a pair of surgical gloves and retrieved the needle and sutures from the kit. "Of course, non-absolvable sutures and a straight needle," she observed. "I'm going to look like the Bride of Frankenstein when this is all over." Unphased, Gwendolyn prepared the suture and brought the needle to the far edge of the cut to pull it through one side of the gash, while closing the wound with her other hand.

While skillfully placing the next stitch, Gwendolyn glanced back to see Ethan's reflection in the mirror becoming increasingly impatient. "Gloria and I were driving in your truck down a road that runs parallel with the road into

McIntosh. There was a birch stand with chaga and I wanted some," she explained. "We went into the ditch and I didn't have my seatbelt on. I was shot out of my seat and my forehead hit the rearview mirror," she said calmly. "It is no big deal. I am fine. We can talk about exactly what happened after the meeting."

"You just drove off the road? You aren't even going to say you swerved to miss a deer?" Ethan asked in disbelief. "The Police Chief thinks there was another vehicle involved," he accused her.

"Yes, Miss Leavitt, I think there was a second truck," Chief Angeconeb clarified from the hallway. "I see you are feeling better. We would like to continue with our questions at the station. Are you just about done here?" There was observable disdain in the seasoned officer's voice.

Tying off the stitch, Gwendolyn asked, "Gloria, can you please pass me the scissors from the kit?" Everyone waited in silence until I retrieved the scissors and snipped the thread where she had it pulled tight. She found Ethan's eyes in the mirror and pleaded silently for help, to which he responded. He understood Gwendolyn wanted him alone and probed into the Police Chief's contempt.

"Chief Angeconeb, I don't know about you, but it has been a long time since I stitched myself," Ethan started and thought, *'and never sober.'* Closing the distance between them, Ethan continued. "Let's give Miss Leavitt a few minutes to collect herself and finish stitching her wound, hmm? Unless, of course, you think Miss Leavitt did something to warrant her confinement."

Situated eye to eye, the two warriors sized each other for a moment with neither willing to yield. Regardless of the Police Chief's sidearm, neither could be certain of who would walk away the victor. Without breaking his stare, Chief Angeconeb said, "You will bring her to the station when she is done here. It won't take long," he said and offered his hand to Ethan. "Unless, of course, Miss Leavitt continues to be uncooperative."

Ethan matched the force of his handshake and said, "Of course, Chief Angeconeb. We will come by after the ratification meeting with Chief and Council and the Elders Circle."

"We should head over to the Roundhouse. I don't want to miss the drumming," I said to cut through the tension building in the small treatment room. "Why don't you gentlemen leave us ladies to finish up here."

"Yes, and Ethan before you go, there is a bag in my truck," Gwendolyn told him. "Can you bring it to me? I need some clean clothes."

Once in the hallway, Chief Angeconeb cornered Ethan and stood uncomfortably close while pointing at both him and Gwendolyn. Although both lowered their voices, I could still hear the exchange. "I will be waiting," Chief Angeconeb warned him. "Don't make me find you. Chief Trout, Gloria and some of the other Elders may trust you and that one in there," he continued, "but I don't. Not everyone is happy you are here."

Without wavering, Ethan questioned, "Do we have a problem? It feels like we have a problem," he suggested. "And it sounds like a problem we should deal with in the parking lot." Looking for justification to give into his anger, Ethan waited for him to react.

The Police Chief took a brief pause and answered without dropping his stare, "No, no problem…for now. We may have a problem later. That depends on you." Chief Angeconeb allowed Ethan one more moment to decide whether his fists were required before he turned to walk out the door with stiff formality. I joined Ethan in the hallway and reminded him that Gwendolyn needed some clothes.

"Yes, right," Ethan responded as he refocused and shortly returned with a gym bag. "Did someone try to hurt you and Gwendolyn?" Ethan asked as he walked back in. "Chief Angeconeb thinks someone ran you two off the road. Reading between the lines of that exchange, I am not sure what happened." He handed me the bag, and I brought it back to Gwendolyn who was waiting to get dressed.

Upon returning to Ethan, I started with a sigh, "David is a purist. He believes we are accepting defeat by partnering with Devlin and lectures anyone who will listen that we must demand the Land be given back to the tribe. *'Just exchanging one white devil for another'* is how he explained it at last month's meeting. He lobbied his clan to vote against signing the agreement," I continued as Chief Trout walked into the Nurses' Station.

"And he didn't have the clout to sway the decision of the Elders," the Chief countered. "The meeting this afternoon will be challenging, as every tribal meeting is difficult regardless of the agenda," the Chief explained. "I am confident today will end with a celebration in the Roundhouse."

The Chief continued with his words directed to Ethan. "We have spoken often of the ancestral rivalry between the clans and the jealousy that continues to plague our progress," he said with frustration. "Chiefs before me hid behind warring clans instead of brokering peace," he observed with disdain, "and Chiefs who follow me will continue to do the same to stay in power." Lowering his voice, he continued as he made his way to the chair beside Ethan. "While they take as much as they can before they are voted out. With two-year election cycles, it is difficult to make unpopular decisions with no immediate benefits to the tribe."

With a deep breath and his hands folded in his lap, he continued. "I trust you, Ethan. Both of you, and I believe in the partnership we are building. Everything that needed to be done to secure the votes for today has been done," he said with resolve. "The four of us will explain the partnership to the tribe and why we should work with Devlin," the Chief declared and patted Ethan on the leg. "Gloria and Gwendolyn are safe. We will find out what happened and deal with them," he confirmed to Ethan with certainty, "when the time is right."

"Agreed. Gwendolyn is safe," Ethan accepted. "But I'm not sure she was the target," he countered. "I don't think someone from the tribe was behind it and even if it was someone from the tribe who drove them off the road, I'm not sure it was their idea. This isn't her first time on the reservation and most of the tribe thinks she still works for the university," he said and looked at the Chief. "Why did they target her and risk hurting Gloria? How could they know she was integral to the partnership progressing? Only a small group knew Gwendolyn authored the agreement that binds our organizations for decades," Ethan asked without expecting an answer. "I let down my guard and my arrogance blinded me," he admitted shamefully. "I told her I would protect her but Gwendolyn naïvely thought everyone would play by the rules. She could have been killed today, and I think they were targeting me," Ethan said through clenched teeth. "That won't happen again."

"We understand there'll be more opposition to this alliance from outside the tribe than within," the Chief interceded. "Your competitors have the same motivations as the Chiefs I described earlier; greed, power, and control of the Land," he determined and hung his head in momentary defeat. "It's an ancient battle we have been fighting for millennia. To control the Land and all its riches, there is little our enemies won't do to have it. We have endured so much violence and brutality in trying to protect the Land," Chief Trout acknowledged. "Each of us has a story, and I hope the partnership we are creating will allow our tribe to heal along with the Land."

As everyone considered their own suspicions and fears, Gwendolyn emerged from the treatment room dressed and ready for the meeting. "What's wrong? What happened?" she asked with worry in her voice. Conscious of our eyes on her, Gwendolyn could see the gravity of the situation. Without waiting for a reply, she cut through the hesitant silence. "Look, I am fine," she said. "The cut will heal and, if I had my seatbelt on, I wouldn't have been hurt at all," she lamented as she reached up and ran her fingers over the bandage on her forehead.

Ethan stood up and walked over to Gwendolyn and touch her forehead as he looked into her eyes. "You should have listened to me. I told you this would be dangerous and not to go anywhere alone," he said softly with a touch of compassion. "It won't happen again. That I can guarantee," he asserted and broke his stare. "I don't trust Angeconeb to guarantee Gwendolyn's safety," he stated while walking towards the Chief. "Let's head to the Roundhouse and review the security plan. I want to go over everything again."

"We have over an hour before the meeting starts and we haven't discussed your experience in the sweat," the Chief said with curiosity as he remained seated.

Ethan winced at the thought of recounting his experience to the Chief, and in front of an audience. While he was still visibly bothered about Gwendolyn, he seemed more affected by the Chief's question. "I think we should prepare for the meeting and watch everyone as they arrive at the Roundhouse," Ethan said firmly and headed towards the door.

"Discussing what you saw during the sweat *is* preparing for the meeting," I told him, which stopped him in his tracks. "We use the tradition of the sweat lodge to purify our minds and our bodies to hear messages from our ancestors and Mother Earth," I explained and continued. "That's why we invited you to join, so our ancestors and Elders that have passed into the Spirit World could communicate with you as well."

"What did you see, Ethan?" Chief Trout asked. "We need to interpret the message you were given before we address the tribe," he continued. "The Elders will want to know what you heard or saw in the sweat before they feel comfortable endorsing the partnership. That is why the sweat happened first," he explained. "It was necessary to secure unanimous support."

Ethan appeared unsettled with having to explain his experience, so I gestured for him to sit back down. With my arm in his, I walked him back to his seat with the hope he would relax and describe whatever it was he saw during the sweat. At the time, I thought he was uncomfortable because he had nothing to tell us. The sweat doesn't guarantee a message from the Spirit World and Ethan wasn't from our tribe. Only Susan was sure he was Indian and even more certain Ethan would receive a message in the sweat that would convince the rest of the Elders' Circle to endorse the partnership. Her powers as a medicine woman were credited with the power to make things happen, both good and bad. Ethan surprised me by spontaneously speaking without further prompting.

"I didn't know what to expect, aside from my assumption that it would be hot," Ethan started lightly, "I figured I like a good sauna or steam, but this was way more intense. I kept thinking *'this has to be over soon'* because it just kept getting hotter," he continued more seriously. "We had been sitting in waves of crushing, wet heat for hours, and some of the men inside were much older and looked to be handling it far better," he admitted. "Every time they poured more water on the rocks, I felt the weight over my entire body and my vision blurred into a haze," he described, almost with disbelief as he continued. "I'm convinced I hallucinated and experienced something akin to a psychedelic trip," he confessed. "I haven't tried acid or peyote, but I have heard stories that sounded similar to what I experienced in college when I took mushrooms."

Ethan continued to explain that colours and rays of light flashed and pulsated just above him with all the distractions of something he called a rave, while the sound inside the sweat lodge turned off. He saw lips moving and the men mouthing chants with the drum, but he couldn't hear them. "Then, I heard birds chirping and I recognized individual calls, like the chickadee, a robin and maybe a finch. It was like background music," he explained. "They just kept pouring on the water and bringing in more rocks. As the steam thickened, my vision narrowed and tunneled with everyone around me disappearing into the blurred edges. I thought I was going to pass out, and I focused on the tunnel, until I saw a light. The longer I stared at it, the clearer everything became. If I didn't experience it, if Gwendolyn told me this happened to her, I wouldn't have believed it," he affirmed. "I felt as though I woke up in a different place and time. I was outside on the edge of what smelt like the ocean and the hot steam felt more like the cool mist in a fog. The lodge disappeared around me and," Ethan stopped and emerged from his recollection in the sweat as if waking up from a dream.

Ethan took a long pause and blinked as if it would bring clarity to his thoughts. He looked up at Chief Trout and held back the rest. "The rest of my experience was personal and I don't want to share it with anyone. The sweat may help me prove Susan's assumption about my genealogy but it is mine to investigate," Ethan stated. "You invited me into your ceremony and I am grateful that you did," Ethan thanked the Chief. "I hope you can understand my request to let me hold back this piece until I understand what it means, to me. We have more pressing matters to handle, and I can't afford to be sidetracked by anything personal," he challenged the Chief. "The sweat was a life-altering experience, but I learned more about the Elders and your tribe during our meetings here and visits to McIntosh. Remind them of the commitments I made and see if you can convince them to endorse the agreement, Chief. We have a small window of opportunity to steal these licenses while Weyerhaeuser is distracted with the appeal and we have some influence over the Governor," Ethan reminded us. "They won't see us coming."

"Take back, Ethan," the Chief corrected. "They stole the Land from us, we are taking back control, together. We aren't stealing anything," the Chief countered and then smirked. "We aren't stealing anything but you may be accused of that by your competitors." The Chief patted Ethan on the leg once more and stood up to look at me. "I am confident in the recommendation you made to the Elders' Circle. They will give you unanimous support and the tribal council will endorse their decision." Chief Trout turned back to Ethan to offer a suggestion. "If you let the ladies deliver your message to the tribe in the Roundhouse and let Gloria speak in our traditional language, you will have your partnership."

The Chief headed to the door and motioned for us to follow. We walked out of the Nurse's Station and made our way to the Roundhouse for the meeting. The Chief stopped to address Ethan, "I received my own personal message in a sweat earlier this year. Truthfully, it was the reason I asked the Elders' Circle to invite you to this one. It wasn't difficult to convince the, uh, ladies to invite you and, well, they drive all decisions in the community," he admitted in jest. "Except the important ones."

Ethan cocked his head in slight surprise and looked over to me as the Chief continued. I held his stare and smiled. It was one of the Chief's favourite jokes and I quite enjoyed it.

"There is an anecdote told at ceremonial sweats when a male Elder is welcomed into the circle. It is tradition within the Jackfish River tribe that men are the decision-makers, when it comes to the important decisions," he paused without a trace of humour. "When it comes to the rest of the decisions, the women decide without the men." Smiling, he finished by saying, "In twelve thousand years of oral history, there hasn't been a single important decision and we are still waiting for the women to tell us when we are needed." While Ethan genuinely laughed, I noticed that Gwendolyn respectfully offered a polite chuckle, dismissing the joke.

The Chief continued to address Ethan as he got into the passenger seat of the truck that was waiting for him, "Maybe at another time and place, we will both be inclined to share what we saw. It may be easier to piece together the message when we truly trust each other," he offered and closed the door.

Returning to the present day on Moose Island…

I stopped on a positive note rather than discuss the part where Ethan was called away by the old man to deal with an emergency. He was forced to return to the office and only had a few minutes to encourage us before leaving. I remember being too nervous to listen to his words and instead watched as Gwendolyn intently absorbed his instructions. Whatever he said, it must have been good. The agreement was later endorsed unanimously by the Elders' Circle and Chief Trout called a vote of the tribal council that ratified the partnership with Devlin. Unfortunately, the emergency that pulled Ethan away was the old man pulling out of the agreement.

"We haven't spoken of that day since. Our world became very busy in the aftermath of the meeting at the Roundhouse and everything seemed to change overnight," I offered, trying to avoid any negative memories. Given the late hour and how much I was enjoying the evening, I left my request for help unasked. "Can you tell me what you saw that day? In the sweat?"

Ethan turned his attention back to the fire and added more driftwood before entertaining my question. We all watched as the flames reached up to the darkened sky and released embers into the air like fireflies. The sparks shimmered in the water as it returned to the cove and my eyes followed them up as they skipped across the stars above us. The sun had fully set, and the tide was returning water to the cove, just as Gwendolyn said it would. Sensing he wanted to leave the rest of that day in the past, I pulled him back to tell me about his vision.

Ethan looked up and spoke to the stars above us, "The stars look exactly as I remember them as a boy, so clear, so sharp," he shared. "When I was young, I always felt safe sleeping outside alone under the stars. I would make a shelter, which was usually more of a fort with rocks and branches built up around me. I would keep building it up until I felt safe enough to fall asleep under the open sky," explained Ethan. He broke his gaze from the sky and looked over to me. "I left the sweat that day with that same feeling of safety, which made little sense." Before either of us said anything, Ethan took us back into the sweat lodge.

"All I could see was a glowing, pale light in front of my eyes and the harder I stared at it, the clearer it became. The dome shelter of the building folded inward and took me to a different place," he described. "And with it, reality seem to bend as well." With little difficulty remembering the details of his vision, Ethan explained, "The landscape in front of me came into focus and I was standing in a clearing surrounded by trees and I could see the ocean off in the distance. Three animals appeared in front of me, a wolf, an eagle and a raven. They were in the middle of a heated argument and I could only hear one part of the conversation; the part spoken by the wolf and he only said, '*I understand.*' The animals appeared as ethereal images, translucent and floating in front of me but something about them were…," Ethan struggled for the right word and I interjected.

"Authentically wild with details you didn't know they had?" I asked, using my own experiences to guide my question.

Finding my eyes, Ethan nodded and continued. "Every hair, every feather, they looked real and I couldn't explain them away. Even when they started talking, everything seemed so natural, except for the voice screaming in my head to snap out of it," Ethan admitted. "Instead of focusing on everything that what was implausible, I let that feeling of peacefulness take over and I concentrated on the message, not the messengers." Ethan broke eye contact with me and turned to Gwendolyn, "Even when I realized I was inside the body of a wolf that was conversing with an eagle and a raven, I let everything happen around me and just listened," he explained while repeating the exchange as the wolf.

Back in time, inside the sweat lodge at McIntosh…

"Do you know what I am doing here?" asked the wolf in Ethan's voice. "What is happening?" Ethan asked sternly.

"Mother Earth sometimes allows humans to bend her rules and shift shape with the wolf to help all living things exist in balance with the Land and one another," the eagle explained. "Exchanging your body with the wolf allows you to establish a connection to the Land and hear messages from the other living things with which you share it," the eagle described and held the stare of Ethan's eyes through the wolf. "It allows you to understand our messages by joining our bodies and spirits to hear us from within," the eagle stated and allowed Ethan to respond.

"That really does not explain why I am out here," Ethan said as he motioned with a paw to the surroundings forest, "and everyone else who should be listening is back in the sweat lodge," gesturing with his snout to point somewhere behind him. "How am I going to help? I'm not Indian," stated Ethan. He was the only white person in the sweat and it seemed illogical that he would be chosen as the shapeshifting human.

"Mother Earth chose you to shapeshift with the wolf. Your people need your help to protect the Land," interjected the raven who paused before continuing. Unsure how to answer, Ethan waited for the looming black bird to finish. "Before you can help them, you need to find your people," he instructed.

"If I am Indian, then I found my people," Ethan said. "Susan told me I am from the Wolf clan. She explained the purpose of the wolf and I will stay to fulfill my duty," he asserted. "If these are my people, I am helping them protect the Land."

"These people are not your tribe. You have helped them protect the Land and Mother Earth needs you to find your tribe to help them," the raven finished.

"Your tribe needs your help, but they have lost their way to you. After you were taken from the Land, your grandfather watched over you. Until he died," the eagle said somberly. "Your grandfather sent a message to you from the Spirit World, *'Go to Moose Island.'*"

"Moose Island? I don't know where that is. What am I going to find there?" As soon as he asked the question, the images of the eagle and raven faded into the background. Ethan floated through the ground and found himself back in the sweat lodge. When he looked down, he realized the wolf's body shifted back into his.

"Wait, how am I supposed to help my tribe if I don't know what I am looking for on Moose Island. Who needs help?" asked Ethan. Before the eagle could answer, Ethan was pulled from the sweat by the Chief.

10 THE ALLIANCE

Leaving the humans on Moose Island, we join all the living things in the Forest of Peace along the shores of the Penobscot River...

Certain he made the right decision to send Elka back, Tuwiye was rattled and uneasy with the feelings that emerged upon her return. While certainty disappeared, in its place he found reprieve and a calming reassurance from Elka's presence and words of support. Elka eroded his confidence by leaving so abruptly and, in her absence, left only the voice of his father repeating in his head.

Her departure left him unexpectedly injured, although he was the one that demanded she leave. Elated with relief, Tuwiye hid his wounds and surrendered as she pulled him from the encroaching darkness from within the cave into the remaining light of dusk. With a peaceful breath, Tuwiye wordlessly took Elka in his arms and nostalgically welcomed the fleeting moment of comfort that accompanied her female embrace. With bolstered confidence, he released her and explained the plan he hastily concocted to fulfill his promise to Cikia.

The plan was dangerous, fraught with unknowns and could easily result in his own death, as it required two Eagles. He earlier dismissed the idea of endangering Elka until she returned and demanded to stay. As he explained, it was a plan that could cripple one bird, while two could collectively shoulder the burden. The belief Kakik was still alive allowed Tuwiye to shield his thoughts from any lingering doubts about his plan. Yet, both he and Elka knew the plan would become exceedingly more difficult if they find Kakik has passed onto the Spirit World.

"Every rescue mission comes with unknowns and that means danger," Tuwiye said, echoing the words of his father. "For that reason, only the strongest are chosen for search and rescue missions." With a softened stare, Tuwiye stepped back and hung his head, while keeping his eyes on Elka. "I should be stronger," he acknowledged. "I was taught to follow my training, which tells me to order you to turn around and deliver that piece of birch bark to my father," the young captain offered with little resolve. Unsure of how to explain, Tuwiye allowed the thoughts in his head to tumble from his beak. "I am so glad you came back and I want you to stay," he confessed as he reached for her wing. "I am a protector and I will keep you safe. The plan will work. I am sure," Tuwiye reassured by squeezing her wing in his.

'Order me?' Elka thought as she unintentionally crossed her wings. From their earlier conversation and his obvious innocence with females, she dismissed her question and softened her steely glare. Elka felt the same way when she was with Tuwiye and held his wing in hers, meeting his eyes with the confidence of knowing he was right.

As Elka walked towards the cave wall, she gestured for him to come closer. "I want to show you something I did not see earlier," she said as her eyes focused on the illustration in front of her. "These messages are significant to everyone in the Land, so I committed as many to memory as possible, so I could recreate them upon my return home. Redrawing each piece in my mind helped me memorize them and, as I retraced the profile of the Eagle, I realized I missed something. We both missed something," she stated with certainty. "Otherwise, you would not have sent me back."

Elka looked up the wall until her eyes found the image that was freshly burned into her memory. She pointed up to the profile of the Eagle with a flame on its chest all contained within the outline of the human. Above and behind the Eagle, the arms of the human encircled the rest of the image. The outline of what first appeared to be one Eagle's head and shoulders was that of two; one contained within the other. Over time, some of the colours melded together and made the outline appear to be a shadow and not the silhouette of two birds. Two birds displayed as one.

"Maybe the colours faded over time and turned the larger Eagle into a shadow of the smaller one but it is very easy to see the two of them up close. I wish I could remember exactly how my Kokum explained the stories to me. I do not remember two Eagles in the legend but she suggested there was more to learn, when I was older," Elka recounted. "She died before we spoke about it again."

Tuwiye mechanically moved his head left to right and up and down to examine the outline from different angles without moving the rest of his body. He hesitated to focus on the two birds and Elka moved in closer to touch the image. "Right here, where it looks like there is a shadow, there is a second Eagle," she said while reaching up to trace the image with her primary feather.

As the tips of her feathers brushed across the etching, she turned to face Tuwiye and opened her beak to explain the rest of her theory when she was overcome by a rush of energy. It pushed the feathers on her head and chest back and forced a deep breath of air into her lungs while images, voices and sounds overwhelmed her all at once and everywhere around her. There was something oddly familiar in the barrage of sensations that summoned memories of her Kokum and eased her resistance to the spectacle playing only for her.

As he watched her body twitched and her lightly shut eyelids bounce up and down, Tuwiye reached out to shield Elka from whatever was happening. The sight of Elka entranced, by what appeared to be the same invisible force that invaded his mind when he met Kakik, startled Tuwiye. Overwhelmed early in his adventure, Tuwiye dismissed the experience rather than understand it and, along with it, ignored the message being sent to him from the Spirit World. Tuwiye waited for Elka to return before reaching out and allowed her to experience the visions without interruption.

Distracted with concern for his new partner, Tuwiye did not register the faint yet familiar whooshing of wings flapping into a soft landing behind them, as the sound was effortlessly devoured by rushing water deeper inside the cave. Tuwiye thought he felt the vibration of crunching rocks beneath his talons and turned his head towards the entrance peering into the dying light of the sunset. In the moment, and dismissing his tactical instincts, Tuwiye ignored the sounds and turned his attention back to Elka, who had returned.

With a few cautious steps forward, Tuwiye gently asked, "Are you back? Elka are you…?" he was unable to finish as Elka abruptly interrupted him, "We need to go, now! Kakik is in trouble. Follow me, I saw the way to the front entrance." Elka started deeper into the cave without waiting for a response from Tuwiye and quickened her pace as she marched into the shadows.

"Elka wait, please," Tuwiye pleaded as he clamoured to catch up. Unsure of his footing, Tuwiye focused on keeping up as Elka gained speed to prepare for flight. "What did you see?" yelled Tuwiye as he forced his wings into flight. As Tuwiye took to the air inside the cave, Elka dropped from sight into the pooling darkness beneath them. Trusting her lead, Tuwiye followed and dove into the swirling winds that tossed him back and forth as his eyes searched for something, anything in the blackness washing over him.

"Follow my voice, Tuwiye. Climb!" shouted Elka back to her companion. "Kakik is on the other side of the waterfall. We need to reach him before the Owls do." It was obvious she was singularly focused on the mission to save Kakik. Following instructions from the flashing images, Elka found a tunnel that would lead them to the front entrance, where Kakik was trapped by fallen rocks and encircled by Owls.

With faith in the rest of her vision, Tuwiye obediently followed Elka and focused on staying close. Uncomfortable following anyone, Tuwiye looked for an opportunity to overtake her. The sound of rushing water grew louder and Tuwiye felt a light mist spray across his beak as he picked up speed. Droplets of water collected and fell from the feathers on his head making it difficult to see. Flying blind into the darkness, his other senses envisioned the path of the mighty river that sliced through the peak and poured out of the Great Mountain. Tuwiye slowed his flight and manoeuvred to where he thought he would be safe.

Surrounded by the roaring water, Tuwiye did his best to focus on finding

Elka. Unable to find her voice hidden in the deafening thunder, he scanned the surroundings for light. Blindly peering towards the rumbling sound, Tuwiye spotted droplets of dull, meandering light from the full moon rising towards the Great Mountain. Moonbeams encircled water droplets in the spray and provided a hazy outline of the falls that Tuwiye could see to avoid. Beyond the mist, Tuwiye could see Elka perched above him, on what he thought to be the tunnel leading outside. Climbing to reach her, Tuwiye avoided the water by landing on a narrow ledge behind the falls and shuffling across to reach her.

Still deafened by the roaring thunder around him, Tuwiye scanned the opening for Elka rather than call out to her again. Losing sight of her while walking behind the wall of water, he flew up to the ledge and landed on the spot where he saw her only seconds ago. Elka could only travel in one direction, Tuwiye followed the tunnel in search of her. As Tuwiye continued down the tunnel he hoped would lead to Elka, his mind shifted to Kakik. His new friend was alone, trapped and surrounded by a formidable and ruthless enemy.

Considered a sinister group of bad and scheming birds, the Owls are feared and misunderstood. Expelled from the Fire Council generations earlier, they were often accused of using trickery, deceit and, almost always, violent means. Most birds and small animals avoided their territory, except for the Eagles, who understood the hierarchy of the Owls and monitored their activities. The Owls policed themselves according to their own rules, which they kept to themselves. Underneath their methods, and often cloaked by aggression and brutality, was a foundation of fairness, a pursuit of retribution, or, ultimately, what is deemed necessary, by the parliament.

From Sentinel training, Tuwiye understood his role to be one of reconnaissance with the Owls, unless intervention was unquestionably required. Tuwiye was trained to observe the Owls cautiously with no quarter for trust or counsel. Eagles and Owls had a bloody history of conflict, unrest and eventual peace through guarded avoidance. Evidence of the hatred for the Owls could be found in every soar and elsewhere on the land. Eagles avoid parliaments of Owls and the Owls avoid soars of Eagles with both seeking habitats in absence of one another.

With the sound of the waterfall behind him, Tuwiye called out to both Elka and Kakik. Moonbeams guided him as he shouted out a name every few steps, hoping to hear something in return. After several unanswered attempts, Tuwiye unmuted his instincts and thought back to the warnings he ignored earlier. He recalled the sound of swooshing wings and the vibration of crunching gravel. It grated on his thoughts and led him to replay everything Elka shared from her vision. Without wasting time, he sought shelter to reassess his plan to save Kakik, and now Elka too.

Tuwiye came to a widening in the tunnel with three different paths from which to choose. The first path was the one he was following, lit by the moonlight, and obviously led outside. The other two tunnels went in opposite directions with the possibility of a dead-end. Elka could have ventured down either of these paths and Tuwiye did not want to risk exposing his position, and that he was alone, by calling out again. Seeking a better vantage point, the trained Sentinel moved towards the moonlight to take a strategic perch and evaluate the threat.

Following the moonlit path in front of him, Tuwiye came upon the rockslide at the entrance. Light piercing through the rubble allowed Tuwiye to clear a pathway out of the cave. Hopping from boulder to boulder, he could feel smaller rocks falling and shifting below his talons. When a larger boulder rolled down the pile outside and off the Great Mountain, Tuwiye heard a muffled sound beneath him. Without giving away his position, Tuwiye quietly asked, "Is someone down there? Kakik, is that you?" asked the young Eagle.

A few moments later, Tuwiye heard the same muffled sound. "Louder! I cannot hear you," Tuwiye said a little louder this time and tersely.

Louder and much clearer, Tuwiye heard, "Quiet, they will hear you. They took Elka with them. You need to get me out of here," a familiar voice demanded.

"Kakik! Are you hurt? Who took Elka? Was it the Owls?" asked Tuwiye.

"They cleared a pathway through the rubble to get out from the tunnel. Follow the moonlight outside and come over to help me. I am trapped and need some help with one last rock. Take care to keep quiet, the Owls left behind scouts," Kakik warned.

Tracking Kakik's voice, Tuwiye found his trusted guide through a small hole he created in the disorganized pile of rock. With his wing, Kakik explained his plan to Tuwiye.

"If you push this rock into the cavern, it will bring down these large boulders here and create an opening above it," Kakik directed as he pointed with his wing where he needed Tuwiye's strength.

"Kakik, this sounds insanely dangerous. I cannot control where this rock will fall and how many others will come down. Let me go back inside and find a safer way to get you out," challenged Tuwiye.

Dismissing the logical questions posed by his understudy, Kakik detailed the rest of his plan, "To avoid being crushed, I will take cover and hope I can get out once the dust settles. When you feel the rock moving, jump from the cliff, in case I miscalculated and some boulders fall towards you," instructed the wise yet scared Raven.

Eager to free Kakik and hear what he knew about Elka, Tuwiye silenced the doubting voices in his mind and readied to force the rock into the cavern. With little warning, Tuwiye pushed the rock until he felt it shift and start to roll. "Stand clear, Kakik!" Tuwiye shouted as he sprang away from the rockslide and dove away from the falling rocks.

As Kakik predicted, the large rock shifted and allowed a wave of smaller rocks to come crashing down that created a large opening above where Tuwiye was standing. When the debris settled, Tuwiye could hear him coughing and complaining. Before he could utter a word, Kakik was expressing his displeasure at the lack of warning he was given.

"Were you trying to flatten me? I nearly died in there. Could you not give an old Raven a wing flap to get out of the way," chirped Kakik. Despite his biting words, Kakik's eyes sparkled with happiness at being rescued. With renewed focus, Kakik descended from the rock pile and walked toward the young Eagle. "We need to find a safe place where we can talk."

"We need to find Elka," Tuwiye stated firmly. "She was leading the way through the mountain when I lost her," he sheepishly explained. "She knew you were alive and exactly where to find you. She thought you were in danger from the Owls."

"I overheard the Owls discussing their *assignment*," Kakik interjected with disdain for the term used to describe the foiled abduction. "They were hired by 'Musquash' to deliver you, alive. For what I could piece together, I think they have been following us since we left the Forest of Peace," Kakik detailed.

"Musquash, as in Elka's soar? If her soar was involved, why was she taken? Why are the Owls involved?" Tuwiye asked in rapid succession. "The Owls only take assignments in the interest of the parliament, or for hire," Tuwiye recited verbatim from his training.

The Owls lived by their own rules, the rules created by the parliament. Keeping their distance from everyone, the Owls operate in the shadows on the fringe of nature, often undertaking tasks no other group would. While all the other living things understood and accepted that the Owls and their services were required, few would admit to hiring them. Young Eagles enlisted to be Sentinels are introduced to the Owls and their organization, reporting structure and regular activities. Tuwiye could not imagine how he and Kakik could be involved in anything that would warrant the attention of the Owls.

"There's more," said the old Raven. "We are not safe speaking in the open like this," said Kakik as he scanned the ground below for somewhere protected. "Let's make camp at the mouth of the river."

Miles away from the base of the Great Mountain and still along the meandering and treed shores of the Penobscot River, Elka paced back and forth under the guard of several Owls. The silhouettes cast by moonlight through the forest canopy above and around them created a shadow menagerie that camouflaged the number of Owls that held her captive. At the base of a large and split sugar maple, two very large and quiet Owls stood on either side of the tree with Elka placed in the tree split. While taken against her will, the Owls handled her with a gentle touch and said very little since ambushing her.

Upon landing on the ledge above the waterfall, Elka did not clear the tunnel for any potential threats. She looked back for Tuwiye and watched him until he faded away behind the water. She did not have time to react when she felt both of her wings restrained in a firm grip from behind and heard a dry, deep voice behind her.

"Easy or hard?" the voice questioned from the darkness. "The boss says it is up to you."

Elka looked towards the voice and locked onto a pair of fiendishly yellow eyes framed by an angry brow that cemented the stare straight ahead. As she contemplated her response, the eyes floated towards her and brought with them a brown face along with pointy dark ears and the horns of an enforcer. She went with sarcasm, leaving both options open for the moment. "For you, or for me?" Elka asked.

The only reaction her question garnered from the enforcer was the further furrowing of his already stern brow as he waited for an actual answer. Without moving or making a sound, the enforcer was flanked by two of his similar-sized colleagues, while the Owl restraining her wings let go and walked her in to join his associates. Beyond the visible enforcers were several smaller Owls awaiting instruction. During her Sentinel training, Elka received the same debriefing as Tuwiye and questioned why the Owls would kidnap her. The kid glove treatment seemed juxtaposed against their demonstrable reputation for brutal tactics and little mercy. "Fine, lead the way. Where are we headed?"

Upon leaving the cave, the Owls escorted Elka a short distance to a sparsely treed section along the shores of the Penobscot River. Eager to warn her companions, Elka dismissed the immediate danger. "Tell me why you were following us," Elka demanded of her captures. "Who hired you?" she questioned, addressing the largest of her captures who remained with his back to her.

Without turning his body, the giant Owl contorted his neck around to face her. She could see that he was not an enforcer like the rest of them. The largest of the Owls, he sported deeply inset eyes that were sheltered by large, feathered halos camouflaged by understated colors that matched the terrain. Decorated with the white markings of a commander just beneath his downward-facing beak, Elka understood he was in charge. Without giving an answer, he crouched while executing two measured flaps of his wings to glide to a stop in front of her, his unnerving gaze unbroken.

The Owl methodically turned his head back and forth to look at Elka up close, as his eyesight was not his most powerful sense. After several seconds of silence, the looming figure broke through the sound of the river flowing next to them with a deep, raspy voice that ruffled back the feathers on her neck. "You are not afraid. Interesting," the giant Owl said while continuing to examine her. "You were not the target. We could decide to hurt you or take you with us as well." He allowed Elka to respond without yielding his ground.

Unphased by his closeness, Elka demanded a second time, "Who hired you?"

"Inconsequential," he said with indifference. "We decided the assignment was worth the risk, given the reward," the Owl answered cryptically. He was impressed by her unrelenting bravado and assumed a more reasonable distance from her. While maintaining eye contact, the Owl continued, "You control your fear well. A valuable trait for a female of your species, especially when you are alone. And with so many of us," he warned, void of any emotion.

Sidestepping the threat, Elka retorted, "I overheard one of your minions lamenting that the assignment was to capture, not kill. If you were not given the latitude to kill, I highly doubt whoever hired you would appreciate you killing me in the process," Elka bargained. "If you hurt me, I will take great pleasure in knowing that my soar will retaliate, and you all will suffer. Let us spare the posturing and feather-waving unless you want to settle this now," Elka threatened followed by a series of intimidating shrieks and whistles that grew into a mantling display.

The enforcer that apprehended her in the cave walked over to his boss and whispered, "She won't tell us anything helpful, boss. We have lookouts perched up and down the river, all around the Great Mountain and we have our associates looking for them as well. We will find the mark," reassured the subordinate. "We can take care of this one so she does not cause us any issues while we search for him."

As he turned away from Elka, the boss conceded, "She is right. We have no justification for hurting her. Killing her will not be worth the price we will pay at the next Fire Council meeting. We still do not know who she is," continued the patient senior. "She could be the daughter of the soar leader or the granddaughter of a prominent Elder. We will deliver her along with our target," he paused as he continued to plan. "He will find us when hears we have her."

"So, we just stay here until her mate comes to save her? That does not sound like a great plan. The boys are restless and need a task to occupy them. Let me send scouts to narrow the search area," the loyal soldier suggested. "We can leave a couple of guards with her and send out the rest to search."

Weighing the effort involved in both scenarios, the boss walked away from everyone towards the river with his subordinate in tow. "She is alone, outnumbered by Owls and does not know why she was taken, yet she continues to be belligerently brave and fiercely defiant. That is unwavering confidence in something," he paused for a moment as he pivoted his neck to look at Elka, "or someone."

He turned his attention back to the water and stared downstream for a long time. The frustrated soldier broke the serenity of the flowing rhythm by asking, "Boss, what are you telling us to do?"

With a stern and impatient stare, the boss replied reluctantly, "Let her go and they will find one another. When they do, we will grab them the way we planned and deliver two Eagles instead of one. She can be the Raven's replacement." He gave his orders with hidden uncertainty. Unsure of who she was and the ramifications of her getting hurt, the authoritative Owl hoped his plan would yield the expected outcome. Otherwise, he knew the Owls would find themselves indebted to the client.

Upstream at the base of the Great Mountain, Tuwiye and Kakik took shelter and water from a protected pool close to the waterfall flowing from the rocks above. Red spruce and white pine trees towered and threw shade over the small pocket of water just down from the landing of the waterfall. The water was cool, calm and hidden from the air. Both birds welcomed the refuge area and allowed their surging adrenalin to temper by taking a moment to centre themselves. Rejuvenated by the fresh water, they were eager to find Elka.

Impatient to share what he overheard, Kakik went first and detailed the exchange to Tuwiye. "The Owls were instructed to capture you and deliver you to a drop site somewhere along the river. If anyone was helping you, they were to be taken as well."

"What payment will the Owls receive for completing their assignment?" asked Tuwiye. "Perhaps that will help us figure out who hired them or why they would accept the assignment."

"There is little the Owls will not do for the right price," Kakik stated with conviction. "Well, most times, it is for the right favor. Something that would be named later and the indebted have little recourse except to comply," explained the Raven. "All we have is the name Musquash. Maybe an Eagle from the Musquash soar hired the Owls? If that were the case, maybe Elka was the mark. Someone from the soar was targeting her for some reason," Kakik offered as a plausible theory without taking a breath.

"What could Elka have done that was so egregious to require someone in her soar to hire the Owls. I could not imagine what problem in the soar could justify that," Tuwiye naively stated.

"Their existence, while loathed by many, is a regrettable necessity for some leaders. Sometimes for the good of a soar, or an unkindness, intervention from an outsider keeps the peace," explained the Elder. "We do not have time to debate the matter right now, Tuwiye. We can argue about the ethics of leadership on the flight home," chirped the Raven. "We need to find Elka."

"I thought perhaps we could reach out to Elka's soar for help but that makes little sense now. Maybe the local unkindness, although we could not trust them either," Tuwiye sighed.

"I could send a messenger back to my unkindness. We could have help here in the morning," Kakik stated with certainty. "All of them will fight until she is safe."

"Or we could just stay right here and enjoy the starry sky above the falls," suggested a voice from the shadows between the trees.

While both birds were initially startled, Tuwiye recognized the voice. "Elka is that you?" he asked as he peered into the darkness.

"Tuwiye! I am so glad to see you," Elka said through laboured breathing. She struggled to regain her composure and did her best to continue. "I was heading back to the peak to look for you but I needed to rest and remembered this pool." In Tuwiye's offered embrace, she nuzzled her beak into his chest and said, "I thought I told you to follow me," as she choked back her fear.

"I am so sorry, Elka. Did they hurt you? Let me see you." He released her and looked her up and down to ensure she was not injured and eventually locked onto her eyes. With his usual tact, Kakik interrupted the moment and bluntly asked "Elka, how did you escape?"

"Kakik, you are alive! My vision was right about you, and the Owls. It has been right about everything up to this point. If it is right about everything, you need to hear the rest of it. Some of it may be difficult to understand," Elka stopped and looked up at Tuwiye.

"First, how did you escape? The Owls are not in the business of letting their assignments go," Kakik asked through thinly veiled suspicion.

"The one in charge sent everyone to search for you and left me with two guards. Both the guards were young and easily distracted. Eventually, the boss left with one of the guards and allowed me the opportunity to overpower the guard when he was alone. I have been flying as fast as I could ever since," Elka explained.

"Were you followed? Did you fly straight here?" Kakik asked nervously. "Did you contemplate the possibility that they let you escape so you would lead them straight to us?"

"Yes, I did," Elka said indignantly. "I flew in different paths and routes away from the river and back to confuse anyone trying to follow my route unless they were close. I doubled back several times to ensure I was not followed and returned to the river to find this pool," Elka explained. "I could not hear or see anything within following distance."

"You really put my associates through a workout," a familiar raspy voice said as the gigantic Owl fell in a silent death plunge from above and landed abruptly. With authority, the imposing Owl, accompanied by several enforcers, surrounded the three companions. "Well, it looks like we will overachieve on our assignment. We will deliver all three of you to Musquash."

"Musquash? How did you know? That is my…," Elka started to say and stopped before finishing.

Her misstep permitted the Owl to press for more. "You are just full of surprises," he said and then paused briefly to consider his next words. "Is Musquash your home soar?" asked the Owl while examining her face for the slightest twitch of confirmation. With the absence of a reaction taken as confirmation, the Owl eased into his interrogation. "The disdain you displayed earlier, for me and my fellow Owls, hypocritical, no? Someone from your own soar, your family, came to us to solve a problem. While brutal in our approach and tactics, Owls are principled and dedicated to the parliament, foremost. We would never go to outsiders. You Eagles cannot say the same, yet you are quick to judge us."

"I experienced many emotions while detained by you and your goons and disdain was only one of them. There was nothing pleasant about being kidnapped and, if my soar hired you, then I can negotiate a new arrangement," Elka countered. "Let us go and the Musquash soar will still owe the Owls a debt. Through me."

The intimidating Owl reared his head and let out a bellowing laugh, startling

Elka and causing her to mantle. He looked over at his number two and nodded towards her. Elka was swiftly subdued by two Owls, which caused Tuwiye to intervene in retaliation. While far beyond his fighting years, Kakik felt the need to contribute as well. Despite a valiant effort, they were severely outnumbered and, eventually, all three companions were restrained by the Owls and heavily guarded.

"Oh, you three are most definitely coming with us now. Regardless of whether you are worth something, you will bring a measure of entertainment to the exchange," the old Owl smirked as he made his way closer to Elka.

"Given the reputation of the Owls, I am surprised you so summarily dismissed my counteroffer," taunted Elka. "If you would tell your goons, your associates, to release me, I can explain just how valuable a favour from me would be to the Owls."

"What could you possibly offer the Owls?" interjected the number two. "We tricked you into believing you escaped and followed you straight to your friends," the younger Owl challenged, as he walked towards her.

As the Owl neared her wingspan, Elka exercised patient precision before knocking over the unsuspecting Owl with her left wing and followed by skillfully gripping his neck in her right talons. Surprised by her adept aggression, the young Owl yielded and waited for her to sever his jugular. The distraction provided Tuwiye with the opportunity to break free from the two Owls holding his wings and maneuvered closer to Elka. Taking the lieutenant under his control, Tuwiye held him down to allow Elka to answer. With a victorious shrill, Elka asked, "Now that I have your full attention, would you like to consider my counteroffer?"

Never using excess words, the old Owl responded by signalling his subordinates to release them with a slow and purposeful nod. Elka held up her wing and checked on Kakik before gesturing towards the Owl to continue, "You have our attention, my dear. What are you offering?"

"First, enough of *my dear*. I do not appreciate the condescension," Elka instructed and continued without allowing a response. "My family are the hereditary leaders of the Musquash soar and my grandmother was a sacred Elder and Medicine Woman with the gift of vision. She could see the future and her counsel was requested by soars from across the land." Elka paused and hopped closer to the condescending Owl. "She was the representative our soar sent to the Fire Council. Like other communities, the Musquash soar felt it imperative to send an Elder to guide fundamental decisions across the Land. At the council, my Kokum was respected for her ability to forecast future events and provided warnings to the birds, fish and animals living in the Land of the Wabanaki."

Elka spoke of her Kokum with the reverence and respect of a seasoned Sentinel yet tempered her commentary with the emotion of a young Eagle who missed her and yearned for guidance. Unbeknownst to her companions, Elka continued with her impromptu strategy of sharing her vision with the Owls to gain their allegiance. A vision that neither Kakik nor Tuwiye heard in its entirety. She wished she had time to confirm the details with Kakik, who was in her vision. Inventing a narrative from the series of disconnected still pictures that appeared on the wall of the Painted Cave, Elka spoke with authority and confidence she did not really possess. Hopeful the details were accurate, Elka pieced together a story that she hoped the Owls would remember.

"Before she died, my Kokum spent her final years telling me stories about the Land and our relationships with other soars and how we interacted with other birds, animals and fish, even the humans," Elka explained. "She told me the Owls were disavowed from the Fire Council during a spring meeting long ago. While the Owls can attend and address the council, the parliament is no longer permitted a vote," Elka paused hoping the older Owl would interject. While she pieced together the best story she could, it was just that, a story

"You are the granddaughter of Elder Muhkati," the Owl concluded and allowed his statement to sink in. "Your Kokum tabled the resolution that eventually was amended to include our exile. While not her intent, it was a disappointing development from months of working with her on a more acceptable resolution." He represented the Owls at the meeting and remembered every word spoken that day. "I do not see the benefit of revisiting the meeting, as it was not your Kokum's fault for what happened that day," the Owl concluded. "I think we can prepare for the flight back to Musquash," he directed and motioned for his subordinates to prepare to leave.

"I can remove the expulsion order," Elka stated with confidence. "I can attend the next council meeting and table a motion to repeal it. She left me her seat and I am to assume it at the meeting on the first full moon following the summer solstice," confided Elka.

The old Owl raised his wing to stop his enforcers from mobilizing their captives. After contemplating her offer, he turned back to face Elka and engaged in the negotiation. "As a point of clarification, you can remove the expulsion order, or you will. You can see the opportunity for a different interpretation of your offer," he sagely pointed out. "I want the terms to be very clear," stated the Owl with little emotion and no room for movement.

"I will," answered Elka. "First, you need to tell us who hired you and help us piece together why. Then, we have a deal," Elka demanded. "I know your code of silence or code of loyalty or whatever you call it to justify hiding the identities of those who hire you. I do not care. You will tell us who hired you and everything you know about the transaction." Elka drew a breath and paused for a moment to choose her next words. "We want the opportunity to face those who mean us harm."

"Is that not a fancy way of saying, 'you want revenge on those who betrayed you?'" asked the Owl. "I am very familiar with that concept. The Owls have made it their means to survive."

Another deflected questioned only confirmed his assumption and Elka concluded her position. "Or you can take us back and turn us over to your client and trust they will make good on their debt," countered the shrewd Eagle as she collectively negotiated for the freedom of her companions and the opportunity to know the identity of the attackers.

The old Owl scanned the eyes of his subordinates that were dutifully looking for direction, as he contemplated the changing landscape. None of them were old enough to remember the significance of the Fire Council meeting that disavowed the Owls. They only knew life on the fringes, struggling alone without the alliances afforded through the council. Owls understand allegiance is to the parliament first and next to fellow Owls. The chain of command through their hierarchy is at the centre of their existence and they depend on it to survive.

The younger Owls patiently awaited a response from their boss as he decided whether to fulfill the original assignment or accept a new one that came with vindication for the parliament. Years ago, it was his personal vendetta to hand out punishment to those that banished the Owls from the Fire Council, especially the Musquash soar. He lusted for the euphoric satisfaction of punishing those who hurt his fellow Owls by taking a swipe at his parliament.

Realizing Elder Muhkati was beyond his punishment diminished his sense of satisfaction. The original price for taking the assignment was for her to explain why she allowed the council to expel the Owls. The mystery behind the anonymous amendment to the motion haunted the Owls and kept them in relentless pursuit of an unknown enemy. It took so long to manufacture an opportunity to gain back a voting seat. Those now serving on council only remember rumours and whispers of what was done to the Owls. To reclaim a seat on the council would provide an opportunity for them to remind everyone.

"I find your terms acceptable," the imposing Owl agreed with indifference. From a few strides away, it was obvious Nebulosa was not finished. He ominously turned his head around to face Elka with his plumage full of air and confidence. Then, allowing his body to follow, he refined the arrangement, "With a slight variation for your consideration. We are scheduled to deliver the Eagle and the Raven to the client at dawn, by the clearing where the boundary of the soar meets the Penobscot River. Instead of a drop off, we can orchestrate an ambush," proposed the Owl with his wing outstretched. "You can exact your revenge and keep it within the family, something every leader tries to do," concluded the Owl.

Before accepting, Elka asked, "To be clear, all I will owe you, all anyone from the Musquash soar will owe you for completing your assignment, is tabling a motion to remove your expulsion order."

"At the next meeting," the Owl further refined the agreement, keeping out his offered wing and maintaining his straightforward stare. "Your job is not done when you table the motion, you need to follow it through and ensure it passes."

"How can I ensure the motion passes? The Fire Council must vote and pass the motion unanimously to invite the Owls back," Elka challenged.

The commanding Owl closed distance with the naïve Eagle, while flashing a smirk of wisdom at her response. Even with his poor vision, the Owl could see Elka was not astute to the protocols of the council or the malicious forces at work within her own soar. "I am sure the Raven can explain how the council works and how to make sure things go your way," he offered as he turned his head to face Kakik. "Isn't that right, Raven? If I am not mistaken, you were there, at the meeting the night we were banished."

Anger and frustration boiled within Tuwiye and, before Kakik could interject, the frenzied Eagle was already in motion. With no thought for the consequences, Tuwiye rocked back onto his forceful tail feathers and sprang up with his left talons, slicing across the eyes of the guard closest to him. No longer in control of his emotions, he continued with his rampage against the captors. With another precise flash of movement, Tuwiye turned to his right and pelted the enforcer standing on his opposite side with several swift jabs of his beak. Before either Kakik or Elka could react, Tuwiye had broken free of all the guards and targeted the Owl in charge.

In response to the immediate threat in front of him, the Owl shook off the invisible restraints that checked his more brutal inclinations. With instructs of a seasoned commander, he expected the rush and used the inexperienced Eagle's energy against him. By contracting his wings to thrust himself upwards, he calculated a viciously accurate side tackle that forced Tuwiye into the tree trunk behind them. Before regaining his composure, the Owl pounced on his challenger to finish the job.

Though still dazed from the impact, the triggered Eagle accepted the opponent he faced might be his last. Before he could call out for Elka and Kakik to take flight and leave him behind, the Owl maneuvered his talons around Tuwiye's neck and squeezed off his air supply. Tuwiye thrashed at the dominant Owl with both talons to break free while his wings landed one body blow after another. As he let his eyelids become heavy, his mind drifted to his companions. If Elka and Kakik returned home unharmed, Tuwiye reconciled his fear with the satisfaction that he defended to the death.

With prompting from several enforcers, the understudy cautiously approached his commander, "Boss, you are going to kill him. We need him alive, remember?"

The voice of his number two caused the Owl to break free from his rage and look down at the Eagle in his talons. Still fighting, Tuwiye thrashed back and forth, exposing his underbelly with the white flame that adorned his chest. As the Owl forced his head downward for a closer look, he released the Eagle's neck and staggered backwards a few steps before bending down and cautiously taking a knee. Confused and unsure why, his second in command followed suit and slowly all the other enforcers paid homage to the Eagle.

Elka and Kakik were taken back at the unexpected show of respect and unsure whether to break the silence. Eventually, the Owl stood up and walked over to Tuwiye. "Forgive my ignorance. I did not see the flame. We didn't know you were a messenger for Mother Earth."

Tuwiye took a few deep breaths to recover before he asked with a hoarse voice, "What do you know of this symbol?" pointing towards his chest.

Hearing only confusion, the Owl realized Tuwiye and his companions were on a mission for answers. Blinded by his lust for revenge, the Owl took his assignment without seeing this possibility. Even when it was clear they were travelling to the Painted Cave, he still did not reach the conclusion he saw now. Already admitting one mistake, the Owl was incapable of conceding another. Instead, the Owl properly introduced himself and his enforcers. As the parliament assumed the messengers had perished and their duty was abandoned, they stopped speaking of the mission, and it was forgotten by the generations that followed.

With a bowed head, he explained, "I am Nebulosa and I rule over all the Owls in the Land of the Wabanaki. We are the sworn protectors of the messengers for Mother Earth. The Owls are at your service and our resources are at your disposal. What do you require from us?"

After a contemplative pause, Elka spoke. "First, we require you to let us go," Elka demanded as she shook free from her guard and moved toward Tuwiye. "Second, we are hungry and thirsty. And we need to rest," the female stated with a motherly tone that stiffened the backs of everyone within earshot, which, for Owls, meant all of them.

"Of course," agreed Nebulosa. "Our parliament congregates in the trees just behind us. We can rest there, while we gather food and water."

Tuwiye was overcome with anxiety and frustration. He welcomed the unexpected turn of events of being alive, yet his confusion was reminiscent of being surrounded by Kakik and his unkindness. "Can someone please just tell me what is happening? Before I started this journey, my life was simple and easy to understand. I knew what I had to do every day and was content in doing it. Who are the messengers? Why is this happening now?"

Without hesitation, Nebulosa described the messengers and why Mother Earth created the Owls. "The Land of the Wabanaki is ruled by the belief that all living things on the Land are connected. Mother Earth possesses the collective and omniscient wisdom from all the Lands, not just the Wabanaki, and she provided the animals, birds, fish and humans with everything needed to survive and thrive from generation to generation. To balance her generosity, the Creator gave every living thing an inherent push to endure and compete with one another. Mother Earth knew it would create a wedge between all of us and the Land," the Owl recited from past teachings. "So, she offered the messengers as a balancing energy that would ensure all living things stay connected to the Land and each other."

"Deciding each clan needed their own messengers, Mother Earth did not choose a single form for her messengers and instead spoke through all living things. She marked her messengers with symbols that took the form of burning flames; an element that spoke to every living thing on the Land," the Owl paused and looked at Tuwiye. "For this message, Mother Earth chose an Eagle. You have very acute vision that is over three times that of a human and your keen eyesight helps you observe what is happening on the Land," explained the Owl. As he stopped to collect his thoughts, he looked at Tuwiye and realized he was still confused.

"I am surprised your father and mother never told you," Nebulosa said, puzzled. "They must have been hiding you since you were laid. I thought they would have explained everything to you by now, especially when the markings appeared. It seems shortsighted on their part, not to prepare you for what would happen."

"My parents were hiding me? From who?" Tuwiye demanded as he sensed something far more sinister at play.

"Not everyone welcomed the coming of messengers. There are many that benefit from a loose connection with the Land and each other. Those that find themselves in advantageous positions over food, water, nesting areas," the Owl explained, "they do not want the change messengers bring. "Those that benefit by abusing power were motivated to keep the messengers a secret and hide the signs of their arrival."

A feeling of dread invaded his chest as he continued to question the Owl, "Who hired you? We need to know who it was. Was it an Eagle from the Musquash soar?" Tuwiye pressed. His instincts pointed to a danger he could not see.

"The assignment came in through our usual channels. Whoever hired us knew the process to reach us, which means they have an influential position in the community. With a messenger in play, it narrows the list," the Owl explained. "Those in power are motivated to hunt down messengers and manipulate messages from Mother Earth to maintain control."

Elka pieced together images from her vision with the information Nebulosa was offering. "What information have you provided back? What do they know about us?" she demanded.

"They provided us with everything we needed to know to find you. They told us where Tuwiye was and who was traveling with him, except you," the Owl stated. "They did not tell us about you."

"There is no time to rest," Elka instructed. "We need to take flight. Everything in my vision has materialized," she explained. "I do not understand all the images and what they meant, exactly. But I am sure that your soar is under attack, right now. We might be too late. We need to get back there and we need to bring help. I will explain more along the way."

Nebulosa turned to his number two and said, "Assemble the parliament and have them organized to depart within the hour. We also need to reach out to all our associates. Cash in every favour, call in every chit. It is time to fulfill our destiny," he continued and then turned to Tuwiye, "which is to ensure you bring your message from Mother Earth. Let's take on some water and then wings up in five minutes."

Unusually quiet for most of the exchange, Kakik spoke up to ask, "Do you think we could stop by my nest? I really should tell Cikia that I am on my way to save the Land. It might be worth an extra beak nuzzle," the Elder offered as comic relief to the situation. With no takers for his humour, the Raven tried a different approach. "I can offer every able-bodied Raven in my unkindness. We can pick them up along the way."

"I need someone to explain the image we saw in the Painted Cave. There were two Eagles, you see," she pointed to the ground where she redrew the profiles with her talons.

"Yes, of course. The image of the messenger is not just one Eagle, in one lifetime. It isn't one form. The drawing had humans, wolves, ravens," Nebulosa recalled. "Messengers in the clans needed to have offspring to carry on their mission. So, the messengers choose mates wisely and with their destiny in mind. This part of the image represents, well you, in this case," the Owl concluded, inferring Elka was mated with Tuwiye.

"Well, we'll just have to see about that, won't we?" Elka questioned as she looked at Tuwiye.

Overcome with questions and uncertainty about the message he was to bring back, Tuwiye found solace and comfort in Elka's eyes. 'Mother Earth is so smart,' he sighed. Feeling heat from her eyes, Tuwiye buried his feelings and shouted to the group, "Let's get moving if we are going to save my soar."

"You heard the messenger," ordered Nebulosa. "You have your instructions. We have a job to do and we will not stop until it is done. I will see you all after, this side or the other," the old Owl prophesized. "Wings up!" he bellowed across his subordinates. With his final statement, the Owls, the Eagles and the Raven took to the skies to defend the Land against an unknown enemy.

11 THE BETRAYAL

Leaving all the living things in the Forest of Peace, we rejoin the humans on Moose Island along the shore of Passamaquoddy Bay…

Ethan continued to rearrange the logs on the bonfire. "I haven't shared that experience with anyone. Not even with you," Ethan said to Gwendolyn as he turned to her. "I told you why I came back home and what I was searching for, but I didn't tell you it was because of a message I received from a talking bald eagle and raven, all while speaking from inside the body of a wolf," he admitted with slight hesitation.

With both dogs at her side, Gwendolyn walked over to him and wrapped her arms around his barrelled chest and buried her head for a moment. While she stood above most of the women in the tribe, Ethan's frame overshadowed hers as he held her in his arms. She turned her head to the side and found me. "I felt so scared that day in the truck with you," Gwendolyn said and then turned to Ethan. "You melted away that fear when you walked into the Nurse's Station. If I had known about your experience, it would have helped me understand why I feel so safe with you," she explained. "You are from the wolf clan and a protector," she said with a smile. "The Spirit World wanted to ensure you knew your role."

Ethan squeezed her back and forced a change in topics. "You ladies got me to tell a story you wanted to hear, and I would like the favour returned," Ethan said brazenly. "You are right, Gloria. After our conversation in the Nurse's Station, we didn't speak alone for a long time and, when we did, we had higher priorities to address," he conceded. "I would like to hear what the two of you said to the tribe that convinced them to give their unanimous support to the partnership agreement."

"It was years ago," Gwendolyn shot back. "We were so nervous. I barely remember the motivational speech you gave us before driving off into the sunset." She stood closer to me as she continued to deflect Ethan's inquiry. "Or, at least I was nervous. I just remember thinking, '*how am I supposed to do this? He is the talker. I offend people just opening my mouth.*'"

Ethan laughed, and the two locked eyes to exchange unspoken words that were interrupted by a quiet and distinctive, '*Hoot-hoot-hooooot,*' with the final hoot much quieter and longer. We all heard it and waited for another call before saying anything. Upon hearing it again, and more clearly, Ethan identified the bird, "It is a Great Gray Owl. I thought I heard it last night up at the house but wasn't sure." A third hoot broke the silence and Ethan decided it was a sign. "Sounds like our friend wants to hear the story, tooooo."

After seeing a glimpse of the Ethan I remembered, I accepted his request. "I know I would love to tell it." Unsure if the owl brought a message from the Spirit World or whether the bird was sent to protect us, the timing of the call suggested there was something in that story our ancestors wanted us to hear. Maybe if Ethan heard what was said in the Roundhouse, he may be more inclined to listen to my request for help and come back with me. While Gwendolyn would be easier to convince, Chief Trout and the tribe broke Ethan's trust and I am not sure he has the capacity to get beyond the wrongdoing. Since I knew Ethan wouldn't be eager to let Gwendolyn return with me on her own, convincing him to come along would be an uphill battle.

Gwendolyn hesitantly began speaking as she turned around in Ethan's embrace to face the fire. "Remember, this was years ago, and it feels like a different life. You were my boss, not my husband and I was completely captivated by your...everything," she offered as she looked up and found Ethan's eyes staring back down at her.

"Husband! You are married? When did you get married? Congratulations!" I exclaimed and walked over to hug them. "Evelyn will be so happy, and Susan will be devastated, nee-hee," I said with a laugh I could not hold back. "I can't believe you're married. Well, I can believe it because I knew you were in love. Please, let me tell this story. Gwendolyn will only play down her role in the meeting," I told them through a chuckle and started before Gwendolyn to offer additional arguments.

Outside the Roundhouse in McIntosh before the Jackfish River tribe signed the agreement with Devlin Forest Products...

We were standing in the parking area near the Roundhouse when Ethan received a call from Mr. Devlin. After explaining he needed to leave, Ethan pulled us aside to remind us of the strategy for managing the meeting. "Gwendolyn, remember that no one actually reads the agreement. Just the lawyers, and there may be some in the crowd, so be ready for them, but do not focus on that document," he said pointing to her bag. "For tonight, it isn't what you say, it is how you say it and who delivers the message," he continued. "We have been open and transparent with the tribe since the beginning. Don't change that now. Answer questions honestly, and be yourself," Ethan instructed and then looked at her and finished with, "but a little slower normal and a little less Gwendolyn."

With knowledge of my dislike for public speaking, Ethan waited until he hugged me to whisper in my ear, "If she stumbles, you need to speak up."

As we watched Ethan drive away, Gwendolyn shook her head and said, "I can't believe he left. I am still expecting him to turn around," she said at highspeed. "Like this is some big test to see if I can keep it together. He can't leave this up to me. What could be so critical that he couldn't stay for the meeting to sign the agreement?" she asked and then stiffened. "It's okay. I have my notes and I wrote the agreement, so I can answer any question," Gwendolyn said, trying her best to appear confident.

With a subtle touch on her arm to slow her down, I reminded her, "It isn't up to you. It's up to us." Relief flashed across her eyes and Gwendolyn took a rush of air into her lungs. "We can do this together," I continued. "Ethan started every meeting by asking new people around the table why they came," I said. "Maybe that would be a good place to start." From her expression, it was obvious she liked my suggestion and nodded for me to continue. "Everyone came to the Roundhouse to hear about the agreement because we told them it concerns the Land. It is the Land that matters to them," I explained. "Describe how you see the Land, exactly as you explained to me earlier today," I suggested. "Then, explain what the Land means to you and how you connect with Mother Earth, as much as you are comfortable sharing. First, explain why the agreement is important to Devlin and finish with how you personally connect with the Land."

"I agree with explaining Devlin's upside in the agreement and why the old man is motivated to sign it. That will naturally lead to describing what happens if Jackfish River doesn't sign it," she agreed. "That is being transparent and a good business partner. To share my personal connection to the Land…I'm not sure I can talk about that with so many people. I don't even know who is here."

"That's what you're asking them to do," I told her and gestured towards the people filling the Roundhouse. "When you and Ethan met with the Elders' Circle, you asked us to share some of our most personal experiences and memories," I enlightened her. "Everyone in the tribe has a personal relationship to the Land and communicates with Mother Earth in their own way. If you share what the Land means to you, I think the tribe will trust what we are saying about the agreement." I refrained from adding the pressure of explaining the outcome of simply diving into her fifty-page agreement.

She stayed quiet for a moment and looked at the crowd milling at the entrance of the Roundhouse. The building was mostly filled with people she just met or will meet for the first time tonight. She fidgeted with her hands, and I could tell my advice was difficult for her to accept. Even if she agreed with my approach, it required her to bare a piece of herself that she has kept hidden. "Thank you, Gloria," she said after reaching a decision. "How long before we start? I would like a few minutes alone to go through my delivery," she asked while adding, "because it sounds like the content has been decided for me," she concluded with a smirk.

Twenty minutes later, Gwendolyn walked into the Roundhouse and headed towards the tables where the Chief and his council waited along with the Elders' Circle. Her energetic footsteps demanded the attention of the crowd, and as she made her way across the room, people stopped their individual conversations while others found somewhere to sit. When she reached the front of the room, Elvis started the meeting with a prayer. At the end of the blessing, Chief Trout introduced Gwendolyn and called her up to speak.

"Thank you, Chief Trout and thank you everyone for coming tonight to hear about a fifty-page agreement that hopes to connect your tribe to Devlin Forest Products," she said to the crowd as she held up a bound copy of the agreement. Removing the microphone from its stand, she walked in front of the head table and tossed the agreement down as she walked by. "I can talk about every page of the agreement because Gloria and I wrote every word after meeting with the Elders' Circle and your leadership. It is long, boring and probably not the reason you came tonight," she pointed out to the crowd. "Before the tribe signs another piece of paper, the Elders' Circle and your leadership want you to understand what is going to happen with the Land," she said without using a negative word like treaty.

As she walked the length of the crowd, Gwendolyn explained that Devlin Forest Products was struggling to buy the wood they needed to run their sawmills. Their competitors were the pulp mills, and they controlled the Land, like Weyerhaeuser who controlled the state forests. They controlled where trees were cut and how many, and they decided how much wood would go to Devlin's sawmills. The pulp mills were trying to put Devlin out of business and take their trees. Gwendolyn pointed out the competitive advantages to Devlin, both in the marketplace and the Governor's office, of a signed agreement with the tribe.

"A recent Supreme Court decision confirmed the duty to consult with Native American tribes when companies want to use the Land. Before this judgment, companies like Weyerhaeuser dodged a role in consulting with tribes, beyond maybe a notification letter addressed to your Chief," Gwendolyn described. "Devlin saw an opportunity and Ethan approached the Jackfish River tribe to partner with the company. Devlin and Jackfish River together can apply to the Governor to take full control of the forest licenses held by Weyerhaeuser; the same company who is hiding behind the state rather than consult directly with you," she said plainly. "Devlin wants to work with Jackfish River to manage the Land," Gwendolyn committed. "If there are questions about the agreement, I can answer them one-on-one after the meeting. Instead of discussing a document that I don't expect all of you to read, I would like to share with you why this agreement is important to me," Gwendolyn suggested as she took in a quiet, deep breath before continuing.

"Minutes before the meeting, I learned I would be talking for my boss, Ethan Travers," she told the Roundhouse. "Everyone knows Ethan is the talker, he is the front man and the one the Elders trust," she conceded. "Like all of you, he has his own connection to the Land. He may have shared it with some of you," she said and looked towards me. "Gloria suggested I share my connection to the Land and, at first, I was anxious. The thought of sharing something so personal with all of you is frightening, and she reminded me I was asking exactly that of you. So, I'll try to put what the Land means to me in words, and I'll start by sharing why I went to forestry school."

With consideration for her words one last time, Gwendolyn started with an open observation. "I don't fit in," she stated bluntly, "anywhere. I don't fit in with my family and I was an outsider in school. It caused me to search everywhere for somewhere to belong." Gwendolyn tried her best to continue without emotion, but her spirit broke through in every word.

"After school, I felt lost, lonely and disconnected from, well, everything. I was directionless and desperate to find my path. Every night, I would go to bed saying I would decide the next day. The next day would come and go, and I was still no closer to a decision," she admitted. "The thought of what to do next eventually consumed me. When I couldn't sleep, I went for a walk. During the day, when I got anxious, I ran in the park or hiked the trails along the lake by my house. The Land accepted me every time I needed her. It didn't matter what I looked like or if I had messed something up. Being so lost and so unsure of what to do forced me onto the Land, over and over," she said with resolve.

"I only ever came close to achieving peace when I was out on the Land. Whenever I was hurt or suffering, the Land made me feel whole and complete. So, I found a job that would allow me to connect with the Land." Gwendolyn looked over and found my eyes before she finished. "While that is true for why I became a forester, my connection to the Land is not my only motivation for approaching your tribe," she admitted. "The rest of it centres on my father, who is not a good man. He works for Weyerhaeuser, Devlin's largest competitor, and they manage the forest licenses we are taking back," she continued as she glanced at Chief Trout. "I believe men like my father work for other bad men and when they are deciding what happens on the Land, its protection is not a priority," she said confidently. "So, I decided the Land and Mother Earth needed one Leavitt in their corner and, if my father worked for Devlin's biggest competitor, then I would work for Devlin and learn absolutely everything I could about how the Land works and how best to protect it. The agreement is significant to me, and, just as your connection to the Land is personal, it is for me too."

With the end in sight, Gwendolyn took a deep breath and looked over at me. She motioned for me to come up beside her to share my thoughts on the agreement, and I was ready. They were the same words I shared with the Elders' Circle the month before when we discussed the agreement. After she called me up, I accepted the microphone from Gwendolyn and settled my nerves before starting. For a moment, I touched my emotions to connect with my ancestors and feel the strength of my tribe as I spoke to them.

"I met Ethan Travers and Gwendolyn Leavitt, first separately when Gwendolyn came to us from the university, and then together when Ethan hired her at Devlin to work on the partnership with our tribe," I explained to everyone. "They have been the same people with the same message since the first visit. Except maybe Gwendolyn," I teased. "I think she changed. She can finally figure out when we are joking and when we are being serious," I chuckled. "Because we're always joking, nee-hee!" I poked. "With a couple of Dunkin's coffees, she still speaks hyper-speed, but she did a wonderful job tonight. I think that was more Nish speed!" A light laughter sprinkled across the Roundhouse and I waited before continuing in a more serious tone.

"Everyone here knows me and how I connect with the Land. I pick medicines and gather food and continue to explore our territory in the shadows of our ancestors. My family in the Spirit World are buried in our Land and I feel them with me every day," I said and touched the memory of my parents and husband that left me years ago. With Gwendolyn still standing at my side, I explained why I wanted the tribe to sign the agreement. "If we partner with Devlin Forest Products, we get to decide what happens on our Land," I said and stopped when I heard some chatter in the crowd about cutting trees.

When everyone stopped conversing, I answered the question concerning cutting. "Yes, there will be cutting and we will plan it together with Ethan and Gwendolyn. Where they cut, how they cut and where they plant new trees," I tried to explain and then looked at Gwendolyn. "She can tell you more about that. I don't understand all of it but I understand how we will work together," I said with a smile. "That is why Ethan and Gwendolyn are here. They are going to listen to us and manage the Land the way our ancestors did. We will protect the sacred places in our territory, and ensure we always have the freedom to hunt moose and deer, fish pickerel and whitefish, gather blueberries and medicinal plants and harvest wild rice."

Back to the present day on the shore of Passamaquoddy Bay off Moose Island…

Leaving the rest of the meeting in my memory, I looked at Ethan and said, "Gwendolyn captivated everyone in the room and they hung on her every word. You would have been proud of her." There was so much more I wanted to say, and still, I wasn't sure how to continue. While I didn't understand so much of what happened next, I couldn't avoid the undeniable fact that Weyerhaeuser ended up with the forest licenses back.

"In that, I have no doubt," Ethan readily accepted. "That was genius," he said through a smile, "having Gwendolyn share her story. What made you think of that, Gloria?"

Thinking back to that day on the reservation, I vaguely remembered Chief Trout prompting me to have Gwendolyn speak to the tribe about why she came to us. With everything that transpired, I was a little nervous that I hadn't contemplated his motivation. "It was the Chief who suggested I ask Gwendolyn to speak and explain to the tribe what pushed her to the Land."

From the corner of my eye, I could see Gwendolyn stiffen in Ethan's embrace. "I never shared that story with anyone, except you. Before that meeting in the Roundhouse, I had not shared that with Ethan or the Chief, only you," she said with a hint of confusion. "How did he know I was going to open up like that? I didn't even know I was going to say it until everything came spilling out."

"He didn't know exactly what you were going to say," Ethan interjected. "It was a safe gamble you would say something perfect," he pointed out to Gwendolyn. "Allowing the two of you to deliver a potentially divisive message to the tribe shows the faith he placed in what we were doing. Unanimous support from the tribe; that was a pivotal moment for all of us. The tribe, and especially the Elders' Circle, understood why you were helping them and it united the tribe behind you," Ethan pointed out to Gwendolyn.

"Maybe it was the Spirit World working through us," I said with a grin. "Maybe that is what he saw in his vision. The one that told him to hang the eagle carving in the Roundhouse before your meeting," I remembered.

"Why are we talking about him like he was on the right side of this?" Gwendolyn asked bluntly. "Because you both trusted him and he screwed over everyone!" Unlike Ethan and I, Gwendolyn didn't have the capacity to trust Chief Trout, and I understood and accepted her limitation. It was something she came by honestly through pain and suffering. "The tribe, the Elders' Circle, Gloria, you…," she listed in rapid fire while gaining steam, "and Devlin Forest Products. They are done, closed, and the old man," she sighed and let her shoulders fall along with her voice before continuing. "I'm not sure he will see what we did as anything besides a betrayal." Despite the strength I felt from her, she was still left injured by what happened.

Ethan walked to where Gwendolyn was standing beside the bonfire. "What happened to Devlin Forest Products was not your fault," he said softly to which Gwendolyn wrinkled her brow. Unphased by her confusion, Ethan continued. "It wasn't the Chief's fault either. The fate of the company was in the hands of the old man. It was his decision, and his alone." He brushed the blowing hair away from her eyes, kissed her forehead and held her face in his hands. "You did exactly what you were supposed to do. You were honest and transparent," he lauded her. "It was impressive how you built trust with the tribe. You can't have it both ways…transparent in some meetings and covert in others," he informed her and released his hold.

"You do it," she challenged him, "being honest with Jackfish River and speaking a different language when meeting with the old man. It took me so long to decipher your language. By the time I understood what was happening, everything changed," she said and let her eyes break his stare.

"You are always unapologetically Gwendolyn," he said and shook his head with a chuckle. "I have watched you flatten everything that stood in front of you. Maybe annihilating is a better descriptor," he teased, forcing her to look up. "You didn't want to change the world, and you did just the same," he said while maintaining her stare. "You didn't try to change Jackfish River to bend them to your will," he pointed out. "You earned their trust by listening and sharing how you felt about the Land. That is how you made change, and I make change in a different way," Ethan said with a smirk and quick glance down to his loosely clenched fists.

"For our tribe, you made change by protecting her," I interrupted. "The very first time Susan met you, she said you were from the Wolf clan. Always alert, constantly looking for danger and protecting the pack," I explained to him while both waited for me to continue. "Remember, you thought it was a bad thing. Susan called you a wolf, and you thought she was likening you to a predator," I reminded him. "You are those things only to those who threaten the ones you love. It took both of you to make the change we wanted to see on our Land," I observed. "It took both honesty and deceit to have our voices and the voices of our ancestors heard."

"I wouldn't say deceit. The wolf has a job to do, just like every other living thing. Sometimes an alpha wolf needs to pick a fight with a stronger predator to distract them from attacking the rest of the pack," Ethan countered and took Gwendolyn's hand before finishing. "Or from attacking one wolf, in particular," he said. With his focus on her and without looking up, Ethan continued. "Now that you're here, we can piece together what Weyerhaeuser used to compel the Chief to sign their agreement. Although, I'm not sure to what end," he acknowledged and looked in my direction.

All I could do was shake my head and tell him what I knew. "I was sent here to find you and Gwendolyn and bring you back with me. The Elders have so many questions and the Chief won't meet with us to explain what happened. When I went to your office, it was locked and looked empty from the outside," I told Gwendolyn. "We didn't know who was involved until trucks and drilling rigs arrived at McIntosh with a work permit issued by the Governor's office at the request of Weyerhaeuser. Given what we have pieced together, I think we need more time than the tide will allow."

Ethan glanced down at his feet and noticed the water inching closer to the bonfire and their chairs. "We're only scratching the surface of a larger story," he confirmed, "and the tide stops for no one. Let's head up to the house and get you settled for the night, Gloria," he said as he gathered the chairs and plates from supper. "We can start fresh in the morning over breakfast," Ethan suggested as Gwendolyn helped me into the side-by-side.

Relieved that Ethan and Gwendolyn seemed willing to help, I happily accepted the offer to sleep and postpone the discussion to tomorrow. As I climbed into the vehicle, the two Goldens looked up towards the house, as if they heard something, and took off running up the road. "I wonder what they heard up there," I thought out loud.

"That's strange, I didn't hear the driveway alarm," Gwendolyn answered and turned to Ethan. "I'll head up with Gloria and see what the dogs are doing. I'll come back down for you."

Nodding, Ethan continued to clean up and move the chairs and propane cooker from the ocean floor back up to the cabin. Gwendolyn climbed into the driver's seat of the vehicle, started the engine and steered us up the hill. As we ascended, I could see headlights turning into the driveway through the trees. First one set of lights and then another and another, which all set off the alarm in Gwendolyn's pocket. In silence, Gwendolyn increased her speed and reached the top to find Chief Trout kneeling to pet the dogs. Behind the Chief were the same three trucks from earlier that day.

As Gwendolyn climbed out of the vehicle, the men she referred to as the Moose Island Police exited their vehicles to join her. Without acknowledging anyone, she shouted, "Archie, Edith! Come!" She yelled it once, and the dogs heeded. Even I heard the change in her voice from relaxed caution to anger. She motioned with her hand for the Moose Island Police to stand down and walked towards the Chief.

"They are beautiful dogs, Gwendolyn, and very loyal," Chief Trout said looking down towards the animals. "I didn't mean to cause a…," and he was stopped abruptly by Gwendolyn's right fist connecting with his upper left jaw. Her blow shocked the Chief and everyone else, including me. I think I may have gasped when I realized what she was doing. "Ah, shoot, that hurt!" Gwendolyn exclaimed, breaking the brief silence. Shocked by her reaction to Chief Trout, I looked to the men that showed up, likely in her defence. They were all silent and motionless, waiting for someone to speak.

Chief Trout, mirroring Ethan's stature, staggered back to regain his balance. Gwendolyn took advantage of the fact that he was looking down at the dogs when she connected. "When I imagined this moment, I thought it would feel way better," Gwendolyn offered. "I hope that hurt," she questioned, "at least a little."

"It hurt," the Chief responded, "and more than just physically." He rubbed the side of his face and reset his demeanour for the greeting he received. "I was hoping to beat Gloria to the punch, mind the pun," he grimaced.

"Why? There isn't anything you can say to justify what you did," she challenged. "You watched Ethan burn every favour he collected and apply all the leverage he accumulated in his career to get those licenses," she accused him. "Dismissed and disavowed from our world for breaking the code," she detailed. "Ethan trusted you and believed every bullshit message and sign from the Spirit World!" she said with sarcasm.

With her distinctive flare, I watched as she unloaded rageful feelings she had buried just beneath the surface. "They fired the entire team the next day, and they needed your signature to do it," Gwendolyn spat back at him. "The power to stop all of this rested with you. That is what we put in the agreement and you knew that. If we couldn't agree on something, the decision went to you," she recited. "And like a coward, you gave it away. Under the first sign of pressure, you succumb to whatever leverage they applied to you."

"Gwendolyn, stop. Please," Ethan instructed from behind her and out of breath from running up the hill. "Hi Merle," he said and turned to the Moose Island Police. "Hi boys," he said and walked over to shake their hands. "How's it going tonight, Jordan?" he asked the one who I remembered as the ferry boat captain.

"Everything's good here," Jordan offered as he motioned for everyone to get back into their vehicles. "You let us know if you need anything. Are you coming with us in the morning? We are meeting at the ferry landing at 5am," the young captain asked Ethan. "We can get Troy to take your place if you are busy," he offered.

"No, I'll be fine to help tomorrow morning," Ethan replied. "But from the looks of this crowd, you better ask Troy to cover me next weekend." With that reply, Jordan nodded and climbed into the cab of his pickup. We all overheard Jordan tell his passenger, "Put down your phone, I get to put this up on Facebook. Send me the video of Gwendolyn cold cocking that guy in the face. The camera on your iPhone is way better than my Samsung," Jordan continued. "I want the highest quality video for this post." The four of us waited for the vehicles to leave before saying anything and, again, Gwendolyn broke the silence.

"When I first got here, you told me to get over it. *'Get over it, or we can't be together.'* Remember that conversation?" she interrogated him. "I know, it sucks being married to someone like me. Someone who remembers everything, word-for-word, from every conversation," she said as she gained speed. As she walked towards Ethan, she rallied on, "I wanted to be with you, so I left what happened in Minnesota back there," she stated while standing in front of him. Gwendolyn continued to address Ethan while turning to face the Chief, "But when it shows up in your driveway, uninvited, it's hard to leave it in the past way back in Minnesota."

With her eyes on us, she asked, "Am I the only one who remembers what happened? What we did together?" None of us seemed eager to silence her, so Gwendolyn continued. "Let's review, shall we? Once the old man found out that Chief Trout attended some meeting with Weyerhaeuser, he pulls out of the agreement because he senses the tribe is going to screw him," she rattled through the details without taking a breath. With a finger pointed in Ethan's direction, she picked up speed, "You were summoned to an emergency meeting, where you were instructed to use whatever leverage you had over the Governor to demand he sign over the forest licenses directly to Devlin," she reminded Ethan. "You refused and resigned on the spot."

Her eyes on the Chief and I, she sarcastically continues with exaggerated gesturing to herself, "No one calls me and let's me know Ethan is gone, and I mean, gone." With a chuckle, she explained, "That was a fun morning, answering questions in rapid fire succession from the other vice presidents about Ethan and why he resigned. As I pieced together what was happening, I was shuffled out the door as the traitor responsible for whatever happened."

"Gwendolyn, maybe you want to take a breath and invite our guests inside" Ethan suggested.

"I am not finished," she shot back without missing a beat. "Somehow, you convinced the Governor that the best solution to the *'war in the woods'* between Devlin and Weyerhaeuser was to issue the licenses to an independent company owned by the tribe," she said in disbelief. "Even as I am saying it, I still can't believe you pulled that off. Except to say that I wish I knew what leverage you held over that narcissistic waste of a pair of pants to force his hand," she said with loathing in her voice for the Governor. "And with one signature, you ripped everything to shreds," she leveled at the Chief with the fury we all witnessed from the Gwendolyn that fought by our side.

"We remember, Gwendolyn," Ethan said with composure. With a gentle grip on her shoulders, Ethan asked, "Did you get it all out? Did you want to hit me now?" Gwendolyn looked at her feet when she realized Ethan saw her deck the Chief. "I made it up in time to see how you welcomed him to the island. I think he gets the message. You're mad." Over her head, Ethan asked the Chief, "How's the jaw?"

"I could use some ice before it starts to swell," he admitted. "You were right about her hook," he said as he rubbed his chin. "But I am curious as to the circumstances that led you to that revelation."

Ethan awkwardly offered an explanation without much success. "We attended some work function for Devlin and part of it was a ridiculous air boxing, relationship-building exercise that I can't begin to explain," Ethan started. "I wasn't paying attention when the instructor explained the activity, and while I am sure you remember," Ethan directed his words towards Gwendolyn, "we don't need to discuss the infamous *you punched me in the face* incident."

"Which one?" Gwendolyn asked with her smirk fading almost immediately. "No, don't do this" she warned. "Don't be cute and make me laugh in a valiant yet futile effort to distract me and make me do something that I don't want to do," and shrugged out of his grip. "We already have to put him up for the night," she acknowledged, still not addressing the Chief by name. "Don't make me treat him like a guest, too."

"I have a hotel room on the mainland," the Chief interjected. "No one confirmed your address, so I took the ferry over just to confirm you were both here," the Chief explained. "We can talk in the morning."

"You can't leave the island until the morning, Chief," I explained. "The ferry shuts down at night and those men that were here," I pointed back to the road where the trucks were still parked and idling, "they run the ferry," I said. As I listened, my eyes widened in disbelief over where the day had taken me from waking up on the reservation that morning. "Can we please get back to what Gwendolyn said earlier?" I asked before the conversation further confused me.

"What did you sign? Why would you fire them?"

"So much for leaving this conversation until the morning," Ethan said more to himself. "Let's go to the house and put on coffee, or tea or whatever we need to stay awake," he suggested. "For some reason, we have all been trying to get to five o'clock when we should talk about why you," he pointed to me, "and you, Chief, travelled halfway across the country to find us," Ethan followed.

Gwendolyn motioned for the dogs to heel and said, "There's meat and cheese in the fridge and lots of snacks in the cupboard beside the fridge." She kissed Ethan on the lips and said, "I'll take the dogs down to the cabin for the night." Walking towards me, she said, "There are two rooms on the lower level, you can take the one on the left at the bottom of the stairs. Snoop around the cabinets and look for whatever you need…toothbrush and toothpaste, towels, shampoo and soap. Use whatever you need," she said with a smile. "Have a good sleep and I will see you in the morning." She hugged me and whispered, "I'm so glad to see you."

She walked to the side by side, opened the passenger door and waited for the dogs to jump up. Looking back at Ethan before walking around to the other side, Gwendolyn drove down the steep road back to the cabin at the shore. No one said a word until her headlights faded into the distance, leaving us standing in the dark.

Ethan turned on his flashlight and started walking along the driveway towards the house before speaking. "Gwendolyn hasn't made her way through all five stages of grief. She's stuck somewhere between anger and bargaining," he observed as he looked back down the road. "All she did was bury her feelings down deep enough to keep them from driving her insane." Ethan guided us towards the house and onto the deck, where he opened the sliding door facing the ocean and invited us inside.

"Grief?" asked the Chief as he pulled chairs from the kitchen table for us to sit down. "I don't understand. Why is this so personal for her?" he pressed. "People get hired and fired all the time. At your level, hers too," the Chief said as he looked towards the water where Gwendolyn had fled. "People come to work one day to find a box on their desk filled with personal items, and a security guard escorts them from the property after collecting their office keys and corporate credit card," the Chief reminded Ethan. "How do I know that?" he continued without letting Ethan answer. "Because you told us. That, and you also warned me I would probably lose the re-election if we weren't successful with the Governor after the old man betrayed us. You told us those were the stakes if we failed."

Ethan filled the kettle at the sink while letting the Chief finish without interrupting and completed his task before engaging. "But we did not fail, Merle," Ethan said slowly. "Gwendolyn is consumed by what happened because we were successful in doing something everyone told us we couldn't. We stole those forest licenses in the chaos surrounding the war in the woods, and while everyone was sifting through the old man's assets, we convinced the

Governor to sign over those licenses to the tribe." With a shake of his head, he continued, "Chief, what it looks like from the outside is that, in one weak moment, you signed it all away."

As the Chief contemplated his next words, Ethan continued to explain Gwendolyn's attachment to the tribe and the agreement. "Every aspect of her life was ripped apart along with Devlin when the old man wouldn't sign," Ethan told us. "For Gwendolyn, it was one betrayal after another until she felt completely alone in the world," he confided. "From her father all the way to me." With a penetrating stare aimed at the Chief, Ethan continued. "When she learned the Governor issued the forest licenses back to Weyerhaeuser, she got on a plane. With her team gone and no one she could trust, she knew she wasn't safe. By the time she found me, her fear had turned to rage," he said as he turned towards me. "Gwendolyn had devised a plan and demanded I come back to help her. It would have worked, except it required unwavering support from the tribe. And I refused to return." Ethan seemed hesitant to dive into the rest of their conversation and with a calm pause said, "You're being awfully quiet, Gloria. How much of the story do you know? When were the Elders cut out of meetings?" he asked and stood to remove the kettle from the stove to make tea.

Before I could answer, the Chief interjected, "What meetings? You have accused me so many times of hiding something from the Elders' Circle," he directed towards me with frustration. "Ethan, you make it sound like I had a choice. When the old man backed out of the agreement, we lost a critical piece of the partnership; the protection Devlin provided to us. It was only a matter of time before Weyerhaeuser made their move with whatever leverage they held over the newly elected Governor."

"The Elders' Circle sent me to tell you what we know and to ask you and Gwendolyn to come back with me," I explained to Ethan. "We don't know how to fight this enemy and they are desecrating McIntosh," I said, knowing I wouldn't have to explain the importance of the site. "But I still don't understand why you would sign something like that, Merle," I continued to press.

For additional clarity, Ethan discussed what was happening at Devlin leading up to the meeting at the Roundhouse. "I was out front at Delvin, risking my reputation and my career trying to broker a deal with the tribe and poking a grizzly bear at the same time," he said. "I'm not whining about it. I demanded the old man let me work with Jackfish because it was the right thing to do. He needed the support of the tribe or the Governor would never have accepted Devlin taking control over so much Land," he admitted. "They would have reissued the licenses to Weyerhaeuser because it was the path of least resistance, a public servant's preferred solution. The Governor was counting on his left-leaning supporters to carry him through the midterms and the partnership with the tribe was the key to securing that vote because it also appealed to the greens."

"We also collected some compromising intel on the good Governor that would have made his re-election without our support difficult," the Chief added. "With so many moving parts, we decided we needed several contingency plans in place. The type of plans we couldn't share with the Elders' Circle or the tribe."

"Most of the contingencies required me to do what I do best," Ethan smiled. "Agitate the situation, grate on everyone's weaknesses and secrets to the point where we had them desperate to sign a deal with the tribe," he said without pride. "Any hold outs we encountered, we intimidated them, we blackmailed them, whatever it took to get the Land under tribal control, especially McIntosh."

Ethan and Chief Trout both gave me time to absorb everything they shared. I took a sip of tea and a deep breath before speaking. Several moments later, I turned to my Chief and asked, "After everything we did to get the agreement signed, and what we all did to get the licenses from the Governor, why would you give them away?" I asked, repeating my only question.

With anger building in his voice as he spoke, "I didn't come all this way with my hat in my hand, or to be accused of selling out the tribe." With a hold on Ethan's stare, the Chief continued. "Do you think I would have signed the agreement if I thought all of this would happen? When Devlin backed out of the deal, it changed everything. We were exposed, alone," he said without giving Ethan an opportunity to retort. "We knew the consequences of taking back the Land," the Chief reminded him. "When you delivered the licenses to the tribe, like Gwendolyn said, you broke the code. It was viewed by the rest of the industry as a declaration of war." With a sigh and glance down at his shoes, the Chief looked up before starting again and with much less confidence. "Weyerhaeuser threatened to support Wade Stonefish in the election if I didn't agree to the terms," he confessed, "by leaking proof to his campaign team that I was stealing from the tribe."

"That would be easy enough to defend," Ethan concluded. "What proof did they offer?"

As Ethan waited for an answer, I searched the Chief's face and waited to see if he would answer the question truthfully. "Did they find your woman, Merle? The one we all know about and don't talk about for Claudia's sake?" The Elders' Circle regarded Chief Trout as a good leader and like all of us, he had his faults. The community is small and there is only one road in and one road out. It is difficult to keep secrets from your enemies and once they are out, it is difficult to keep them from spreading off the reservation.

The Chief broke the uncomfortable silence and reluctantly answered. "Yes, they found Anne and threatened to expose our affair by releasing my credit card statements. Before I was elected, I didn't have a bank account or a credit card," he admitted, which came as no surprise. "I have been using the tribal card as my personal card for years. I pay the bill every month," he defended. "Even though I can show no funds were misappropriated, it is much easier to believe their narrative that I was funneling the tribe's money to my mistress."

The Chief took a deep breath and continued with his story. "All I had to do was get rid of Ethan. If I agreed to dismiss him, the statements would go away and they would transfer control of McIntosh to the tribe. Nothing else would change and that was supposed to be the end of it," the Chief said remorsefully.

"But that isn't where it ended, Merle," I challenged him. "They fired everyone working for us, from Gwendolyn down to the office assistant, who is your cousin," I reminded him. "You're right, we gave you the mandate to protect McIntosh, but not at the expense of everything else."

"Merle, why didn't you come to me? We could have…" Ethan started when I cut him off.

"No, Ethan. Let me finish," I demanded. "We already protected McIntosh. Once the forest licenses were issued, Ethan convinced the Governor to give the tribe some kind of letter that made sure anyone wanting access to McIntosh and the surrounding forests had to obtain the consent of the tribe," I told him. "That is why the Elders' Circle sent me to find Ethan. We need confirmation on the letter. You would have known this if you had agreed to meet with the Elders' Circle or read any of the updates we sent to your office."

"What are you talking about? You ambushed me with that '*secret*' meeting in the Roundhouse," the Chief accused me.

"We did that because of your stonewalling. We couldn't get through to you or the other councillors," I said and continued my rant. "You are rarely available on the reservation and never without an appointment, which we could not get."

"You never answered my phone calls or texts," Ethan reinforced. "Your emails bounced back to me as if they were blocked. I can be persistent but I don't chase people. When I smelled something, Gloria defended you."

"Yes, I said if you signed an agreement with Weyerhaeuser, it was because it was a better deal for the tribe," I informed the Chief. "If it is a better deal for the tribe, why are bulldozers and drill rigs parked at McIntosh?" I asked. "How is the tribe in control? We are on the outside again with a blockade that could give state troopers and federal officers an excuse to invade the reservation."

"How could neither of you reach me?" the Chief asked. He retrieved his cell phone from the chest pocket of his blazer. A very traditional Chief, he was wearing jeans with a suit blazer embroidered with colourful images on the lapels and a large bear embroidered on the back. While his name was Merle Trout, he was from the Bear clan, the same as Susan, as they are the medicine people and healers. "I will call Maryann in the morning and figure out who was keeping your emails and phone calls from me."

"The same Maryann whose uncle just defeated you in the election?" Ethan further recalled. "Gwendolyn still follows the tribe's Facebook page and saw the results posted last week."

A larger plot may have collectively played us, even from within the tribe. As I continued to contemplate convincing Ethan to come back to Minnesota, the Chief dropped his shoulders and let his eyes soften. "Regardless of my mistakes and shortcoming as a man, the immediate threat is McIntosh. Gloria is right, if the tribal police can't control the blockaders, it will set our relationship with state and federal law enforcement back decades. Not to mention the uproar in the tribe if they drill through the graves of the bodies buried under the church and the unmarked graves across the property."

Sounding more like the Ethan I remembered, he asked, "What does your agreement say? What are your lawyers telling you?"

"Hank missed a clause about subsurface mineral rights when reviewing the new agreement with Weyerhaeuser. His only experience with these types of agreements was our work on the state forest license, which were silent on mineral rights as they typically remain with the state," he continued. "In the agreement, there is a clause that gave control over McIntosh and the old boarding school site to the tribe, except, '*should the state relinquish mineral rights within the area,*'" the Chief recited as if the clause was committed to memory. "Since signing the agreement, the Minnesota state legislature passed a bill that transferred the mineral rights to Weyerhaeuser. With gold, silver and rare earth metal prices soaring, the company is exercising their rights to the minerals."

"A standard negotiating practice for Weyerhaeuser, especially when sitting across the table from Robert Leavitt," Ethan asserted. "It was Robert that approached you, correct? Gwendolyn's father?" Ethan questioned. "How did Hank miss something as significant as mineral rights?"

"Yes," the Chief said with disdain and brushed off his last question. "Robert approached me to discuss a '*proposal,*'" he said regretfully. "He spun a narrative about Gwendolyn being his mole inside Devlin and that the agreement we signed was a template she accessed when working as an intern in his legal department," the Chief recalled. "When I asked for some time to consider the proposal, he put a clock on the offer and it expired as soon as I stood from the table," he finished.

Looking off into the distance, Ethan voiced his frustration with the Chief. "When Weyerhaeuser replaced Gwendolyn and her team, Robert hired a security firm to come to the reservation and escort them from the office," he said without raising his voice. "Regardless of whether the new agreement gave them full control, Weyerhaeuser took over and no one tried to stop them. Not even the tribal police," Ethan took a breath and said, "because you agreed to bench your enforcers."

Familiar with his hockey analogies, I could see Ethan's anger wasn't directed towards us. "Mason was able to confirm that Weyerhaeuser transferred all responsibility for the forest licenses to existing staff in the Minneapolis office. He hasn't been able to get any answers about what is happening around McIntosh, except for what we heard in the news," I added, hoping Ethan's understanding of the history at McIntosh would compel him to help.

The Chief seized the opportunity to poignantly asked, "Will you come back with us? I am not sure I will be able to find this letter or even point our lawyers in the right direction," Chief Trout continued. "There are so many questions we can't answer about our previous agreement and the purpose behind several clauses. Now that I have lost the election, it will be even harder to unite the tribe and the Elders' Circle on a path forward," he lamented. "It will look like I am trying to fight the results of the election and redeem my reputation by implicating the new Chief, who will be sworn in at the end of the month."

"He had to be involved," I said with confidence. "Why else would Robert threaten to support him if you didn't agree to his ultimatum?"

"If that was even true, Gloria," the Chief countered. "After all, they were trying to blackmail me."

"Who are they? I thought you said it was Robert who approached you," Ethan asked, noticing the subtle inconsistency.

"He brought his number two with him," the Chief answered. "His name was Faulkner or Fletcher, something like that," he recalled. "I can't remember his first name; it could have been Chris or maybe Eric. He said he was a classmate of Gwendolyn's and made it seem as if she was on board all along." As the Chief continued, he could see the muscles in Ethan's jaw ripple. "I knew it wasn't true…," the Chief was interrupted midsentence by loud shrieks and shrills from outside.

After waiting a moment to see if it would subside, Ethan got up from his seat and walked outside to see what was causing the stir. "It's two eagles circling low and right above the driveway," Ethan informed us from outside. As we joined him on the deck to see the pair, the shrieking grew louder and more panicked with no signs of stopping. Both eagles were mature enough to have their white heads and tails with glorious chocolate brown feathers over their bodies in contrast. The birds of prey were hovering low enough to see their eyes darting between us and the water below.

"Something must have scared them," I said. Without looking back at us, Ethan started walking out the driveway to greet his two dogs who were running towards the house.

"Archie, what's up boy? You need a petting?" he asked as he bent down to comfort his dogs. "Edith, come get a belly rub. Come here, girl," he said to calm down the excited animals. "Where's mom? Where is she?" Ethan encouraged them. "She is going to be worried when she sees you are gone." With the dogs inside the house, he looked at the Chief and said, "Gwendolyn needs to be part of the solution," he said. "She deserves to hear all this, too. You can get settled in your rooms while I bring her back up to the house. We can pick this up in the morning," he stated and walked out the driveway towards his truck.

In a moment alone with the Chief, I took the opportunity to list several of the demands from the Elders. "Merle, the Elders want Gwendolyn and Ethan hired back. We need to challenge the agreement you signed with Weyerhaeuser, and it is critical that we find Doug Price, Ethan's friend in the Governor's office, to confirm the letter he gave us for McIntosh," I rambled. "Weyerhaeuser is contesting the letter and with the Republicans in the Governor's office, he is demanding the letter be verified by Doug or we have to find some other proof the letter is real."

Despite trying his best to follow, the Chief looked away in the distance. "Doug, Doug Price? Why does that name sound familiar? Did I meet with him as well?" he asked.

"No, none of us met him. Ethan and he were classmates at Bentley University out here somewhere and played hockey together," I remembered, mostly because Bentley is the name of my oldest grandson. "Doug was a big reason Ethan travelled to Minnesota, and they both worked for Devlin with Doug eventually moving to the Governor's office." The Chief had picked up his cell phone and was tapping the screen. "Are you listening, Merle?"

"Yes, I am," he said without looking up. "That name is familiar and I can't remember why," he said as he continued to stare at his phone. A few moments later, he said, "I can't find whatever article I was reading. I just know I heard that name somewhere today." He took in a breath and said, "It has been a long day and this has been a lot to process. I am not avoiding any of your demands, and my last official act as Chief of the Jackfish River tribe will be to hire back Ethan and Gwendolyn," he said with conviction. "Until Chief Stonefish takes over, we will work on stopping the mining company at McIntosh and reinstating our forest license. Between now and the end of my term, we need to understand who our friends are and who needs to be seen as our enemies."

"Agreed," I yielded, and gathered my things from the back door where Gwendolyn had placed them earlier. As I walked over, my foot knocked the Chief's satchel and a file of papers spilled onto the floor. The file folder had '*Travers*' written across it in large, black letters. As I gathered the papers, he explained the file.

"You went to the National Congress to find Ethan and Gwendolyn," the Chief said. "Darrell gave you the address, but the file hadn't arrived yet. It came via fax to the tribal office, and I thought the information in it would help you convince Ethan to come back."

Looking for permission to read the file, the Chief nodded. "It contains pieces of Ethan's family tree but the file is incomplete. When you contacted the congress to access the investigative team, they ran Ethan's pedigree information through the national database. An intern didn't realize he wasn't native and thought it was a standard search," he explained. "Turns out, Susan was right. Ethan is Native American. He isn't Anishinaabe; he is Wabanaki from right here, which tells me Ethan is searching for his birth parents. I thought we could use this file to motivate him to help us," the Chief proposed. "There are enough leads in here to help Ethan track down his family."

The file was thick with excerpts from handwritten censuses, along with photocopies of microfiche newspaper announcements and birth and marriage certificates. The first page was a summary that explained the file's contents:

'Investigative team identified male subject TRAVERS, Ethan, as a potential match in the Native American database for a NEC relocation. One of the last births subjected to the mandate of the NEC and tracking efforts ceased in the late 1980s. Potential identity for: unnamed male birth June 9th, 1969, taken from

Pleasant Point Passamaquoddy reservation by NEC for relocation in Charlotte County. Current address provided by the Passamaquoddy Tribe is 45 Deadman's Harbour Road, Moose Island, Maine. No registered phone number or email. Investigation needed to confirm match: location and registration of birth for unnamed male birth and adopted male named Ethan Travers. Male subject TRAVERS, Ethan was not contacted, as per the request of Jackfish River Indian tribe.'

At the end of the paragraph was a bulleted list of documents, like Ethan's birth certificate and baptismal records, with checkmarks or empty boxes beside each item. My first instinct was to scold Merle for not simply offering Ethan the information without asking for something in return. Before I could, Ethan exploded in through the backdoor and grabbed the landline from its cradle. He dialed a number without looking at us and started barking as soon as someone answered, "Jordan, is the crew still on the boat?" he paused waiting for an answer. "Wake them up and tell everyone to get out on the water and stop any boat from leaving the bay," he paused again for Jordan to speak. "Yea, she's in trouble; she's gone. She went back down to the cabin for the night and the dogs came back up to the main house without her," listening to Jordan, Ethan paused for a few seconds before continuing. "I don't know how long she's been gone, so we might not catch them on the water." Listening intently, Ethan looked at us and motioned for us to get moving outside. "Thanks, Cap. My cell phone will work as soon as we are at the ferry landing, so keep me updated. Maintain Moose Island Police protocols, no staties. I want local boys only. We keep this quiet and get her back on our own," he demanded and hung up the phone. "Let's get moving," Ethan barked. "I'll explain the plan on the ferry. The crew is fired up and waiting."

The Chief and I were following Ethan when he stopped and turned back inside. He carefully lowered a lock box from the shelf above the coats by the backdoor. After he punched four numbers into the keypad, Ethan retrieved a handgun from inside with one hand and two magazines with the other. With skill, he loaded and cocked the weapon before placing it in the back waistband of his pants. Walking purposefully towards his truck with the dogs in tow, Ethan let them into the back.

As we caught up with him, he turned back to me and said, "Gwendolyn came here because she was scared," he explained. Ethan jumped behind the steering wheel and the Chief helped me into the front seat then climbed into the backseat. Ethan could see my wrinkled brow while he turned the truck around. "Well, that's not the only reason she followed me here." He didn't stop as he left the driveway and found the floor with the gas pedal when he reached the main road. "A long time ago, you asked me if I loved Gwendolyn," Ethan recalled. "Do you remember?" After I nodded, he continued. "I lied to you that day and said '*No, I would die for her.*'"

"I remember," I said with a smile. "Actually, you said you would lie down in front of a train for her," I remembered and smiled. "I knew you loved her back then and figured you needed time to realize it for yourself. It was so hard to keep from telling Gwendolyn," I confessed to Ethan. "She labelled her love for you as infatuation and tried to dismiss it. She didn't talk about it often, but she confided in me several times that she always felt safe with you."

Slowing down to maneuver the truck through several sharp turns, Ethan sped up on the straightaway. "I knew it from the moment she first put me in my place, and I kept falling harder the more I worked with her," he confessed. "She should be leading a research team working on curing cancer or sitting as a Supreme Court Justice," he praised her, "not banging it out with neanderthals in boardrooms that function more like back alleys," Ethan described to us. "Look, I'm no dummy, but I can think like the criminals on the other side of the table," he confessed flatly, "and stay ahead of them. It's the only way to protect her," he said with certainty. "Gwendolyn mistakenly believes there is right and wrong left in the world, and thinks she is protected by being on the right side when both sides are wrong."

"Gwendolyn doesn't strike me as a woman in need of protection," the Chief said in earnest as he rubbed his chin. "She walks with an air of confidence that women from the tribe do not have and acts as if she isn't afraid of anything," the Chief observed. "You make it sound as if we are negotiating with the mob or a biker gain; no rules, no consequences," the Chief questioned Ethan. "Even if that was the case, would her father's reputation not protect her?"

After finding the Chief's eyes in the rearview mirror, Ethan asked, "Have you ever spoken to Gwendolyn about her father?"

The Chief shook his head slightly, "We spoke once about her father, briefly. She told me she wasn't on speaking terms with him since accepting your job offer," he answered. "I asked her how long she was going to let that go on before repairing the relationship."

With a knowing smile as to Gwendolyn's response, Ethan turned to me and asked, "You never told him why Gwendolyn sought work with the tribe in the first place?" Shaking my head, Ethan continued, "Her father accumulated a lifetime of enemies by screwing over everyone in every deal," Ethan detailed, "and when Gwendolyn enrolled in forestry, she showed up on each one's radar." At the ferry landing, Ethan stopped the vehicle and shifted the truck into park.

He looked at the Chief and continued, "Then, she graduates and she ends up being brilliant and beautiful and terrifies every one of those neanderthals across the table. She made her own list of enemies, some influential ones…governors, CEOs and pretty much every single male colleague," he embellished to drive home the point. "When Robert had security walk Gwendolyn out of the office without warning, he sent a message to everyone that it was open season on his daughter." After opening my truck door, he said, "Stay here, I will be right back."

"We must think of Robert Leavitt as an enemy," I said to the Chief. "I don't want to share anymore of Gwendolyn's secrets until I have spoken to her," I stated, unwilling to discuss the matter in her absence. "You need to understand that Gwendolyn's father is not a good man. She knows it and has been trying to expose him. We need to help find her."

Ethan returned to the truck to hear the Chief ask, "Are we sure her father is capable of something like this? Of hurting his own daughter?"

"Robert can justify saying anything to anybody, and somehow it's always the truth," Ethan answered. "I didn't think he was capable of physically hurting her either," he admitted, "but he could justify kidnapping her if he felt it was for her own good. To get her away from me."

I looked at the Chief who had the same confused look on his face. Ethan shook it off and said, "I don't have time to explain everything tonight," he barked. "Take my truck across on the ferry. I am going with the rest of the crew to scan for boats in the bay. You are in good hands with Jordan, and I will see you on the other side." We watched as he ran towards the wharf and hopped into a waiting boat that immediately carved a path in the water away from dock. I was filled with dread as the last thing I saw was Ethan check his handgun, along with two other men in the boat.

Jordan honked the horn, and the Chief moved to the driver's seat of the truck to start the engine and drive onto the ferry. Alone on the boat, we sat in awkward silence and both looked out our windows at the encroaching darkness. I could see two other boats heading in opposite directions from the landing, presumably searching for Gwendolyn as well. I opened my door and stepped onto the deck and when I did, I could hear a voice over the speakers, "Hello Gloria and Chief Trout. I am going to turn on the spotlights at the back of the boat as well," he said. "Watch the stern for any boats on the water."

I obligatorily turned my attention to the water behind the boat. The large engines created dark swirling pools that hung onto the back ramp. Beams from the boat's lights sliced through the water attracting fish closer to the surface. It was relaxing to watch the water rolling rhythmically until I remembered what I was doing. Frustrated with finding my friends only to lose them again, I looked back to the truck to find the Chief standing beside me watching the water as well. Filled with questions, I opened my mouth to speak and wasn't sure what to say. The Chief's eyes said what I felt, and I wasn't sure there were any right words for the moment. Before I could summon any statement, the ferry horn honked.

"She's here!" Jordan yelled over the speaker to us. I looked up and saw Jordan waving and pointing, "Gwendolyn is at the landing!" he shouted. I laughed with relief and made my way to the front of the boat where I waved to Gwendolyn who waved back while holding a cell phone up to her ear. Following her eyes to movement down at the wharf, I saw Ethan's boat tying up to the dock. Before it came to a stop, Ethan jumped out of the boat and sprinted up the walkway to where Gwendolyn was standing. As the ferry landed, Ethan reached Gwendolyn and picked her up with both arms. They walked down the slip together and Ethan was well into his interrogation by the time they reached the ferry deck.

"Why would you agree to go with them?" Ethan demanded. "How did you not have time to get the shotgun? One shot in the air and I would have been there before they had time to load you in a boat," he pressed.

"They were waiting inside the cabin," she answered. "One of them found the shotgun and shells and placed them on the desk for me to see. They weren't messing around, so neither did I," she said plainly. "I tried sending the dogs, who were too busy making friends with the intruders and wouldn't leave," she explained. "I wasn't sure when they would make it back up to the house to warn you."

"Actually, the eagles beat them to it," I interjected to diffuse the rage building in Ethan's eyes.

"Okay, you got in the boat," Ethan said through clenched teeth. "Where did they take you?" he demanded.

"We walked down to our dock and they put me into a boat where I was blindfolded," she explained. I was surprised by her calm demeanour and noticed that her composure was easing Ethan's anger. "I know there were three boats; not sure how many men," she said. "The other boats went in different directions, I guess as a distraction?" she offered. "Since I was brought here in a truck, they must have taken me straight across the bay to the basement of a building. They kept me blindfolded when they asked me questions."

"Was Robert there?" Ethan asked. "You would have recognized his voice," he muttered. "Did you recognize any voices? Anything familiar about the building?"

"I don't think this has anything to do with Robert or what's happening back in Minnesota. First, they addressed me by my married name, Mrs. Travers," she started. "That's partly why I felt safe with them. If Robert had sent them, he wouldn't have given them my married name. He doesn't know."

"You said, first," Ethan prompted her.

With an annoyed look, she continued with her explanation. "Second, the questions they asked were all about the documents I requested from the Charlotte County archives," she said to Ethan. Turning to me, she continued. "I have been researching Ethan's genealogy to find his birth parents. When I built his tree on Ancestry, most of the documents were sourced from the Charlotte County archives, which is about 40 minutes from here," she continued. "I couldn't find copies of the documents on microfiche and needed to make a formal request for the original documents."

"So, that's how they found us?" Ethan asked. "You left our address with them?"

"No, I left the P.O. Box in Calais, like the rest of our mail," she retorted. "They knew a lot, Ethan," Gwendolyn said with apprehension. "They knew we were married; they knew about our work with the tribe, and they seemed to know all about you. And farther back beyond Devlin. They knew about Bentley and your hockey scholarship," she said with a crinkled brow. "They asked me about my document request, our work with Jackfish River and why you left Minnesota."

"What did you tell them?" Ethan asked. "Did you mention the search for my birth parents?"

"No, I gave them a plausible answer about writing a research paper on the Wabanaki, similar to my research at UMD with Jackfish," she explained. "The rest of the questions centred on my research on foreign companies buying up land and forest companies in the United States and Canada."

"The research that we agreed you wouldn't pursue once we left Devlin?" Ethan questioned with his tone soaked in aggravation. "Because it was too dangerous to continue without the protection offered by an organization like Devlin?" he continued as he searched her eyes for an answer. "You didn't leave it alone, did you?"

While her eyes betrayed her, she shook off his final question. "We can talk about it on the flight back," she said as she took his hand. We all waited for her to continue because there was something she wasn't saying. Gwendolyn lowered her voice before continuing, "We need to go back to Minnesota, Ethan. My Mom died and my father is burying her tomorrow at two o'clock."

I reached out to embrace my friend and saw the ship's deck lights illuminate the tears forming in the corner of her eyes. Shaking her head and with her voice cracking, she turned to me and said, "I am okay, Gloria." Her words aside, I wrapped my arms around her and she bent down into my embrace. "I lost my mom a long time ago and grieved the loss. She is at peace and her suffering has ended," she whispered so only I could hear.

While in Ethan's embrace, she rested her head on his chest and said, "Let's get back to the island so we can pack and find someone to take care of the dogs." Upon exiting his arms, she took a deep breath and turned to face us. "The ferry ride will give us adequate time to discuss how we are going to stop what is happening at McIntosh," she declared.

"We can put business aside tonight, Gwendolyn," the Chief suggested solemnly. "You can take tonight to put your mind on positive memories of your mother." Keeping his distance, the Chief motioned Gwendolyn back towards the truck. "We have time to devise a strategy following the service. You need time with your family, and space to mourn."

With a slight shiver, Gwendolyn made her way back towards the truck and opened the front passenger door. Before stepping up inside, she turned back to face the Chief and said, "My mother was all I had left in Minnesota. The fear of embarrassing her was the only thing that kept me from exposing Robert's skeletons." With a mournful voice, Gwendolyn shared a glimpse of the secrets she carried with her. "You see, Merle, I know where all the bodies are buried. I know everyone's dirty little secrets. Because they've all confided their deepest fears and most humiliating mistakes to me. Secrets they'd never reveal to another person, regardless of whether I wanted to know. Several of those skeletons belong to influential individuals, and they'll be eager to keep them buried."

She climbed into her seat and waited until we were all inside before continuing. "I've kept my powder dry long enough," she asserted by repeating the instructions Ethan gave her before walking into difficult meetings. "After my mother is laid to rest, we'll apply pressure on every secret to ensure McIntosh is safe," she said with defiance. "With Robert, his skeletons are personal. When we knife him, he will know I was involved," she said without emotion as she looked out the window for something in the darkness. "It shouldn't come as a surprise to him. He spent most of my life sharpening his blade on me."

To be continued...

ABOUT THE AUTHOR

GC Hennessey is an author with a passion for exploring the intersection of nature, culture and resilience. With a background in mergers and acquisitions, GC crafts narratives highlighting the bonds between the human and natural worlds.

Her experiences in the forests of northern Canada inspired The Painted Cave, book one of the Legends Lost trilogy. GC spent her career working as a registered professional forester at the side of the man who would later become her husband.

At the insistence of her husband, GC invested early in Bitcoin and a company named MicroStrategy. These strategic investments allowed the couple to retire on their own terms and shed light on the foreign takeover of land and resources across North America through series like *Legends Lost*.